A
Covering
Of
Honey!

British Library Cataloguing in Publication Data
A catalogue record for this book is available from the British Library.
ISBN 978-1-8381235-1-2

Cover Design by Christopher Burtenshaw

Printed and bound in the UK

Acknowledgements

I would like to thank my husband Christopher for creating the cover
design of this book. Also, for his help in the layout of the content.
And for all his support, patience and encouragement during my time of
writing.
Not forgetting my dear friends, Anne and Lyn, who have encouraged
me with both their enthusiasm and interest.
Thank you!

Dedications

This book is about families and siblings.
Therefore, I dedicate it, with much love, to our children:
Sarah, Jonathan and Felicity.
And to their spouses, Dave, Ruth and Rich.
Also, to our grandchildren:
Jordan, Evan, Chloe, Evie, Xavier, Edward and Alexander

1

The Prologue.

A young girl sits at the kitchen table. Her mother sits opposite. The older children have left for school and the youngest is missing them already. Both mother and daughter are unaware of the significance of the moment, which will remain to impact the child throughout her life. It is only a small, domestic happening of no apparent importance, yet it will remain with the child forever; setting her life on a course, which in this moment, she has neither the understanding nor will to comprehend.

The crumbs of the older childrens' breakfast litter the table. The butter dish is empty as is the marmalade jar. There is only one slice of bread left in the crumpled wrapper and the mother toasts it for her little girl. She is not listening to the child who chatters endlessly, for her mind is preoccupied with other matters. She wonders how she should react to these and so absorbed is the mother in her thoughts that, she forgets the toast; until the smell of burning alerts her and she rushes to save it.

The child begins to cry; she is hungry, and this is the last slice of bread. The cereal box is also empty and there is little milk in the jug. However, the mother smiles brightly, speaking quietly, not betraying the apprehension she feels. 'Now Phoebe, let me show you something magical.' The child's tears stop: her attention focused on the promise of magic. Her mother takes a knife and begins to scrape the blackened surface of the bread. Intrigued, the child watches, as it gradually changes through lighter shades. She claps her hands, a mixture of surprise and anticipation, still innocent enough to believe in magic.

'There!' Says her mother. The relief in her voice unnoticed by the child, whose delight is short-lived. 'But mummy there's no butter!' For a moment her mother pauses, before reaching into one of the kitchen cupboards; she emerges holding a pot of honey. The child smiles reassured; but when the mother opens the lid, her smile disappears and she hopes the scraping of honey, left at the bottom of the jar, will be enough.

She turns to the child, still smiling brightly and, begins to spread the honey, her knife jingling in the almost empty jar. The child gazes intently, as her mottled bread gradually disappears beneath a smooth, golden, pool of honey. Thankfully, there is enough to cover the meagre slice thickly. The honey has spread much further than expected.

The child bites into her toast, eagerly anticipating the satisfaction its delicious, sweetness will bring. No longer is it a burnt offering, but a sweet savour. 'Mmm!' murmurs the child, as her eyes close in enjoyment.

Her mother smiles, her expression relaxed, her thoughts no longer preoccupied. 'Always remember Phoebe, honey is a lot like love. It only takes a little to spread much further than you expect!' The child nods, her eyes still closed, enjoying the pure pleasure of honey, oblivious to her mother's meaning.

Chapter 1

A storm was brewing; Frances had heard the forecast but hadn't anticipated its arrival until later in the evening. She peered anxiously through the windscreen at the gathering grey above, where the clouds were staining the landscape an inky black. Suddenly, the sky ripped open releasing a streak of lightning, which twisted to earth like a fallen angel breathing fire. A crack of deafening thunder split the sky; her grip on the steering wheel tightened; she hated driving in rain and wondered if she would be able to make it to the farmhouse before the storm broke. Something had been hit and she watched the flames, like hungry tongues on the far horizon devouring the shadows. She heard sirens screaming in the distance. Nervously, Frances swung off the road, deciding to sit the storm out; thereby revealing her tense, yet cautious nature.

Sitting there, shivering slightly, she wondered if any of her siblings had arrived yet or would she be the first. Uneasily, she drummed her fingers on the steering wheel; she wasn't looking forward to this family holiday, which had been in the planning for the last six months. How would they all manage to survive a week together in the country? How would she get on with Cynthia after all this time? Would she be able to continue her pretext in the face of her sister's smug contentment? She'd been sceptical from the first when Phoebe had suggested what a great opportunity it would be for them all to spend some time together. Phoebe, who was always trying to unite a family otherwise fragmented both emotionally as well as geographically. Frances jumped, as another electrifying clap of thunder tore the heavens apart. A sign which during a past age was thought to signify the anger of the Gods'. Today though, it was she who was angry; with an anger that had grown over many years, but with which she'd learnt to live, to suppress and control. There was still time to turn back she told herself. She wasn't superstitious, but the storm had unsettled her, and she wondered if another type of storm might also be lying in wait for her, or perhaps even for them all?

Phoebe strained to keep her eyes open, her lids stalked by fatigue; she was aware of the dangers and decided to pull in at the next service station. The youngest of the four siblings, she also lived the furthest away from their holiday destination, but after a busy day in her London office, the long drive to North Wales no longer seemed the good idea it once had. Since her mother had died, they had all seemed to drift further apart and she found herself cast in the role of trying to unite disparate individuals with the concept that families matter. To date, it had been hard work.

She breathed a sigh of relief when the lights of the services, shone like welcoming beacons, across the frenetic lanes of traffic. Now, seated with a mug of black coffee and a pack of chicken sandwiches, she texted the others she was going to be late and not to wait up for her, but to leave the door open and she would see them in the morning. She smiled to herself, remembering how security conscious Henry was; he would probably be sitting up waiting for her, the protective, older brother. Henry had always been the one to fight her battles, guarding her against either the merciless teasing or bullying of her sisters'. He'd also taken her side in any argument and even into adulthood she still relied on his defence. Strangely, such thoughts began to ease her tension and she found herself beginning to relax at the prospect of the long drive still awaiting her.

However, Henry hadn't left home yet. Rather, he was sitting wearily on the side of his bed, wondering what he should pack. He still could not come to terms with the fact that after twenty-five years of supposedly contented married life, Anna had announced she was going on holiday with her best friend Lizzie, for the half-term break. He and Anna were both teachers, their twin sons away at university. Anna had packed her case the night before and left earlier that afternoon, for the sunny beaches of Spain. But as the headmaster, Henry had stayed later to tie up all the loose ends of the term.

'Why?' He'd asked Anna.

'Well, why not?' She'd replied. 'We're always together, it will do us both good to have a change. Besides, Lizzie is still getting over Stephen's death. She needs a friend's support; it will be good for her. Whereas, you and I have the summer holidays to look forward to, haven't we darling? Also, the boys will be home then too. Don't be unreasonable, please!'

Henry didn't think he was the one being unreasonable; after a hectic term, he'd been looking forward to a relaxing time alone with his wife. Nevertheless, he knew it would be pointless to press the matter further, he always lost any disagreement with her. Besides, perhaps she was right, a change might be good for them both. He'd wondered if Jeremy, the deputy head, might be free for a spot of fishing, only to discover Jeremy was spending half-term helping out with his grandchildren as both their parents were working. This announcement had made Henry reflect on the changing roles of men in society, far removed from his own father's generation and the example he'd set Henry; always expecting more from him, than his three daughters: treating him harshly for small misdemeanours. Chiding Henry for any display of emotion and considering a handshake the greatest display of affection between father and son. A far cry from the hugs and kisses exchanged between Henry and his sons whenever they met. He sighed, even now at his age some of these memories were painful and he didn't want to dwell on them. He hoped he'd provided a better role model for his sons in an ever-changing society, yet felt he too, had also failed in many ways, leaving his children with a far from perfect example of fatherhood. Nevertheless, he hoped his sons knew that both he and Anna were there for them, in a way his father hadn't been for him.

Now, he considered his unpacked case. He'd almost reconciled himself to his home alone state, when Phoebe had rung, suggesting the family week away. For some reason, she'd left him until last for, as he was later to discover, his sisters had been asked some months before. Why he wondered? Was it because Phoebe had hoped for an all-girls-together getaway or perhaps, much nearer to the truth, she'd taken it for granted dependable Henry would always be there for her at short notice?

He hadn't been sure at first, after all, the four of them hadn't stayed under the same roof together for over twenty-five years! However, it seemed a better idea than spending the week alone; he felt the need for a complete break, yet wasn't sure a family holiday would provide what he currently needed. Therefore, as he carefully packed his clothes, he couldn't shake off the thought, he was making a huge mistake.

The road was ill-lit, but the lights of the farmhouse blinked through the darkness. Cynthia was glad she'd brought the satnav. However, Roger thought them unreliable and preferred maps: insisting she took one with her, just in case. It had taken a lot of persuasion on her part to get Roger to agree to this holiday alone with her brother and sisters for a full week. 'After all,' she'd said, 'It might be my last opportunity.' Eventually, but nevertheless reluctantly he'd agreed: with the proviso she call him if needed. 'It will be fine! This is something I have to do and I need to do it alone.' Even as she answered, he'd raised both hands in resignation. 'Okay if you must!' With that he'd left the room, unhappy and worried. Cynthia understood all this and felt a sense of guilt for harassing him with her insistence, but this was something she had to do in preparation. She knew he didn't understand this; nevertheless, she still found the determination and strength to, somehow, see this challenge through.

The whitewashed farmhouse was set like a huge mother of pearl stone, into the hillside overlooking the coastline, which stretched across the water to Anglesey. She felt exhausted from her drive and was grateful to pull onto the rough track leading to a muddy parking area. There had been a recent deluge leaving debris and twigs scattered across the route, which struck the car's undercarriage as it slowly ascended. Finally, she pulled on the handbrake and rested her weary head on the steering wheel: trying to gather her strength to meet the family.

Unknown to Cynthia, Frances, the first to arrive, was the only person waiting patiently inside. Tired and tense she'd arrived an hour before, to find the house almost in complete darkness. The owners had left the key in the door and a hall light on, but she had to make her way up a steep, grassy slope slippery and sodden underfoot to the flagstone steps of the entrance. There were no outside lights and she'd tripped on the first step, twisting her ankle and gashing her knee. After which, she'd decided to stay put and leave the rest of her bags in the car until morning. Unfortunately, these were the ones containing the comforts of home; but Frances was stoical as well as pragmatic and therefore willing to make do.

She'd stumbled and fumbled through the various rooms, turning on lights, hoping her efforts might blaze an easier pathway for her siblings to follow.

The kitchen was huge with grey stone walls and a dull slate floor. Nevertheless, it was well equipped, and the owners had left tea, coffee, milk, and Welsh cakes. Fortified by a cup of tea and a cake, she'd made her way slowly up the steep staircase to the bathroom where, to her surprise, she found a first-aid kit complete with bandages and antiseptic to treat her injuries. Probably, I wasn't the first to fall on those wretched steps, she'd thought, wondering why there were no outside lights. She'd just finished binding her ankle when she heard a car arriving. Frances hoped it wouldn't be Cynthia; the last thing she wanted now was to be alone with this particular sister.

Phoebe had spent longer than intended at the service station, enjoying the comfort of relaxing for the first time that day. She even felt tempted to take a room for the night but felt this would only provoke the others, as she'd been the one to persuade them all to make the effort to come: largely against their will. She knew them all too well to expect them to be understanding if she didn't arrive until the following day. All accept Henry of course, he'd understand, but from the outset she didn't want to upset either Frances or Cynthia.

At least the traffic had eased and Phoebe turned on the radio and began to hum. However, her mind was on the week ahead and how they would all get on together. She was aware there was always some underlying tension between her sisters, but had never discovered the root cause. However, more than this concern, she'd some news of her own to tell them and she wasn't sure how they would react; so, she began to hum more loudly, as if trying to block out any disturbing thoughts.

Phoebe had been the unexpected child of her mother's mid-years, but nevertheless, a welcome addition to the family, even though she'd later learnt, her father had initially not been quite so happy at the prospect of adding to his ever-growing brood. However, her arrival had changed all that and she became his favourite child, a fact not unnoticed by her sisters. Her mother indulged her autumnal daughter as she called her; partly due to her being born in October and partly due to her own late fruitfulness.

Phoebe, a sensitive child, had been close to her mother and with an awareness beyond her years, she seemed to imbibe her mother's hopes as well as her struggles. Intuitively understanding both her moods as well as her attitudes. Often, they ate breakfast alone together after the others had left. Phoebe loved these times, especially when her mother would spread honey thickly, straight onto the crisp slightly burnt toast, without adding any butter. When she'd eventually asked: 'Why?'
Her mother replied. 'Honey spread like butter is like love which covers many faults.' Phoebe had looked at her quizzically. 'You see, nobody is perfect, just like this piece of burnt toast. But, when you take a spoon of

honey and spread it thickly a transformation takes place. When we love people, we don't focus on their shortcomings or failings but choose to see beyond these. In this way we cover them with our love.'

Her mother's didactic metaphors, once understood, had left her with an amount of uncertainty. She knew a single bee, could produce the equivalent of a teaspoon of honey in its lifetime which in human terms, added up to a lifetime of loving! A lifetime of giving! Surely then, more than a teaspoon would be needed! She thought of the bee and the investment of its life; its instinctive efforts and diligent labour; yet doubting her own capacity to produce the necessary, human equivalent. Nevertheless, her mother's analogies apart, Phoebe could remember the pleasure of biting into the hard, crispness of the toast and the soft, smooth, sweetness of the honey on her tongue, as she listened to her mother's words, not understanding them. However, they had often returned to her in adulthood as she remembered those times with affection. Causing her to gradually understand her mother's meaning as well as her desire for maintaining their family relationships. This had been her reason for suggesting the holiday together, but she was already anticipating her need to spread honey and wondered if she would have enough in reserve; for this blend of honey needed to be spread unconditionally and this was the hardest part of the challenge, almost like dying to one's own considered rights and dignity!

Henry, two hours later than planned, was at last on the road but his mind was on his immediate family. He still couldn't understand Anna's decision. He understood Lizzie was a good friend and grieving for her husband, but surely, she had family who could support her? He knew she had adult children living in Sussex and a cousin in Essex. She also had sisters-in-law nearby. Therefore, why rely on Anna when he needed her? For the last few months Anna had seemed quieter than usual, more tired, more irritable, her moods alternating between brooding melancholy and unbridled anger. True it had been a demanding term for them both; she'd often brought schoolwork home, sighing as she marked long essays late into the night. Also, discipline within the classroom had been an ongoing scourge and three students from her literature classes had been suspended, due to the disruption they'd caused. Parents had complained to the school board that their children were the victims rather than the perpetrators and what about the mock exams they were missing out on? Their futures were being jeopardised through Anna's lack of classroom control. Consequently, she'd been under observation for the last month. She came home moody and depressed. He'd become increasingly concerned about her mental health and then they'd discovered their sons Jack and Jake had been using drugs. This had led to them missing lectures and failing last year's end of term exams. They'd both received counselling as well as permission to resit in six months, adding to the expense of their tuition fees as well as concern for their well-being. At first, Anna, just like the parents of those students in her classes, couldn't believe their sons would have resorted to drugs. Hadn't they been brought up with an understanding of substance abuse? They'd been warned how soft drugs could lead to harder addictions and their boys weren't fools! It had only been when Jack and Jake, rather diffidently admitted: 'Yes we've taken drugs! At first occasionally, but then more regularly.' Suggesting it had helped them to cope with the stress of university without giving no thought to the consequences either in terms of their education or the damage to their longer-term health. They were now hopefully back on track and taking their studies more seriously. Jack in the school of science and Jake in the school of humanities. So different in character and ability despite being twins. However, although they'd seemed to come through this setback, as parents their trust in their sons' attitudes had been seriously undermined and these events combined, had taken their toll on Anna. Perhaps she'd been right after all. A complete break from family might be just what she needed. Henry sighed. He loved his wife, but lately she seemed more distant, uninterested in sex and, no longer sought out his company. She'd always been more independent in her decision making. He hoped this was just a passing dilemma, simply a hiccup in their relationship; the thought he might be losing her was just too unbearable for him to consider.

Gratefully, he pulled off the motorway, leaving the chaos of noise and lights behind. The velvety blackness of the lane wrapped itself around him like a blanket. The motion of the trees swaying in the breeze seemed to wave him forward and something akin to relief descended upon him. Unfortunately, this was short-lived; there were only a few miles left before he'd reach the farmhouse; he felt himself beginning to relax a little; his journey would soon be over and it would do him good to see his sisters again. He was especially looking forward to seeing Phoebe; he'd always felt closer to her than the others. Somehow, Phoebe seemed more vulnerable and he'd always felt the need to protect her from the robust and resilient challenges his other sisters always seemed to impose on her. He hoped her time in London had made Phoebe more self-possessed, more independent and, more confident in her own decisions. He couldn't always be there for her as in the past.

Suddenly his thoughts were interrupted by the smell of acrid burning, which seemed to have seeped into the car and, turning the bend he came to a sudden halt. A barn in a nearby field was ablaze and fire engines barred the way. A policeman approached him. 'Fraid you'll have to turn back sir, too risky for you to proceed. A barn hit by lightning you see; the fire has spread to some of the other outbuildings: it is going to be a long night!' Henry groaned inwardly, it had been a very long day already and he felt exhausted both emotionally as well as physically. However, he curbed his frustration and tried to speak calmly.

'Can you redirect me then; I'm on my way to Llanbryn Farm?' The policeman shook his head.

'Sorry sir, this is the only direct route from this point; you'll have to travel a fair few miles in the opposite direction, then take a more circuitous route before you'll reach the farm.' Henry swore under his breath. Then the policeman added. 'Alternatively, you could spend the night at the local inn if you wish. It's just about four-hundred yards back and then you take a right turn and you'll find the White Swan Inn a couple of hundred yards down on the left-hand side. We should be finished here in the morning.' Then by way of explanation, he continued. 'Unlucky for Jones the farmer, will he survive yet another disaster, I wonder?' Not only unlucky for Jones; Henry thought as he tried to swing the car around in the narrow lane, hearing the hedge growth, like the long nails of an unseen predator clawing at the paintwork, as he did so. Heavy with both tiredness and misgivings he decided to take a room at the inn and set-off again in the morning, hopefully in a better frame of mind.

Frances had heard the car arrive and wondered which of her siblings it might hold. She hoped it wouldn't be Cynthia, who she didn't want to face alone. It was easier to cover her antipathy with the others present; so much easier to avoid those unwanted conversations, which might lead to further distress. Superficiality was the order of the day, served on the platter of necessity whenever she and Cynthia met; for them both, it was the only acceptable terms of their meeting and the same dish they had both served one another on many occasions: unpalatable to the taste and difficult to digest.

Waiting in the narrow hall to greet whichever of her siblings it might be. Frances gave a silent gasp as Cynthia entered. She hardly recognised her sister and momentarily was lost for words, caught somewhere between shock and incomprehension.

'Help me with the bags, will you Fran?' Frances moved quickly forward not speaking but relieving her of what looked to be the heaviest load. 'Thanks.'

Cynthia walked slowly following Frances into the dimly lit lounge, where she sank gratefully into the first available armchair. Frances had never seen her so thin; she looked exhausted and her skin appeared jaundiced, almost like parchment stretched thinly over her bones. 'You're not well.' It was more of a statement than a question, but Cynthia didn't answer or even look at her; instead, she grimaced slightly and holding her side, she bent to rummage in her bag for a small container of pills. She emptied two into her hand and swallowed them quickly. 'Glass of water?' Frances asked hurriedly.

'No, I'm fine, but think I'll go on up.' Cynthia wavered slightly as she stood, before slowly climbing the steep stairway. Frances carried her luggage up for her but neither sister spoke again. Cynthia had just taken her bags from Frances with a brief dismissive nod before closing her bedroom door, leaving Frances alone on the landing. Frances was still in shock; this wasn't the meeting she'd anticipated. This woman, once so robust, now so diminished, was more of a stranger to her, than ever.

Chapter 2

Henry had passed a comfortable night at the White Swan as well as having enjoyed a full English breakfast with extra toast. Now he was once again back on the road, refreshed and actually looking forward to the prospect of meeting his sisters. It was a bright May morning and the countryside was wearing her early summer colours. The trees were now fully in leaf providing canopies of shade for the grazing cattle, already staking their claim beneath patches of dappled shade. The windows of the car were open and he could hear the birds singing in the hedgerows; while crows called from above as he passed. The world seemed a better place this morning.

However, his newfound ease was soon disturbed by the same smell of smoke filling the car as it had yesterday. He slowed down remembering the events of the night before. Henry knew he must be approaching the farm and realised for Jones the morning would be far from bright. Rounding the bend, his thoughts were confirmed. The results of the fire were still smouldering the barn now no more than a pile of dusty ash beneath the blue sky. Several of the outbuildings including a stable block, had been partially gutted, their remains no more than a chaos of blackened beams and bricks. A pair of greys whinnied nervously in the paddock opposite tossing their manes as a man, presumably Jones, leant on the fence, speaking softly, as he tried to calm them. Henry pulled over and walked towards them. 'Morning!' He called. The farmer turned enquiringly, his face drawn and weary: grey with tiredness and smudged with soot. By way of explanation, Henry spoke: 'I saw the blaze last night: had to turn back.' The farmer didn't answer but turned away gazing beyond the horses towards the surrounding hills. Henry felt awkward, rather like some sleazy voyeur entertaining himself with the misfortunes of others. 'Sorry, I shouldn't have intruded.' However, his words seemed to be consumed in the ether as the farmer appeared to be lost in his reverie. Henry rested a hand on his shoulder, before turning to leave, but this too was unacknowledged by Jones, apart from a deep sigh, which spoke more loudly than words. Henry turned back to the car; his heart not as light as it had been a few minutes earlier.

'Henry is here!' Phoebe the last to bed and the first to rise had been watching for him. Now she was rushing downstairs and out onto the muddy car park waving happily at his approach. He smiled when he saw her. 'Bee!' He began with mock seriousness. 'I expected a more dignified welcome from you. Haven't your months in London done anything for you?'

She grinned. 'Well actually they have, but that's another story for another time. Now come here and let me hug you.' His jumper smelt of tobacco, sweetly aromatic and familiar. It comforted her, but until that moment she hadn't realised she needed comfort. Could she be in denial she wondered? 'Still smoking that smelly old pipe? Don't you care it's clogging your lungs with tar?' But before he could reply she was pulling him towards the house. 'Come inside, the others are waiting; you can get your bags later. I should prepare you though, Cynthia looks terrible!' She turned and hugged him again, almost as if his presence was the panacea for everything unpalatable.

They'd all been shocked at Cynthia's appearance and all had tried unsuccessfully to broach the subject with her. However, Cynthia wouldn't be led. She'd promised herself what needed to be done, she would do in her own time when she was ready. For as she'd said to Roger, it wasn't an easy task ahead of her either for herself or her siblings. More than this, she felt it was her prerogative to choose when and with whom, she was to share her secret. A secret which she knew it would be impossible to hide for much longer, if at all.

Henry's room enjoyed a view over green sloping fields speckled with sheep. Slate rooftops and grey-stone walls laid the boundary of the village and beyond this the pebbled beach stretched as though smiling in a wide grin around the bay. In the far distance sailing dinghies, their coloured sails rippling in the breeze, were floating leisurely like toy boats on a park pond. He raised the sash window and imagined he could hear their halyards tinkling as the boats bobbed and bounced on the waves.

It was a calming scene, a soothing moment and for the first time, he became aware of how tense he'd become over the last few months. His work was demanding and Ofsted together with continuing government interference with the curriculum had added much to the ongoing demands of running a busy, comprehensive school; as well as managing staff, pupils, parents and a budget which was continually being cut. All this before he could even begin to think about his own family cares. Perhaps it was time for him to consider his options? He was still only in his mid-forties; he knew several teachers, both older and younger, who had made such career changes successfully, without regret.

However, Henry wasn't somebody who easily gave up; besides he loved teaching, despite the pressures that came with it. Nevertheless, he knew everyone has a breaking point and he wondered how far away he was from his? Just then his train of thought was broken, by a quick knock on his door. 'Henry it's Bee! Feel like a walk?'

The ascent was steep, yet terraced in the rough style of Welsh mountains, riddled with sheep tracks, rough roots, rocks and bracken. Gorse, yellow in bloom, tugged at their clothing as they squeezed through narrow ways. It was as if the foliage sought to entangle them slowing their progress, yet the sun was warm and the bleating of the sheep pleasant. Phoebe was pleased to have Henry to herself, they were the only walkers. Unsurprisingly, Cynthia hadn't felt up to the walk, which was really more of a climb and Frances, still nursing her recent injuries, said she'd stay and rest her foot. A situation which suited everyone.

For the first forty minutes, they'd walked in silence, enjoying the views and the beauty of the landscape. Both seemed to be deep in their own thoughts, whereas in truth they were each gradually unwinding, as they lowered the defences which they had daily built around themselves in their differing lifestyles. The sun and distant lull of the waves soothed their nerves and slowed their pace. They both experienced an inward melting, a mellowing of mood as their anxieties and concerns lifted from them in the charmed atmosphere of late spring meeting early summer. A buzzard mewled overhead its shrill cries piercing the mellifluous flow of a skylark's song, extravagantly squandering its joy on the blue above.

Henry paused to remove his jacket and wiping the sweat from his brow he inhaled deeply, as he surveyed the panorama, spread in all its beauty before them. Phoebe unrolled a picnic blanket and they sat in silence for another few minutes before Henry spoke. 'Well little Sis, what have you got to tell me?' Phoebe looked down pulling at a coarse blade of grass.

'What makes you think, I have anything other than my usual boring news to tell you?'

Henry smiled. 'I know you too well. For instance, I know on the one hand you're dying to spill the beans, but on the other you're not sure how I'm going to react.' Phoebe shifted uncomfortably. Henry was right, he'd read her thoughts perfectly; he'd always understood her better than her sisters. Although she reflected, perhaps it was also something to do with his long years of teaching experience, which had made him so discerning. He noticed her discomfort. 'Of course, I don't want to pry; you don't have to tell me anything you know, but I'm here to listen if you want to talk.'

Phoebe looked at him; his face was red with exertion and yet kind, the first wrinkles of age spreading from the corners of his eyes as he smiled at her. She took a deep breath before blurting out: 'I'm pregnant!' If he was surprised, Henry gave no sign of it.

'I see, how do you feel about that?' Phoebe grimaced.

'Spare me the rhetorical counselling approach, please!'

'Sorry, didn't mean to keep you at a distance.'

'I know, I'm just a bit touchy, guess it must be my hormones.'

'Now you're using your pregnancy as an excuse for your sensitivity.' He smiled.

'Okay, point taken! I must remember not to use my baby as an excuse for my irritability.' Her response warned him he was on sensitive ground.

'I'm teasing you; seriously though how do you feel about it?'

'Well I'm not sure, but of course I'm pleased!' Henry looked at her, his gaze simultaneously concerned, yet full of gentleness. He wanted her to carry on speaking so waited, but then he noticed her tears welling and reached over to take her hand squeezing it in the warmth of his own, as her tears began to fall.

Frances and Cynthia, far from keeping one another company, had both retired to their own rooms as soon as the others left. Now they both lay on their beds remembering the past. For Frances this was painful, but for Cynthia bitter-sweet. The past had been kinder to her but nevertheless, had also left her with a sense of guilt. Although, as she so often told herself, it was not entirely of her own making, for Roger had colluded with her. However, apparently, Roger had never shared her guilt; neither had he been willing to take any of the blame. 'After all, such things happen despite ourselves.' He'd told her. However, Cynthia hadn't been so sure.

Frances too, was dwelling on the past an activity she increasingly seemed to return to the older she grew, yet the pain was always magnified when in the company of Cynthia. The past had driven itself between them like an immovable wedge, permanently cutting them off from any real understanding or tolerance of one another. In their own way, they both regretted this, but each failed to find a way forward; both were incapable of making the first move in terms of reparation and, as a result, both suffered in silence; outwardly barely tolerating one another, but inwardly longing to be free from the grim consequences of their estranged relationship.

As Cynthia lay on her bed, she listened to the silence of the house; assured that Frances was also in her room, she struggled to sit up. The sun was warm and the farmhouse had a veranda where early honeysuckle crept and bloomed. This overlooked the bay beyond, and Cynthia knew it would do her good to sit for a while in the fresh air, but what she didn't need at this moment was Frances's company. She'd have to make her move stealthily and this she managed; as on their return, Henry and Phoebe discovered her dozing in a wicker chair.

They stood for a moment gazing at her ashen face. Her eye sockets were deep-set and dark half-moon shadows rested beneath them, drawing attention to her prominent cheekbones. They looked at one another, their expression caught somewhere between shock and sorrow. Until that moment neither had realised the severity of their sister's illness; but now, her face in repose revealed what she'd managed to hide in her waking moments. For in sleep Cynthia had put on her own death mask. She opened her eyes, sensing their presence, slightly startled and anxious as if she intuitively knew her secret had been unwittingly stolen as she slept! Looking into their faces she understood, at least as far as Henry and Phoebe were concerned, she only needed to fill in the details. 'I see you've both guessed.' They nodded and unsure what to say each laid a hand on her shoulder. 'Please don't tell Frances, I want to tell her myself.'

'Don't tell me what?' Came a voice from behind, where Frances was walking towards them smiling and looking refreshed from her afternoon nap. However, the smile was superficial revealing the white of her teeth but never reaching her eyes. Moreover, her voice was sharp, stretched by the tautness of vocal cords under strain. Phoebe and Henry exchanged looks; the sort that communicated both a mutual awareness as well, as a mutual dread, of what was about to ensue. Henry forced a hearty chuckle, the falseness of which was noted by them all. 'Cynthia was just saying she didn't want to be caught napping!' Now all three of us have caught her!' Frances didn't look convinced; however, she too wanted to avoid any conflict, especially so early in the week. 'I see.' She said, leaning on the rail and looking out to the semi-circle of blue beyond. They were all surprised when Cynthia spoke again. 'Actually, there is something which I need to tell all of you, but I prefer to do it on a one-to-one basis, as it will affect you all in different ways.' Henry cleared his throat as though about to say something, but then seemed to think better of it. Whilst Phoebe, who was ever ready to smooth over creases in relationships, responded too quickly. 'That's fine Cynthia, we all understand, don't we?' She looked pleadingly towards her other siblings. Henry cleared his throat again. 'Of course! Absolutely!' He blustered. Frances however, remained silent. The last thing she wanted was to be left alone with Cynthia, especially if she had something significant to say. Who knew what she might come out with? Also, more importantly from Frances's point of view, how would she react if left alone with her sister? 'I really don't understand why you can't just say whatever it is, whilst we're all here and get it over with.'

'When did you ever understand me Frances?' Cynthia was speaking to Frances's back as she still leant over the rail, apparently enjoying the view, but in reality, fuming inwardly. She didn't answer, but instead turned away and walked inside without speaking. 'Well, what a magnificent view we have from here!' Said Henry with forced jocularity as he took Frances's place leaning on the rail. Nobody else spoke: eventually though they all wandered inside, separately and silent.

Cynthia, never one to be opposed, remained the most unruffled of the four. Nevertheless, she felt the need to hear Roger's voice; safe within her room she called him. 'Darling!' She noticed the apprehension in his voice, as he answered. 'Is everything all right?'

'Of course, I'm just a bit tired after the journey.' Roger remained silent; they both knew this was an understatement as well as Cynthia's own

flavour of denial; a denial, which only served to cloak her inner despair and so avoid those necessary and inevitable conversations with others. 'I just wondered how things were at home; are you and the girls managing?'
'We are! Missing you though!' Then he cleared his throat before adding; 'I'm especially missing you sweetheart.' Cynthia felt her mood soften. For a few seconds, a poignant silence drew them closer, followed by Cynthia's querulous voice. 'The weather is good here, but certain relationships are just as bleak as they have always been.'
'Cynthia,' Roger's tone was steeped in a masked plea; one simultaneously marinated in both love and concern. 'You must put the past behind you, you're only tormenting yourself!'
'Am I? Is that what you really believe, Roger? Well is it?'
'My belief is only for your good. I don't care what anyone else thinks. This is not the time for you to be raking over the ashes of past events. You need to live in the present for your own sake, as well as mine. The girls and I need you!'
'Is that what you really believe? What about your own contribution to that pile of ashes? Has the fire truly burnt out or is it still smouldering?'
She heard him sigh: a long, slow expiration of resignation. 'Fine! Have it your own way. I'll be here if you need me.' Cynthia was shocked. For the first time in their lives, her husband had hung up on her. She sat thinking of him, perhaps beginning to understand for the first time, how circumstances had taken their toll, not only on herself but also on him. Why did she always seem to push people away? What was it within her that insisted on her meeting life alone, shunning the comfort and refuge others wanted to give? Was it pride, independence or just wanting to prove she was stronger than others perceived her to be? Cynthia never offered sympathy or even empathy, she didn't know how to and she certainly didn't want anyone to offer her any.

There was a knock at the door. 'I'm resting!' Phoebe was outside and not put off by her sister's curtness. 'Cynthia, could I come in just for a few moments?' Now it was Cynthia's turn to sigh.
'Well! I don't expect I'll get any peace if you don't get your own way, as usual. But only for a few moments.' Phoebe poked her head around the door and smiled.

'I just wanted you to know, Henry and I do understand and want to support you as best we can.' Cynthia turned her face, flushed and angry towards Phoebe.

'How could you possibly know or understand what I'm going through? You, always mother's favourite: spoilt, pampered and always excused!' Phoebe felt as though a bag of refuse had been thrown over her. She stood staring in shock at Cynthia, not knowing how to respond. Her eyes filled with tears, but she remembered she mustn't let her hormones get the better of her. 'I'm sorry if that is how you see me? Perhaps you might try looking beyond your resentment of a fictional past, to the present reality of a family that both loves you and wants to be involved in your life, whatever might be happening in it.' Cynthia's eyes burned with both fury and fatigue. 'Leave me! I need to be alone! None of you understand me!' Phoebe, to her own surprise, stood her ground. She spoke gently.

'Perhaps if you let any of us, find the way to come closer to you then we might understand.' Her words burnt into Cynthia's already inflammatory mindset, causing her to let out a sound, more animal than human. Phoebe quickly withdrew, closing the door noisily, but not before quietly saying. 'You're wrong Cynthia, terribly wrong. Have you ever thought that it might be *you* who hasn't really understood the rest of us?'

This was too much for Cynthia. 'Get out, get out!' She shouted, adding as Phoebe quietly withdrew. 'You understand nothing, nothing at all!'

This wasn't the reception or the holiday, Phoebe had hoped for. Spreading honey thickly like butter, wasn't an easy task; suddenly she felt daunted like one who needs to conquer a mountain but without the right equipment.

Chapter 3

Roger was agitated; he paced to and fro occasionally pausing to run his hands through his dark hair. Cynthia was wrong; he still carried the guilt of his unfaithfulness to both sisters. Frances and Cynthia were both casualties of his narcissistic behaviour. He knew both carried the scars of his selfishness, both still had never forgiven him even though Cynthia insisted she had. Nevertheless, he knew deep within her she still cradled her hurt. And now, when she needed him more than ever she still kept this distance between them. Would she ever forgive him? Would she ever let him into her trust again? Time was so short, her life was ebbing and he realised in another sense, his life was ebbing too. What would life hold for him without Cynthia?

Roger was not alone in his soul searching. Phoebe too was trying to find a way through the labyrinth of her thoughts and emotions. Her attempt to share her heart with Henry had fallen short of her expectations. At least he knew her secret, which did bring her some comfort. He'd received her news well, apparently without judgement, but also without knowing the circumstances with which she was now struggling. It seemed Henry was no longer able to solve all her problems as he once had. Now, she was a woman in her own right and responsible for her destiny. It was immature of her to expect someone else to make the momentous decisions facing her. Yes, they could offer support, advice even, but only she could find the way forward. Phoebe had never made any momentous decisions alone and now she was facing perhaps the greatest of her life.

Her thoughts were interrupted by a slight flutter within; unconsciously her hand slipped down as she caressed her abdomen; she smiled. How could she feel herself alone with this new life, fragile and yet simultaneously robust within her, budding, blossoming with vigour, little by little until the time when it would burst upon the world, dependent solely on her love, acceptance and, resourcefulness. Her thoughts turned to Mason, where was he now? What was he doing? This life within her was a part of him too, but of which he knew nothing. He was on the other side of the world sheep farming in New Zealand, following in his father's well-worn groove. 'It's in my blood. I have to go back, it's expected, but

more than that, it is what I want to do!' He'd hung his head when he'd made that last comment, unable to look her in the face. If he had, then he would have seen the devastation written there in her eyes and drained complexion. She hadn't realised about the baby then, rather it was the shock of finally appreciating, she hadn't understood the nature of their relationship. For Mason, she was only a girl he'd met during his year as an intern in London. He'd wanted to combine travel with a type of work completely different to home, just for the experience. He'd wanted to know if there might be another option for him. Was he capable of anything else apart from what he'd grown up with, before taking up the reins alongside his father? The answer had been: no! Phoebe hadn't understood. It wasn't as if Mason had deceived her; she'd known from the start the length of his stay and the reasons behind it; but had expected his plans to change, as their intimacy had deepened. She'd never felt this way about anyone before and she'd assumed he'd felt the same. Her heart told her this would last a lifetime and so she'd ignored the whisperings of her reason that, this wonderful new way of living would last only for a few months. There were times when her conscience shouted warnings, but with Mason warm and breathing deeply in sleep beside her, she'd managed to silence the doubts, pushing them away focusing only on the present. For the last year, she'd lived her life in moments each one centred on Mason. He'd become like a drug censoring her reason, heightening her emotions, binding her to a dependency she'd never dreamt possible. 'Penny for them love?' Phoebe jumped; her reverie broken. Frances stood close beside her. She'd overheard Cynthia's angry retort and had come in search of Phoebe to offer comfort. 'Cynthia has always been touchy, don't let it upset you. I guess she's feeling none too good. She certainly doesn't look it, does she?'
'No! She doesn't!' Phoebe shifted pulling slightly away from Frances's closeness. She couldn't remember her older sister being this affectionate before. Frances, who'd never married, never had children. How could she possibly unburden herself to her? This cautious, stoical woman, whom she felt she hardly knew. How could she understand the complex emotional mix that was Phoebe's world at the moment? Nothing in Frances's experience would have equipped her to respond empathically to Phoebe's situation. More than likely she would simply walk away,

shocked into silence by her younger sister's predicament. It wasn't as though Frances was malicious, only insensitive and inflexible. She hadn't even seemed to realise how ill Cynthia was. Frances lacked the life experience to be able to identify with the dilemmas of others. Frances's life had been problem-free and therefore the difficulties faced by others were beyond her comprehension. This was Phoebe's reasoning as she pulled away from her sister's embrace, choosing not to take her into her confidence. Better to let her believe, Cynthia was the cause of her anxiety.

Frances tried again. Something unsettled about Phoebe's demeanour had touched her and she wanted to be the older sister able to bring support of some kind. She began to search among her thoughts like a secretary searching for a particular file, under the heading of 'comfort', but the words were as elusive as a mislabelled file. 'Oh well!' She said, which sounded almost like a sigh of relief as she turned to walk away. 'Soon be time for lunch!' She spoke as if this might be the panacea to all problems. 'I'll be there in a minute.' Phoebe answered as she stood, continuing to rest her hand on the hidden life within; her thoughts far away on the other side of the world searching for Mason.

Frances felt unsettled; she realised she'd failed to connect with Phoebe and not for the first time, confirming her sense of inadequacy. It had taken her a few days before agreeing to come on this holiday. She'd been taken by surprise when Phoebe had rung suggesting it. However, Frances had long come to terms with her distant family relationships. Her siblings thought her cautious yet stoical; but in reality, she was simply someone nursing a deep hurt, who'd turned in upon herself as a form of protection. Her stoicism was really a form of resignation to a perspective which viewed life as both hard and lonely. Frances blamed Roger for this, not Cynthia, not herself, only Roger.

Henry was feeling unsettled too. Anna hadn't been in touch, not even to let him know she'd arrived safely. He'd tried phoning her several times, but her mobile always seemed to be switched off. This wasn't like her at all and Henry was worried.

The holiday wasn't turning out to be the relaxing break he'd hoped for. He'd hidden his concern when Phoebe had told him about the baby and he hoped she hadn't detected how shocked he'd really been to hear her news. Nevertheless, swamping any form of shock was his concern; how was she going to manage as a single parent? She hadn't mentioned the father and so he assumed he was absent. He didn't believe his younger sister, with her limited life experience, had any real understanding of what it would mean to cope alone. He'd also been rocked to realise the seriousness of Cynthia's condition and Frances's seeming lack of awareness. The tension between these two was tangible and he'd some insight as to the cause but as nobody had ever openly spoken about it, he didn't want to be the first and wondered what good it would do anyway, so long after the event. Roger had chosen Cynthia over Frances. Roger had married Cynthia and not Frances! He swore under his breath, as he thought of Roger's attitude towards his sisters, before reaching for his jacket and deciding to take himself off to the pub.

Cynthia was feeling bad. Her head ached and she felt nauseous but it was the exhaustion she found most difficult to cope with. Her lack of energy crippled her days and she grieved for the time wasted; she understood there was little time left to her and she felt frustrated she couldn't use it the way she would have liked to: her fatigue squandered her motivation dissipating her hours. She was also upset at losing her temper with Phoebe. 'Poor kid!' She'd muttered to herself, remembering the pain in her eyes, as she'd left the room. It was actually Roger who she was angry with; a truth she now realised, she'd been ignoring for many years, suppressing it, hoping it would go away, pretending, even to herself she'd forgiven him. Was there a way out of all this mess, she wondered? How was she to find her way forward, so late in the day?

On his way to the White Swan; Henry slowed as he passed the farm, remembering the night of the blaze and the following morning when he'd tried to speak with Jones. An unnatural stillness seemed to have settled over the farm, which Henry found disturbing, causing him to pull over onto the verge. He sat listening to the silence, noting the empty paddock. It was a sultry day and he opened the car windows hoping for a breath of breeze, but none came. He wiped the perspiration from his brow and wondered why he was there; in Wales with his sisters and now at the farm. This isn't where he wanted to be. Rather he wished he was at home with Anna and his boys. He regretted being there and wondered how the girls would take it if he was to leave tomorrow. Then, as if from nowhere, a clear shot sounded, causing a cacophony of crows to rise in an avian cloud from the nearby woods; their raucous ascent shredding the stillness. Suddenly, led more by instinct than reason, he threw open the car door and tore in the direction of the shot. The smell of burning still hung in the air and he noted the blackened beams of the barn and the remains of another outbuilding, which although still standing on two sides, stood as though branded by misfortune. He carried on running his breathing noisy and shallow now, but the sound of horses whinnying and hooves clattering on concrete urged him to run faster. He rounded a corner and stopped, stunned by what he saw. The two horses, each tethered by a short leash, were trying to rear in their makeshift stables, their eyes rolling in fear, whilst their hooves thundered deafeningly on the rough concrete, their bodies crashing against the sides of their makeshift stalls in their panic. Jones was holding a gun pointed in their direction, tears were streaming down his face, his sobs causing the rifle to shake in his hands; at his feet, a dog lay in a pool of blood. Deeper in the shadows Henry could just make out a noose hanging from the rafters, with a chair beneath. Forgetting any crisis counselling skills, he'd learnt over the years, he shouted: 'Stop! Don't do it! Nothing is that bad!' Jones swung round, pointing the barrel at Henry. 'What would you b****y well know about it! Just get off my property and mind your own b****y business!' Henry didn't move but he did begin to speak, more quietly now. 'You're right I don't know what you've suffered or what your feelings are in this moment, but I do know that killing your horses and then yourself is not the answer.' Jones stood staring at Henry, who wondered if the farmer had heard anything he'd said. The man seemed almost insane; what could have happened to have pushed him onto this fearful precipice? He continued. 'Look, give me the gun Jones and let's talk. Afterwards, if you still want to kill the horses and yourself included, I'll give it back to you and walk away.' Jones was still staring at him continuing to sob and shake at the same time. Henry regretted his words and inwardly rebuked himself. What an idiotic thing to have said, whatever made me say that? He felt afraid, inadequate and daunted. How would Jones react? Would either of them get out of this alive? The horses continued to stamp and clatter. Momentarily, Jones looked towards them and Henry took his chance rushing towards him, knocking him over. Henry grabbed the gun and threw it outside, where it landed in the hedgerow. Jones tried to stand, cursing and sobbing, only to fall again. Defeated, he lay face down on the floor, his hands moving like claws amongst the damp and dirty straw. Then he tried to stand but fell again to his knees and began crawling slowly, painfully, towards the dead dog. Henry could see he was trying to gather any source of energy still left within him and wanted to look away, unnerved by the pathos of the moment and overcome by something akin to, embarrassment, but found himself unable to do so. Rather he was mesmerized with fear and grief; it was as though he was unravelling inside racked by emotions, he hadn't known he possessed. Still, he couldn't draw his eyes away from the misery of the scene unfolding before him. Eventually, after what seemed like an interminable time, Jones reached the dead body and laid his head gently, face down, on the dog's back. His crying turned to deep, shuddering groans. 'What have I done? What have I done? What harm did you ever do me? Always at my side. Oh! My faithful old girl, what have I done?' Emotion welled in Henry as he watched; whether of grief or relief he didn't know, but he felt as though he'd just weathered a storm, if not on the scale of Jones's, at least close to it. All his own doubts and anxieties seemed to descend on him and rather like Jones, he felt as if he was unravelling from the inside out. For a long time neither man spoke or moved; both were locked in their individual worlds of pain and yet breathing the same air fresh off the Welsh hills. Henry managed to calm the horses, speaking softly and stroking them gently. He also cut down the menacing rope hiding it from sight. He felt drained as if he'd walked through a living nightmare, which he hoped would soon end.

Eventually, Jones became silent and Henry helped him to stand. 'Come on Jones, let's get out of here.' Jones allowed himself to be manoeuvred into Henry's car. His lion of a rage replaced by the docility of a lamb. 'I think we both need a drink!' This was all Henry could say as he turned on the ignition and drove off in the direction of the White Swan.

Cynthia was woken from her troubled sleep by the sound of footsteps pacing to and fro across the bare floorboards above; she knew it had to be Phoebe. Cynthia struggled out of bed and noticed it was only four in the morning; she knew she should really try to go back to sleep in order to have enough energy to face the day ahead, but her conscience troubled her and she wanted to make up for her outburst yesterday. So, pulling on her dressing gown she struggled towards a shabby armchair and sighed heavily as she almost collapsed into it. Then she texted Phoebe to come down and have a chat.

Phoebe hadn't been able to sleep. Her thoughts were heavy and indecisive; for the first time in her life the future appeared intimidating. Henry was wrong in thinking she had no concept of what would be involved in raising a child on her own. Phoebe was only too aware as one of her close friends had tried to do exactly this without the support of her family; the child had eventually been relinquished for adoption and she'd witnessed the emotional turmoil, which even now several years after the event, still relentlessly pursued Jasmine. How many times had she tried to comfort her, assuring her friend she'd done what was best for the child, as well as herself; but now Phoebe had doubts, very real doubts, which had begun to steal her sleep and torment her nights. More than this, was she doing the right thing in not letting Mason know about the baby? Surely it was his right as well as the baby's but would he be resentful, if he knew? Perhaps even coming to despise her as a result?

These had been her thoughts, just as Cynthia's text had summoned her attention but Phoebe wasn't keen to respond. Cynthia's cutting remarks had left their scars. She'd tried, for her mother's sake, over the years, to build family relationships, but now it was evident to her these efforts had been in vain. Her siblings were only interested in their own lives; they had all grown too far apart and no amount of honey, albeit spread ever so thickly, was going to bring them together again. In fact, Phoebe wondered if they had ever really been a close-knit family. Each of them seemed to carry wounds in one form or another. Perhaps, she was deceived by an ideology all of her own imagining. It was time, like the others, to start focusing just on her own life. After all, nobody else seemed interested in maintaining the family bond so why should she? With this in mind, she texted Cynthia saying she was going back to bed.

However, she hadn't reckoned on her sister's tenacity and was surprised, just as she was drifting off again, to hear her bedroom door open as Cynthia almost stumbled in: pale and short of breath. She jumped out of bed and grabbed her, just as she was about to fall. Putting her arm over her shoulders she helped Cynthia into bed, propping her up with pillows and, climbed in beside her. She felt nervous listening to her struggling to get her breath; her pallor had taken on a bluish tinge and she held her hand over her heart. Phoebe wondered if she should phone for an ambulance, as well as Roger, but as she reached for her phone, she felt Cynthia's hand on hers; 'My bag! Bring me my bag!' She gasped. Phoebe tore downstairs and returned within seconds. 'In the side pocket there are some pills, pass them please!' Phoebe fumbled about and with relief found the container; she went to the basin and filled a glass with water, which Cynthia began to sip slowly. Half an hour must have passed before she partially recovered and was able to speak. 'I had to talk to you Phoebe, I'm sorry for shouting at you earlier, you didn't deserve it; it's not you who I'm angry with.'

'Who are you angry with then?' But Cynthia couldn't reply, the effort of climbing the stairs had exhausted her and sleep had now reclaimed her. Phoebe pulled the covers up over her and went to sit by the window as the new day began to break over the distant horizon. However, the beauty of the moment was lost on her, for she was tired and wondering what the next few hours would bring.

The new day brought Roger! His arrival announced by a rumble of tyres below in the rough courtyard. Henry had been drinking his morning coffee on the veranda and he waved to him as he walked towards the house, but Roger didn't wave back. Instead, he strode in long strides, his jaw tense and his face set determinedly, like a man ready to face his nemesis.

Frances had been watching from the lounge window and gasped when she saw who it was. Forgetting her injuries, she mounted the steep stairs two at a time, like someone caught in a flash flood trying to reach higher ground. Slamming the bedroom door behind her, she leant against it trying to catch her breath.

She hadn't seen Roger for several years and had promised herself she wouldn't ever have to again. The memory of their last meeting was always indelibly present in her mind, a painful pleasure she seemed unable to relinquish. Now she listened for his footsteps on the stairs. She sat on the edge of her bed trembling, her heart beating erratically, wishing she was anywhere but here. She felt like a cornered wildcat without an escape and nowhere to hide. Suddenly her door was flung open and Roger stood on the threshold. Frances jumped up her face crimson yet unable to speak. Roger was shocked; he looked exhausted as well as embarrassed by his blunder. For seconds neither spoke, they both stood immobilised like a downloading video caught in mid-streaming. Then he spoke; 'I'm sorry, truly sorry for interrupting you!' Then he closed the door quietly behind his retreat as though silence was all that was needed to cover his misdemeanour. Frances heard him open the door to Cynthia's bedroom and her sister's angry exclamation as he entered, but the door had been quickly closed and she was unable to hear anymore. She was left alone confused and troubled with only her imagination and memories for company. Had his apology simply been offered to cover his intrusion today, she wondered. Alternatively, had he been referring to the greater interruption his intrusion had caused in her life, stretching over many years?

Against her will, Frances was remembering her last meeting with him. It was a little like reassembling the missing pieces of a jigsaw puzzle, which had been angrily swept off the table; the anger had been hers: the table her life.

Ironically their last meeting had also been in a bedroom, one almost as impersonal as the one she now sat in, with the exception, this time she'd been there long enough to unpack. She stared at her hairbrush laying on the scratched surface of the dressing table, where she'd discarded it earlier; she noticed the stray strands of grey hair trailing from it and remembered the last time in that cheap room beside the motorway when her hair had been thick, dark and wavy and she couldn't help remembering how Roger used to love running his fingers through it. He would bury his face in it and tell her she carried the fragrance of the meadows with her. Without realising what she was doing she picked up the hand mirror and examined her face, noticing the wrinkles radiating from the corners of her eyes; others stretched irregularly across her forehead and the deep lines etched downwards from the corner of her mouth resembling those of a ventriloquist's dummy.

On that remembered occasion her complexion had been smooth, without blemish. Frances had never been a beauty, but she'd once been an attractive woman, everybody had said so. She dressed with a certain flair and had been able to pay for the quality clothes which had defined her elegance. 'What happened?' she asked herself as she looked down at her shapeless, practical, blouse and leggings; but of course, she knew the answer. Roger had happened! After he'd left, the Frances of that era had almost imperceptibly vanished, before gradually transforming into this woman of today, who still trembled slightly as she coldly considered her reflection.

Henry had felt reassured when he saw Roger arrive; the sense of responsibility he'd felt for Cynthia, since discovering her secret, shifted from his shoulders. He'd felt Roger should have accompanied his wife here in the light of her condition and not left her to make such a taxing journey both emotionally and physically on her own. Henry had guessed his sister's reason for doing so; nevertheless, he felt it was Roger's place to intervene, rather than his own.

Thankfully, he'd continued sipping his coffee, finding a new freedom to reflect on other matters. He'd enough problems of his own what with Anna's unusual behaviour and his own concerns for his sons. Added to these were his thoughts about Jones. He wondered if he should tell somebody about the farmer's state of mind, a GP perhaps, but felt unsure this was the answer and what the repercussions might be if he did.

Their time at the pub had not gone as well as he'd hoped. They'd driven in silence the air thick with their own muffled thoughts. Jones had sat slumped in his seat, head down, sighing deeply on occasions as his breath parted the air in a gentle wheeze. Aware of the farmer's weakened state of mind, Henry felt the risk of the unspoken words which hung over them both, like the sword of Damocles waiting to fall. Words and meanings appeared to be a gamble and he wasn't willing to dice with death after what had just happened. He felt shaken and the responsibility of what he had witnessed weighed heavily upon him.

They must have looked a strange pair as they entered the White Swan. The landlord had called out to him with a cheery wave: 'Can't keep away, can you Henry?' And then noticing Jones following behind continued his banter. 'What's your poison today Jones?' Henry had winced, while the friendly barman continued: 'The first tipple is on the house for you both, to welcome our new guest and to cheer up our old friend.' He'd stared at Jones who hadn't appeared to hear any of this but rather had dumped himself onto a chair as if he'd been a sack of potatoes. 'Fire got to you has it, Jones? Well, you settle there and I'll bring you something to put some fire in your belly!' Henry winced inwardly again, the barman certainly wouldn't win any medals for tact and diplomacy, but no doubt his heart was well-intentioned as he set down two glasses on the table and waved away Henry's offer of payment. 'This one is on the house. We look after our customers here, don't we Jones?' But Jones seemed to be lost in the labyrinth of his turmoil and didn't reply. The barman had knowingly patted Henry's arm and nodded, as if to communicate his understanding of the situation, and as Henry looked around several others had raised their glasses in his direction, to let him know they too knew Jones and understood his silence.

So, the two men drank without any conversation of their own; whilst the soft lilting, lull of the Welsh language whirled gently around them acting as an effective sedative, offering to soothe their frayed nerves.

Henry had driven Jones home. The farmer only spoke once as they arrived back at the farm. 'Come in with me, will you?' Henry had been looking forward to his bed but felt he could only oblige this broken man. Surely, it was little enough to see him inside, perhaps to even stay a few minutes. But he'd forgotten about the dog still lying on the stable floor. However, Jones hadn't; he began to speak, but more to himself than Henry, his tone low and his voice halting. 'Bonnie was always here see. Throughout Bronwyn's illness, even when Tom left after his Mam's death, Bonnie was still here. She was gentle, faithful and hardworking.' Henry wasn't sure if Jones meant his wife or his dog, but he listened knowing it was good for Jones to be speaking at last. He continued and Henry listened to a list of tragedies, which began with his wife's battle with cancer, the failure of his dairy herd, as the price of milk fell, his son leaving home and stating he hated farming and everything to do with it and culminating in the night of the fire. Jones had lived through the horrors of the Foot and Mouth outbreak having to slaughter his own cattle and sheep; also, the failure of cereal crops due to the freak weather conditions of the last few years had cost him lost labour and money. He was a man on the verge of bankruptcy both emotionally as well as financially. Even before the fire and Henry's timely arrival; Jones had thought it a kindness to kill his dog and then his horses, before killing himself. He broke off in mid-sentence as if he'd just remembered something dark at the edge of his mind. 'Bonnie! I must bury my lovely girl, my faithful friend!' He exclaimed.

'You can wait until the morning, surely Jones! You've had an exhausting day. It will be easier for you in the light of day.' But Jones wasn't listening; he was already walking out into the darkness again and Henry could only follow. The last thing he saw and heard before leaving, was Jones bent in the light of a hurricane lamp digging and the ring of the spade as it sliced through the earth and hit a stone.

Chapter 4

Now as he sat on the veranda, he knew he had to go back to the farm. He tried to tell himself this was supposed to be a holiday, time spent with his sisters. It would perhaps be better to go back to the White Swan and let the locals know Jones's current mood. After all, they knew and understood him better than he did, but he was unable to shake off the conviction, he should return and quickly. As he stood, he was surprised to see Frances coming towards him. She looked flustered. 'Henry, are you going out?' He nodded. 'Can I come with you?' He wasn't sure if this was the right thing to do, but at least it was an opportunity to spend some time with her and he knew he welcomed her company. Besides, she'd looked at him pleadingly, perhaps it would be good for her to get some fresh air as she hadn't left the house since she'd arrived. However, more than this, he wasn't looking forward to meeting Jones alone and couldn't be sure what he might find on arrival. He would have to explain to her in the car, the events of yesterday. Frances was a stoic and would cope, of this at least he felt certain.

Cynthia was more shocked than Frances when Roger burst into her room. Unlike Frances, she'd not been aware of his arrival and more than this she'd believed Roger would have respected her wishes to do this last task alone. His presence was unwelcome and would only complicate matters, especially where Frances was concerned. Cynthia knew her time was running out and she desperately needed to repair the past with her siblings, if this was at all possible, whilst she still had the strength and courage she needed. So far, she hadn't managed very well, worn down by pain and weakness. Now with Roger present her attempt at a reconciliation was further limited. It wasn't that she didn't understand his distress created by her condition. However, he failed to understand this was her time and she needed to use it wisely. Roger's presence was far from helpful and she felt her anger rise at his presumption and unwanted interference. He moved forward to embrace her but she pushed him away. She tried to control her voice. 'Roger, please leave! I understand why you've come but please believe me when I say I must do this alone; even if it is the last thing I do. If you really love me, then please try and understand, but even if you can't, please respect this is not only what I want, but what I need to do!'

'Darling!' Roger tried to embrace her again but she moved away, uncertain of her resilience if she relented. Cynthia would have loved the comfort of his arms but this wasn't just about them anymore; for too long they'd lived within the comfortable confines of their family life. But now, Cynthia's own suffering had raised her consciousness of a wider suffering beyond the boundaries of her own experience; developing a newfound empathy for others, as well as the awareness she had also been the cause of pain to many. A pain she hoped she would be able to relieve, if not wipe out, before her death. She wanted to be able to die with a clear conscience. This had been the only reason for her coming on this holiday, to try and erase her regrets and if this was to be denied her, then she needed the comfort of at least knowing she'd tried. However, it hadn't gone well so far and now with Roger there, she knew she would be bound to fail in her last endeavour. 'Please Roger, go home! Do this one last thing for me, won't you?' Roger sighed, again running his hands through his hair. 'This is madness, Cynthia. I don't pretend to understand. Don't I mean anything to you?' Cynthia felt her resolve begin to weaken.

'Idiot! You mean everything to me, but others matter too and I must have something left for them and this time might be all that I have to offer.'

'But what about me? Don't my feelings matter?'

'Of course, they do, and I have given myself faithfully to you for all these years. My being here today doesn't change any of that.' Roger had felt his teeth clench at the word 'faithfully'. He wondered if it had been a reproach and just for a moment, he hung his head. His unfaithfulness was the reason Cynthia was here and he was being sent away. But he also understood Cynthia was here because of her own unfaithfulness too, which she was also trying to put right. 'Alright, I'll go, but promise me you'll call me if you need me.'

'I already have!' Cynthia said, her voice heavy with weariness. Involuntarily, she moved towards him and soon he was holding her close. Her head nestled under his chin. Slowly he stroked her hair, gently kissing the top of her head.

In the car, Henry explained to Frances the events of the previous day. She listened in silence, but her face expressed shock and apprehension.

'I saw the fire on my way here.' She said. 'I saw the lightning strike, heard the sirens, but I was too far away to see what had been hit. Poor man, he must be devastated!'

'He is and I need your help, Fran.' She turned to look at him surprised by the plea in his tone as well as the abbreviation of her name, which he hadn't used since they were children. 'You don't think I'll be in the way then?'

'No! You're just what we both need.' Frances wasn't sure he was right; nevertheless, the need to be needed was strong within her and because of this, she overcame her reluctance to get involved. She silently assured herself she would say and do nothing other than quietly support her brother.

As they drew into the farmyard, Frances noticed the greys. 'They're beautiful!' She exclaimed, more to herself than Henry. He nodded, remembering if he hadn't arrived on the scene when he did yesterday, they would both have been shot and now laying as still as poor Bonnie: rather than prancing gracefully around the paddock, their tails and heads held high, as they whinnied into the breeze.

Frances had always loved horses and, in her earlier years, enjoyed riding. However, she'd been far from proficient; nevertheless, those gentle canters through the countryside had always lifted her spirit after the weekly slog in a dim and stuffy office. For her, riding had been a kind of therapy setting her up for the week ahead. The muffled thudding of hooves on damp turf, as the sweet keenness of the breeze tousled her hair, always energised both her heart and soul; as if with each breath fresh energy and strength were beating a new pathway of hope through the lethargy of her life.

'I'll stay here and watch the horses.' She said as Henry pulled up beside the burnt-out barn.

'Perhaps that would be best.' He said, still wondering what he might find inside. He knocked, almost timidly, at the weather-beaten front door and waited. Nobody answered. So, after a minute he tried the door; it wasn't locked. Hoping this was a good sign he called. 'Hello Jones, it's only me, Henry!' I sound like an old friend he thought to himself, but this man is a stranger, so what the hell am I doing here? I'm supposed to be holidaying with my sisters, not playing the Good Samaritan!

Jones was seated at the kitchen table an empty cup and plate of crumbs in front of him. He was wearing the same clothes as yesterday, hanging crumpled and loose upon him. Henry realised he must have slept in them, but it looked as though he'd at least taken the time to shave, which was another good sign. Jones still hadn't spoken as Henry eased himself on to a rickety chair beside him. They sat in silence for a while and Henry wondered if Jones was aware of his presence; a few seconds later it was clear he was: for unexpectedly he began to speak, as if to the air. 'I've decided to sell up.' Henry wasn't sure what to say so remained silent. However, Jones seemed to have found his tongue and he continued as if the dam of grief within him had at last broken down, now to pour out in a garbled torrent of decision making. 'I have no insurance to claim on, no liquid assets and no taste for weathering more disasters. I just want to cut my losses and move on.' Henry wondered who would be willing to invest in such a catalogue of catastrophes, but wisely didn't verbalise his reservations. No doubt the land itself still held value, but for what he couldn't be sure. 'Do you think it would be good to give yourself more time to think this through?' His voice was tentative and sounded unconvincing. With a brief, derisory laugh Jones answered. 'No, I've had plenty of time to think, more than I've wanted or needed.' The whinnying of the greys caught their attention and they both looked towards the window offering a view of the paddock. Frances was leaning on the fence and both horses were there nuzzling her, hungry and looking to be fed. 'Is that your wife?' Jones asked, turning towards Henry for the first time. 'No, my sister, we're here on holiday staying up at the old farmhouse.' 'She seems to like the greys.' Jones said. 'Yes, she used to ride a bit when she was younger, but could never afford to keep any horses of her own.' 'Tell her she can ride them anytime; I don't ride you see; it was Bronwyn who used to do that.' 'Bronwyn?' Henry queried. 'My wife! My dear wife!' Jones's voice trembled as he spoke. 'Thank you, I'll let her know.' Henry stood up; he was thinking of Anna. He longed to walk out into the sunshine and leave this room of shadows behind. He'd done what anyone would have, but now he just wanted to be free of any further responsibility for this man, which had begun with his instinctive sense of care, but which nevertheless he still reluctantly carried. Jones seemed in a better frame of mind than yesterday and Henry didn't know what else he could do. He touched Jones on the shoulder and said goodbye starting to walk towards the door where he suddenly turned as he heard the scraping of a chair on the flagstones. To his surprise, Jones was walking towards him his hand outstretched. He took Henry's hand in his and looking directly into his face said. 'How can I ever thank you? I owe you my life!' Henry was touched but in an uncomfortable way. He felt he'd really done so little and even that he'd done reluctantly, with a sense of compulsion as though not to betray his own integrity, his sense of responsibility and basic human compassion. 'Anyone would have done the same, it was nothing.' The clasp of Jones's grip tightened.

'Friend, it was everything!' As he spoke his eyes moistened and Henry felt embarrassed. He withdrew his hand and again reached out to touch Jones's shoulder. He wanted to shake this man off, to free himself and walk away out into the new day clothed in all its finery. Therefore, he was surprised to hear himself say. 'Come up to the farmhouse and join us for dinner tonight; we eat at about seven.' Jones didn't answer, but Henry thought he detected an almost imperceptible nod of assent. He closed the door behind him and stood for a few seconds breathing in the fresh air. It was good to be alive; so good to be able to walk away. Soon he and Frances were in the car, both unaware of Jones standing watching them through the window. The broken dam of his heart now flowing freely.

On the way back to the farm both brother and sister sat quietly occupied with their thoughts. Roger's arrival had not only shaken Frances but had carried her back into the past.

Chapter 5

When spending time with the horses Frances had been remembering her youth and the first time, she'd brought Roger home to meet the family. It had been after an afternoon of horse riding, in the countryside. They'd been dating for six months and both had begun to realise the seriousness of their feelings for one another. Roger suggested she take him home to meet the family, whilst she would have preferred to wait another few months; nevertheless, she'd agreed: a decision she'd lived to regret.

It was painful to remember that particular evening; at first, there had only been her parents and a very young Phoebe seated around the dinner table. Her mother had taken extra care in laying out her best cutlery and cutting a posy of white and pink roses to grace the table. However, her father had worn a sour, defensive, expression and said very little. Whilst her mother, trying to compensate for her husband's taciturn welcome, spoke hurriedly in stilted sentences which framed many questions with a smattering of small talk. Phoebe, too young to have grown any social skills, had dropped her cutlery on the floor and after bending to pick it up had managed to also knock over her drink, which spread in a flowing pool of creamy milk, soaking the table cloth. They'd all quickly stood, interrupting their dinner, while her mother mopped up and changed the tablecloth. Frances remembered scowling at Phoebe, who'd immediately burst into tears and run upstairs.

However, worse was to come. Cynthia arrived home from her date; she'd burst into the room twirling and humming her face flushed from the warm night air. Even now Frances was able to recall how beautiful she looked, her dark, wavy hair shining under the lamp as she twirled about the room. Suddenly, she'd become aware of Roger's presence and stopped; blushing and apologising. He'd simply raised his hands and beamed at her, apparently lost for words. Frances had looked at him and crumbled inside as she recognised the look of startled admiration in his eyes. From that moment she knew he was lost to her forever. The evening had changed them all. As they drew up at the farmhouse Henry let out a deep sigh. 'I've invited Jones to eat with us tonight.' His eyes were on Frances, wondering how she'd react.

'What! Why ever did you do that? Aren't there enough tensions in the house already?' Henry shrugged.

'I've asked myself the same question and I don't know!'

'Do you think he'll come?'

'I don't know; I think he gave a nod.'

'Whatever are we going to talk about? You said the man was deranged!'

'I don't think I said deranged; he has just had a lot to cope with.'

'But it has affected his mind; he's disturbed in some way?'

'Well it would, wouldn't it? When bad things happen to us it is disturbing!'

'Oh, Henry why do you always feel you have to rescue everyone!'

Frances was annoyed, she was wondering if Roger was still there and wasn't looking forward to trying to avoid him for the rest of the day. Having to cope with Cynthia was more than enough. Henry was also irritated, both with himself and Frances's reaction. This definitely wasn't the holiday he'd imagined and certainly not the one he most needed! He slammed the car door.

Phoebe was also beginning to wish she'd never suggested this family getaway, which seemed to be turning into yet another family head-on collision. She'd heard Roger's arrival and thought it a good thing, following last night's incident; until she heard the ensuing clash of wills behind closed doors: filtering through the floorboards up into her bedroom. Later she'd seen Roger leave and wondered at the wisdom of his decision. She felt uncomfortable and it wasn't just because she was concerned for Cynthia.

Her thoughts had recently been much with Jasmine. Her own pregnancy had presented the facts to her in a new light. Would she be able to give *her* baby up for adoption? Was she being fair to the child who would have no say in a matter, which would set the course of its destiny? Also, was she being fair to Mason? Didn't he have a right to know he'd fathered a child? The decisions she'd to make seemed momentous, impinging on both the future and fortunes of others. It was difficult enough living one's own life, how then could she make such huge decisions on behalf of two others? How could she give away her own flesh and blood? More than this, who was she to give away the flesh and blood of her ex, without his knowledge? The enormity and weight of the life she was carrying lay heavy not only in her womb but also on her mind.

Not one of his sisters was happy about the possibility of Jones coming to dinner that evening. Cynthia announced she would eat in her room and Phoebe said she'd join her. Cynthia seemed about to protest, but then apparently changed her mind. 'That's fine with me; give us a chance to catch up!'

Phoebe looked surprised and Frances raised her eyebrows. Momentarily, she thought about joining her sisters, but seeing the look of dismay on Henry's face she decided to support him. She understood he'd invited Jones from a sense of compassion and not from any real choice of his own. She'd seen how nervous he'd been on their approach to the farm and again the need to be needed rose within her. 'Looks like it will just be the two of us and Jones then.' She said, forcing a smile in Henry's direction. She saw the relief break on his face and was glad. Nevertheless, she wasn't looking forward to the prospect of dinner in Jones's company and called over her shoulder to Henry. 'You're going to have to do the cooking; I'm off for a walk.'

'I'll come with you!' Called Phoebe, not waiting for an answer as she headed off to find her walking boots. Frances hadn't expected this and felt resentful. She wanted some time to herself following the shock of seeing Roger that morning; time alone to think, to remember, to process these newfound emotions which were unsettling her. However, the aim of this holiday had been for them all to spend some time together and she hadn't the heart to say no to Phoebe, who she thought was looking a bit peaky and somewhat strained; no doubt a walk in the fresh air would do them both good. At least she hoped it would. Nevertheless, whatever Frances had been expecting it wasn't the bombshell Phoebe was about to drop!

They had decided to walk to the village as Frances thought there would be less chance of turning her ankle again in the lanes. Her foot was healing, but still tender when walking.

They walked slowly in silence for a while, both conscious of the gulf separating them, aware of their lost intimacy, which the long intervening years had created.

At first, it was enough to relax into the bared beauty and slow bustle of the countryside. The hedgerows were alive with the rustlings of small birds; the soothing rhythms of their soft chirping seemed to steady their pace, filling the gap of their lost years, drawing them closer. The gentle bleating of the sheep, rising from the soft contours of the green hills, also lulled them both into a sense of well-being; as if the honeysuckle, fragrant and bright, threading the lanes with its delicate offerings of tranquillity, entwined the sisters in the peace of the moment: breaking down the barriers which the wasted years of minimal contact had built.

Frances was the first to speak. 'This is nice!' Phoebe smiled remembering her English teacher who had always discouraged them from the use of such an insipid adjective. Nevertheless, she understood Frances's meaning exactly. 'Yes, it is very nice!' Her answer was followed by a deep sigh as if she was discharging the heavyweight of indecision, which had built within her over the last few days.

They began to talk, sharing their mutual memories of childhood. 'We weren't the perfect family, were we?' It was Frances who spoke and Phoebe was quick to answer.

'No family is perfect Fran.' Again, the use of her name expressed in the affectionate terms of childhood softened her heart. 'We're all flawed Fran, surely you realise that by now?'

Frances hesitated before replying noticing Phoebe's sideways glance in her direction. 'I do, but I think my expectations of others are always too high and I can't help hoping for more than people are able to give.' Phoebe was surprised at her frankness and for a few moments wasn't sure how to answer. 'I guess because none of us are perfect our expectations are imperfect too. On the other hand, I can see, it is good to expect the best of others, but we all have to accept each other's limitations as well.'

Frances wrinkled her nose: 'That sounds a bit too precious for me!'

'Is it Fran? Or might it just be offering others a bit of slack, in the same way, we might need them to do the same for us on occasions?'

'Being realistic you mean?'

Phoebe thought for a moment. 'Yeah, sort of, but also understanding we're not all in the same place in terms of life experience or even opportunity.'

'So, let me see. You think we should go through life trying to understand those who put us down, cheat on us and kick us in the teeth?' Frances's voice had risen and so had her colour. Her eyes were bright and she was glaring at Phoebe, although in her mind's eye she was seeing Roger as she had that morning: polite and cold. Phoebe looked surprised. 'Whoa! Steady on Fran, what's your problem?'
Frances felt foolish; she hadn't meant to direct her anger at Phoebe. Conversely, she wanted to get to know her younger sibling and renew the family bond, which had once united them. 'I'm sorry! You're not the one I'm angry with.'
'Do you want to talk about it?'
'No! But thanks all the same.' Frances looked at Phoebe whose eyes were questioning.
'Look I'm sorry. I guess you cut me some slack then.' Phoebe shrugged. 'It's partly about accepting folk where they are and not where we would like them to be.'
'Quite the philosopher, aren't you little sister? Just wait until you've lived as long as me. People can't be relied upon in the way you seem to think.'
'Perhaps that's my point.' Said Phoebe, who was beginning to feel awkward. She couldn't remember having seen her sister this angry before and it mystified her how anyone could be so angry in such a peaceful and beautiful setting. 'I guess someone must have really hurt you in the past?' This wasn't the response Frances had expected. For some reason, she hadn't reckoned on her sister being so discerning. She felt unnerved and ashamed of her outburst. Emotional, but lost for words, she didn't know how to answer, so instead, she linked arms with Phoebe hoping this gesture would speak louder than words, as they continued walking in silence.

Neither spoke, but nevertheless, began to walk in step with a newfound intimacy. Both sisters were unsure what had happened, but somehow, they'd begun to find one another again and each was wondering where this greater sense of belonging would lead them?

Phoebe's first impression of the village was grey; the walls bordering the neat gardens were built of grey stone. The houses square and solid were built of the same, their slate rooves also grey, as were the pavements on which the two sisters walked. A dismal contrast to the natural beauty of the vibrant countryside, but nonetheless possessing a charm all of its own.

Suddenly one of the grey doors flew open and a little boy ran screaming into the front garden; a young woman ran out carrying a crying baby. 'Owen, you come back here now; do you hear!' Her hair was long and dark, held off her face with an Alice band, which looked as if it should have been worn by a little girl rather than a nursing mother. Her blouse was partly unbuttoned and had slipped off her right shoulder, exposing an expanse of white flesh. She'd obviously been breastfeeding before being interrupted by her older offspring. The young child tugged at the iron gate, and when it refused to open flung himself onto the ground in a paroxysm of tears, kicking and rolling on the gravel pathway crying even louder as the gravel pressed into his chubby, bare legs. His mother bent down and tried to pull him up with her free hand, but he wriggled, pulling away. She noticed Frances and Phoebe passing and shrugged her shoulders. 'Terrible twos, what can you do?' She spoke by way of an apology and tried again to lift the child unsuccessfully as her blouse slipped even further down exposing her bra, wet with milk. She hurriedly tried to cover herself, but again unsuccessfully. Red with embarrassment she tried to coax her little son to his feet, but he yelled all the louder, bringing the neighbours out as each grey door slowly opened. His yells causing them to wonder what all the commotion was about. 'It's about time you learnt to look after your kids properly Dinah!' Called one particularly cross looking woman dressed in dark colours. 'You know I do the best I can Blodwyn, but it isn't easy with my man away most of the time.'

'Put away, more like!' Blodwyn retorted her broad arms folded across her bosom, as she looked to her neighbours for support. She was rewarded by a thin ripple of laughter. Other neighbours were tutt-tutting and speaking in low tones to one another, but no one offered to lend the harassed Dinah a hand. All except Phoebe, who had noticed the mother's look of combined exasperation and humiliation; without thinking she opened the gate, gently lifting the baby out of its mother's grasp allowing her to pick up her still wailing infant and carry him indoors. Phoebe followed, the baby now quiet in her arms, looking into her face, its blue eyes wide with astonishment. The fragility of this tiny form sent a current, close to maternal longing through Phoebe causing her to shiver. She'd acted purely on instinct and not thought about Frances left standing alone with the group of sniggering neighbours. Now, as she surveyed the gloomy interior and the threadbare carpet, she wondered what had possessed her. The little boy was quiet now sitting on a ragged sofa and sucking his thumb. Phoebe handed the baby back to its mother, who immediately pressed the infant to her breast where it was soon sucking noisily. 'Thanks miss, much appreciated!' Phoebe nodded and made her way out, feeling the loss of the child in her arms. She touched her bump as if to reassure herself there would soon be another to fill them, not realising, that at the same time she was making the decision, which earlier she'd found so difficult to do.

Frances waited impatiently for her; the neighbours had once again disappeared behind their grey doors and so she was alone when Phoebe emerged, as one still caught within a web of dreams. 'Whatever possessed you to interfere?' She demanded.

'I just wanted to help; that's all!'

'You should have kept walking; we don't belong here; it's not our business!' Phoebe was still feeling the emptiness of her arms, devoid of the trembling so dependent little life. 'If there's a need and we can help then I believe it *is* our business. At the end of the day, I did so little!'

'So how would she have managed, if we hadn't been there?' Phoebe heard the edge in her sister's voice. 'But, *we were there* Fran. That's the point! Let's not make an issue of it, please.' Suddenly, Phoebe felt tired, weary even, of having to justify her decisions. Was this to be her future existence she wondered; not only seeking to justify her decisions, but also the very existence of her child? Frances sensed her irritation, realising it was best not to take the matter any further. Instead, she said: 'Come on let's find somewhere to sit down and have a drink, my ankle is killing me!'

They were seated outside the Admiral's Arms. Yet another grey building, but one from which, in every window box, there streamed a descent of early, summer blooms. Both had a full glass and a packet of crisps. 'I'm glad I never had children.' Said Frances, bending for the third time in as many minutes to rub her swelling ankle. 'Do you think it would have been different if you'd married?' Frances looked vague for a moment, she was thinking of Roger and Cynthia and their two girls, who she hardly knew. 'I don't know; it's hypothetical. How can you know what you haven't lived through? I've never felt any desire for children; I suppose I'm not the maternal type. Although, I imagine in a marriage you have to agree, probably before marriage, on something so life-changing!' Here she unconsciously sighed and wondered briefly if she would have felt the same way had she and Roger married. The sigh was not lost on Phoebe, who interpreted it as a silent regret for what now could never be. 'How about you, do you want children eventually?'

Phoebe raised her glass and drank before answering. Following her earlier decision, she'd deliberately steered the conversation in this direction and was now regretting it. 'Actually, the decision has been taken out of my hands.'

Frances gave her a questioning look. 'Whatever do you mean?'

'I mean I'm going to have a baby.' Frances frowned; 'I suppose you mean you want children in the future?' Phoebe bit her lip and again drank deeply, the icy flavours of the juice, seemed to help her speak. 'I mean in approximately six months. I'm pregnant; you see.' Phoebe couldn't look her sister in the face, but rather looked down at her emerging bump as if cradling the foetus with her eyes. 'You idiot!' At that, she did look up and saw the fury in her sister's eyes. 'You little fool! Whatever were you thinking?' This wasn't the response she'd expected. Now it was her turn to feel angry, but it was a defensive anger, the anger of a mother rising to the defence of her unborn child. 'You're judging me Fran and you have no right!'

'I'm your sister!'

'So, you feel that gives you the right to tell me how to live my life?'

'Well, it seems I'm a bit late for that!'

'Exactly! Where have you been for the last ten years? Too busy to visit? Too busy to phone or send a text?'

Phoebe was angry. Frances was fuming and stood up quickly as if to leave. However, the impact on her ankle was too much and she let out a cry, sitting down again quickly. Phoebe was at her side. 'I'll get some ice.' She said, but before she could move a battered jeep braked suddenly and did a quick reverse. A man, probably in his mid-fifties, got out. His jacket was frayed at the collar and his boots caked with mud. He looked in need of a shave and ran a calloused hand over his chin as he approached them. He hesitated before speaking, taking a moment, as he scrutinised Frances's face. The sisters looked at one another their expressions slightly amused: but also questioning. 'You're Henry's sister, I saw you at my farm today.' So, this was Jones! Again, they exchanged glances. Phoebe was the first to speak. 'I'm Henry's younger sister Phoebe, and this is Frances. Henry has mentioned you.' She held out her hand, but he seemed to have forgotten this simple gesture of civility. Embarrassed, Phoebe quickly withdrew it wondering what he wanted. The tension between the sisters had evaporated with the stranger's arrival, but both were at a loss to know how to continue. Surprisingly, it was Jones who spoke first, as he pointed to Frances's ankle. 'I saw you had some problems and wondered if you needed a lift back to the farmhouse?' Again, the sisters exchanged looks; both were thinking of the erratic driving display they'd just witnessed, as well as wondering at his state of mind. However, it was obvious Frances wasn't going to be able to walk back. Phoebe answered. 'That would be great thanks!' Frances wasn't happy with this, but she was a pragmatist and the pain in her ankle was increasing. It would have been churlish to refuse.

Within fifteen minutes they were back at the farmhouse. They had driven in silence, with nobody feeling the need to talk, but all feeling the awkwardness of the situation, which only increased as Jones insisted on lifting Frances out of the jeep. 'Won't do your ankle any good if you jump down.' His tone had been as flat as his statement, but the gentleness of his touch communicated a kindness beyond words. Frances flushed as he set her down. She held out her hand as she thanked him, but again the gesture seemed alien to him. 'Well, I'll be off now!' Was all he said, climbing into the jeep and leaving in the same erratic way in which he'd pulled up outside the pub. 'Here, lean on me.' Phoebe said, as together they hobbled towards the house.

'Did he say if he was coming to dinner or not?' asked Henry.

'He seemed in a hurry.' Said Phoebe.

'Oh well, we'll just have to wait and see.'

Henry had spent most of the afternoon cooking his version of a cottage pie, made with prime minced steak and laced with red wine. It was as though he hoped to put new strength into Jones by adding a touch of luxury to the ordinary. This was the kind of man he was, but perhaps his hopes were a little too rich even though well flavoured!

Phoebe wished she could have been at the table when Jones arrived. But the pallor of Cynthia's drawn face kept her to her word. She'd heard a car pull into the courtyard below when seated in Cynthia's room; both held a tray on their laps. The food looked delicious and Phoebe was famished, but Cynthia looked at her plate as if to eat was the greatest challenge life had posed her. She toyed with her food, pushing it to and fro with her fork, like an infant trying to find the picture on the bottom of the plate.

However, Phoebe emptied her plate with relish; while Cynthia set hers aside almost untouched. Phoebe understood why. So, she drew her chair closer to Cynthia's taking hold of her cold hands. 'Come on Sis, spill the beans!' She spoke gently, yet nervously. She was the younger speaking to comfort the older and this was new to her.

Cynthia squeezed her hand. 'You're pregnant, aren't you?' Phoebe hadn't expected this and nodded. 'How did you know? Did Henry tell you?' Cynthia gave a weak smile.

'I've had two of my own; I could read the signs; you'll be needing bigger clothes soon your bump is beginning to show.'

'I suppose I just haven't thought about new clothes yet.'

'Are you and the father still together? Assuming you haven't been artificially inseminated, that is?' For a moment Phoebe felt assaulted by her sister's candour and blushed.

'No, we're not!'

'Does he know about the baby?'

'No! He doesn't.' Cynthia frowned.

'Don't you think he has a right to know after all the baby is as much his as yours?

'It's difficult.'

'How so?'

'We parted before I knew about the baby. He's gone back to New Zealand to help run his father's farm.'

'That's hard for you. Are you going to contact him?'

Here Phoebe faltered. This was exactly what she wanted to do, but wasn't sure if it was the right thing.

'I haven't made up my mind yet. I need more time to think. I'm still trying to come to terms with the situation myself!' Cynthia nodded.

'I understand; I'm still trying to come to terms with my imminent death, which nobody wants to talk about.' Phoebe's hand unconsciously touched her bump; she realised the incongruity of the situation, caught somewhere between the beginning and end of life. She wasn't sure how to answer or even if an answer was needed. 'I don't know how to talk about death, but I can listen.'

Cynthia didn't answer, as silence hung between them: filled with their unspoken thoughts.

Then Phoebe spoke encouragingly.

'I know it must be difficult for you, but I'm here.' Cynthia sighed; she really wanted answers to questions she knew Phoebe couldn't answer. Nevertheless, she began to speak. 'We all know we're going to die, but we're all too busy living to recognise our own mortality. It approaches by stealth, at first completely unnoticed; until it is suddenly there, threatening our existence.' Phoebe noticed the white-knuckled clench of her sister's hands; it was as if she was trying to hold on to life, with all her remaining strength. She didn't know what to say, but it didn't seem to matter, as Cynthia continued. 'You never think it is going to happen to you; death I mean and all its wretched causes!' Here she looked directly at Phoebe; 'I thought I had years left to live; there is still so much I want to do! I always thought I would grow old with Roger and live to see my grandchildren!' Her eyes filled with tears, but she didn't cry. 'We were going to travel, once the girls were established.' Here she smiled as if remembering the plans they'd made. 'We even thought of buying one of those motorhomes.' The smile faded as her eyes filled with sadness. 'I've had two years of treatment, which I've been grateful for, but there is nothing more they can do. I have, if I'm lucky, three months to live and yet so much to do before I can let go!'

Phoebe swallowed hard as she struggled to control her own emotions. Although she'd realised her sister's time was limited; it was still a shock to hear that time defined in Cynthia's anguished tones. She sought to find the right words, but they evaded her. In the pause of the moment, she felt the inner flutter of her child moving. She moved to Cynthia's side, placing her sister's hand over her womb. Cynthia gave a little gasp as she felt the weak movements, causing her to smile. She would probably never see this baby, but despite this it had brought her joy! 'Life goes on!' Her voice seemed stronger and Phoebe noticed. It was as if hope had entered the room, filling it with life instead of death. Both sisters sat watching the gentle, almost imperceptible movements of Phoebe's bump, laughing with each tiny quiver. The unborn child had managed to bring a sense of peace to both women, providing them with the timely gift of reconciliation.

However, downstairs Henry and Frances were trying to relieve the awkward silence of their meal, with comments designed to start a conversation, which always seemed to die on their lips after the first sentence. Jones was not an easy guest!

Frances was pleased to see Jones had tried to spruce himself up a little, for the meal. His shoes were mud-free and he wore a clean, opened-neck shirt. He'd shaved and washed his hair, which was brushed back revealing a peppering of grey. They were halfway through the main course when Henry thanked him for giving the sisters a lift home. Jones shrugged; 'I was on my way to the estate agents and recognised your sister in passing. She seemed to be in pain.' He resumed eating and it was obvious he was enjoying his meal. 'You're definitely going to sell the farm then?' Jones finished the last mouthful, wiping his mouth with a paper serviette, before speaking. 'Yes, I don't have any other options. The land alone will provide me with a reasonable amount to live on and, if I need to, from time to time I can perhaps get some farm work. I should have done this years ago and then things perhaps, wouldn't have turned out as badly as they have. I know when I'm beaten, don't I?' There was a note of resignation in his voice which Frances heard, causing her to speak despite her resolution just to support Henry. 'Don't you think you're giving up too easily? Many farmers are having to diversify and turn their business around by thinking creatively. There are always other options!' Jones was silent for a moment or two and then noisily scraped his chair back as he stood, throwing his serviette carelessly onto the table. 'I have to go! Thanks for the meal.' He spoke only to Henry, who tried to detain him. 'There's still dessert to come.' However, Jones was already at the door.

'No thanks!' Again, his focus was only on Henry and the next moment he was gone. Henry rarely became angry, but he'd worked hard to help Jones and in just a few words, Frances had undone all his hard work. 'Well, that went down well, didn't it?' He said, noisily gathering up the dirty dishes and walking out to the kitchen.

Frances followed him; 'I was only trying to help.'

'Don't you think it would have been better to have said nothing?' After all, neither you nor I know what he's had to cope with.'

'Perhaps, but I didn't expect him to get up and leave! That was rude!'

'He is grieving, remember.' Together they cleared the table in silence; Henry frustrated his efforts had been to no avail and Frances because she felt resentful. She wished she'd never agreed to this holiday, which was turning out to be a disaster. She remembered the sense of foreboding she'd felt on the journey there; the storm as well as the lightning, which had personally involved her in a drama she'd no wish to pursue. Henry had a good heart but was too soft for his own good. He'd been just the same even as a child, trying to be the peacemaker between his stubborn sisters. It was one of the things she found most endearing about him, but also the most infuriating.

The table was cleared, and the kitchen set ready for the morning. Frances was tired, the day hadn't gone well, her ankle throbbed and she longed for bed. Therefore, when Phoebe suddenly appeared announcing Cynthia wanted to talk with her, Frances was annoyed. 'Can't it wait until tomorrow?' Phoebe was still struggling with her own emotions and shook her head. Henry, who'd been silent throughout, asked if he could go instead. 'No, this time, it's Frances she needs.' Again, and not for the first time that day, something in Frances aspired to her own need to be needed. 'I'll go!' She said and like a lamb to the slaughter walked quietly out of the kitchen. Raising their eyebrows, Henry and Phoebe looked at one another and shrugged.

Chapter 6

Frances spent a lot of time alone; she knew the family perceived her as independent and in need of nobody's help. However, although her exterior presented a strong woman, inside she was a vulnerable personality. Her independence had been borne of necessity rather than choice. Consequently, she found it hard to open up to others, especially family, as she didn't want them to know how wrong they were in their judgement of her. It gave her some protection to be thought of as a stoic; someone who could rise above the waves of self-doubt and swim safely to the shore, without drowning. Perhaps, it was because of this, people never seemed to share their lives with her; believing she'd have little empathy or time to share, with those who weren't coping as well with life's challenges, as she appeared to be. Therefore, it was a rare experience for Frances to feel needed and even this she viewed as a weakness, rather than simply a part of her basic human nature. Nevertheless, whenever such isolated occasions arose, her defences came down and she generously gave of herself. It was this inclination, which had transformed a tired, angry woman into the attentive and willing listener who entered her sister's bedroom.

Cynthia sat on the side of the bed; her dressing gown tightly drawn around her. She appeared to be shivering and her face was ashen. For the first time, Frances realised how ill she must be and this softened her mood further. 'Why don't you get into bed Cynthia? You look frozen.'

'I'm fine!' There was a note of antagonism in her voice which Frances recognised. She tensed in response. 'You wanted to talk?'

'Yes, I want you to be honest with me.'

'What about?' Frances genuinely had no insight. Cynthia pulled her dressing gown closer around herself. 'Do you really mean to tell me you have no idea?'

'That's right.' Perplexed, Frances looked enquiringly towards her sister. 'I want to know what happened between you and Roger twenty-nine years ago. Did you sleep with him?' Frances felt as if a thunderbolt had hit her. She had no idea Cynthia knew anything about that one occasion. Roger must have told her. Suddenly, she felt like a defendant before the judge and jury. However, by the look on Cynthia's face, the verdict and sentence had already been passed.

Again, she made herself look at Cynthia; to be met by the pain in her eyes and the pale set of her jaw. Her whole body braced to resist the information she was so eager to hear. It would have been so easy to walk away, to withhold the truth, hide her shame, but she was unable to do so; something deeply intuitive kept her rooted to the spot. Rather, she understood time was running out for them both and, at last, she was free to make the confession they both needed to hear.

She sat down, grasping the arms of the chair, as if for support. Yet still, she focused on Cynthia's face, knowing this was not the time to look away. 'What do you want to know?' Now they had reached this point, Frances wanted to get through her story as quickly as possible. 'Everything!'

Frances tried to search for the right words, but they eluded her. Her memory clouded the insignificant details of the affair and yet she remembered clearly, too clearly, the pain of love re-found and love re-lost. Life hadn't been kind to her, now it seemed ready to humiliate her again. 'I'm waiting!' Cynthia's voice was venomous; her body seemed to recoil like a snake preparing to strike. 'Get on with it!' She almost hissed, her voice toxic with emotion.

Frances knew deceit had cornered her and now only the truth would set her free. She sighed deeply, releasing her hold on the arms of the chair; instead, she clutched her hands nervously in her lap, her fingers intertwined like long pale eels twisting and writhing. At last, finding courage she didn't know she possessed, she began her confession.

'It was when you were ill; you'd been in and out of hospital for so many tests and then eventually surgery. Mum was looking after the girls at home and Roger had just been made redundant.' Now Frances looked down at her hands, she couldn't bear to keep looking at the expression on Cynthia's face, so accusing, so bitter! She continued. 'Roger and I met in the town one day.' She heard the sharp intake of Cynthia's breath.

'You'd planned to meet?'

'No, we sort of bumped into one another.'

'You expect me to believe that?'

'I can only tell you what happened, not what I expect you to believe.'

'Hmm!' Frances took this as a sign she should continue.

'As you know, I hadn't seen Roger for a long time and so I was shocked to see him looking both thin and drawn. He was obviously distressed and asked me if I'd have a coffee with him.'

'How am I to know you hadn't seen him for a long time? I suppose you thought it was my fault he was so stressed, as well?'

'I don't remember what I thought; I was just concerned about the change in him. We simply had a coffee together and he talked, while I listened.'

'What did he talk about?'

'You mainly and the girls. He was worried sick about your health and, having been made redundant, his self-esteem was low.'

'And you were there, a loving shoulder for him to cry on?'

'That is not how it was.'

'That's how it sounds!'

'Do you want me to carry on?'

'Of course, I do!'

'Then stop interrupting, this isn't easy for me you know.'

'You surely don't think it is easier for me, do you?'

'You're the one who wanted to hear; shall I continue?'

Here she did look up, but it was Cynthia's turn to look down and brush a tear away as she nodded. Frances tensed; her stomach felt tied in knots and her throat was taut. She didn't want to add to Cynthia's pain, despite her own; rather she wanted to bring her relief and if possible, peace. 'We met on three more occasions; twice for coffee and once on a weekend.' Out of the corner of her eye, she noticed Cynthia tense again. 'The second and third were a repetition of the first. Roger talked, I listened. I thought I was helping.'

'Yeah, I bet you did! You never forgave me for loving Roger, did you?'

Now it was Frances turn to feel a fresh surge of pain as she relived the memory of Roger breaking off their engagement, with the announcement he'd fallen in love with Cynthia. Something within her which had passively lain down, for so many decades, suddenly rose up like a dragon in fury! The intensity of its fire, burning her heart, scorching her will to continue. It was Frances's turn to feel cheated, denied, robbed of the only precious thing she'd known in her adult life: Roger's love! She wanted to retaliate, to wound, to stir up jealousy on the level which she herself

had experienced; but once again as she looked at Cynthia's wasted form, she felt her inner dragon lie down, as silently as a kitten. Cruelty has only pain to give and nothing to gain. Part of her wanted to cause pain, just as both Cynthia and Roger had caused her so much, over many years. But simultaneously, now she was confronted with this wreck of a woman struggling in extreme weakness, she felt something akin to compassion, a desire to alleviate rather than to crush. Cynthia was dying, this was obvious, but Frances didn't want to be the one, who dealt her the death blow. How could she live with her conscience, with her siblings, if she gave in to this desire to wound and perhaps even destroy? The intensity of her feelings appalled her. She shrank from this inner revelation of what she might be capable of. This woman who everyone thought of as being so strong and resilient. The conflict within her was great, as she struggled to master her emotional turmoil. 'What happened on the weekend, did you sleep with him?' Again, that question thought Frances. For the moment she ignored it and continued her story. 'You were still in hospital and Mum and Phoebe were going to stay at yours for the weekend to be able to visit you, as the girls had gone to Roger's parents. I was working away and staying in a motel overnight. Roger had phoned asking if he could talk to me again and when he heard where I was, he booked into the same motel and we had dinner together.' She didn't have to look at Cynthia to feel her tension as the atmosphere was steeped in it. 'He just wanted someone to listen; he needed someone to talk to; that's all.'
'Did you both go back to your room?'
'Yes, for a while!'
Frances was still struggling inwardly, torn between the desire for retribution and compassion. It would be so easy to use her words to bite and even devour her sister, like some predatory wildcat on the loose. She didn't reply but rather gazed at her sister's diminished form staring at her, exposed and vulnerable in her weakness; waiting, to hear those words, she dreaded to be spoken and yet not withheld, after so many years of silence. Taut with tension, Frances felt poised, ready to pounce on her prey but where would be the victory in that? She asked herself. Would the words once spoken to destroy, then turn back on herself, if not immediately then in later years. Her sister was in enough pain already, both mentally and physically, what would she, Frances, gain by adding

to it, except more pain for herself? 'I see!' Said Cynthia, but her tone and body language were like that of a whimpering dog, crouched in fear before a furious owner, whose hand was raised ready to deliver a beating. Frances found herself wincing and wondered if Cynthia had noticed. Apparently not, for she continued to stare at Frances, her features frozen in fear of what she was about to hear.

Something deep within Frances broke, releasing her inner torment, in a barely audible sigh.

'No, I don't think you do see!' Frances knew Cynthia believed the worst of her, but now the opportunity for revenge was open to her, she found herself unable to take advantage of it. Instead, she stood and took a deep breath, as though preparing herself for something sacrificial. She noticed Cynthia shrink within herself as if she had no other means of defence, against what she was about to hear. It caused Frances to falter slightly, giving her time to draw on her reserves of stoicism with which others always accredited her. 'Right I'm going to be open with you. If Roger had wanted to sleep with me, then I would have slept with him!' Cynthia gave a sharp intake of breath. 'I knew it! You did sleep with him!'

'You're not listening! I said I would have if he'd wanted to, but he only saw me as a sister-in-law in whom he could confide. I'm telling you Cynthia; your husband is besotted with you and your girls! He loves only you!' Once the words were out of her mouth Frances felt deflated, spent, exhausted. She moved towards the door, but Cynthia was standing and walking towards her, tears streaming, arms outstretched. As they closed around Frances, she felt her sister's frail body, almost skeletal beneath her touch. She felt her rigidness begin to melt as she responded to Cynthia's embrace and for a reason, she could not fathom, she found her own eyes were also moist with tears, which she unsuccessfully struggled to hold back.

Henry was on his way to bed. He paused outside Cynthia's room. He could hear sobbing and opened the door slightly, amazed to find the two sisters, who for years hadn't been able to tolerate one another's company, with their arms around each other, sobbing and laughing at the same time. He was closing the door gently; when he heard Cynthia say. 'What a fool I've been all these years!' Henry smiled as he closed the door behind him, his thoughts turning immediately to Anna and the boys.

Chapter 7

This holiday was turning out to be unexpected at almost every turn, not the quiet, sultry days of relaxation, he'd hoped for. He hadn't heard from his wife or sons during the last few days having been preoccupied with other people and their lives. He felt empty as if he'd given away all the love inside. He needed to both see and hold Anna. To reach out and draw his sons in close. Where were they now and why was he here in this place, so far away from them all? His heart ached and it was a relief when sleep reached out and drew him into oblivion.

Henry was dreaming; he could hear Anna's animated laughter, full of energy challenging the demands of the day with her usual strength; the way she used to be before those demands became too personal, too painful. It was just as if they were sitting across from one another at breakfast. He could see the auburn tints of her long hair glinting in the sunlight, and smell the aroma of coffee, as she poured it dark and strong into their mugs. This glimpse of past domestic bliss made him smile; he turned in his sleep murmuring, before abruptly waking, shading his eyes from the bright sunlight pushing its long golden rays through the bedroom curtains. Was he awake or still asleep? He could hear Anna's laughter and the smell of coffee rising from the veranda below and in an instant he was at the window. Anna was seated opposite Phoebe and Frances. She was laughing and talking loudly as if she'd imbibed the energy of the morning sun, like some elemental tonic, poured into her coffee. Moments later he was on the veranda. Anna stood quickly; she moved towards him smiling and within moments they were both entwined. Phoebe and Frances tactfully feigned an interest in the remains of their breakfast. They needn't have bothered though as the couple, arms around each other, wandered off to the garden below. There, in a sequestered summerhouse, Henry's amazement gave way to a flurry of questions which gently fell, dissolving the distance between them, as Anna replied with renewed warmth.

Anna had arrived half-an-hour before, having driven straight from an early morning landing. After only five days in Spain, both she and her friend Lizzie decided to return. Anna was missing Henry and her friend felt she could better come to terms with her loss by confronting her grief at home, rather than trying to escape it.

Anna was holding Henry's hand. 'You see darling we both realised the pain we felt was on the inside and simply changing things on the outside wasn't the answer. Lizzie especially needed to work through her grief, rather than trying to suppress it.' Henry nodded.

'I know last year was very difficult for you too.' Anna sighed.

'For us both!'

'Yes, as far as the boys are concerned, but you've also been under a lot of stress at school.' She nodded.

'Concerning that, I've decided to work my notice, which means I'll be leaving teaching at the end of the summer term.'

This was a surprise to Henry, but he hid it well. 'Are you sure about this?'

'Yes!'

'But you've always loved your work, until recently. Are you sure this is what you really want?'

'Yes, it is actually, I feel relieved now I've made the decision. I'm sure it is the right thing to do.' Henry wasn't convinced, but wisely just smiled and said nothing. For the moment he was just grateful to have her there, smiling and relaxed beside him. Temporarily, at least, he felt reassured and dismissed his previous concerns about their relationship as imaginary; no more than the result of overwork and over worry!

Phoebe looked at her watch; it was almost 11:00 a.m. and Cynthia hadn't been down for breakfast. She knew there had been an emotional exchange between her two sisters the previous evening. However, she didn't know what it was about, but Henry assured her the outcome had been good. Therefore, it couldn't just be that Cynthia was avoiding Frances; more likely, she was exhausted. With this in mind, fifteen minutes later, carrying a tray of scrambled eggs and toast, she gently opened Cynthia's door.

The curtains were still drawn: the room steeped in silent shadows. Cynthia's form was barely discernible beneath the bedclothes and for a moment Phoebe wondered if it would be kinder to let her sleep a bit longer. However, the heavy stillness disturbed her and with sudden agitation, she set the tray down and rushed to the bedside. 'Cynthia! Wake up!' She almost shouted, shaking her sister by the shoulder. But, there was no response. Phoebe began to panic but still had the presence of mind to feel Cynthia's pulse: it was still beating. Snatching her mobile from her pocket, she rang for an ambulance, before racing to the top of the stairs and shouting down to the others. Within moments they were there. Frances strode to the window and flung the curtains back allowing the sunlight to stream in bringing hope with its light. Then she turned her sister on her side making sure her airways were clear. Henry was on the phone to someone and Frances realised, with a sense of misgiving, it was Roger. 'Don't you think we should wait and see what the paramedics advise before we call Roger back? After all, he was only here yesterday and Cynthia sent him away.' Henry looked at her in amazement.

'Are you crazy? If anyone should be here it's her husband!'

'Of course, I just didn't want him to have a wasted journey.' Henry looked at her strangely, there were times when he just couldn't fathom what was going on in Frances's head.

Phoebe, Frances, Henry and Anna sat in silence. The paramedics arrived and Cynthia was hospitalised. They'd all followed the ambulance and waited anxiously for any news, but none was forthcoming. After several hours and numerous cardboard cups of coffee, Roger had arrived frantic and pale.

At a glance, Frances took in Roger's state, anxious, lonely, close to despair. It reminded her of the time when he'd turned to her for comfort and she felt a deep-seated pain rise within her akin to grief, for what now could never be.

Henry offered to sit with him, but he said he preferred to be alone. Henry nodded, he was concerned about the others. They were all still in shock, estranged from the comfort of normality they all needed. He felt both their courage and resources were about to be challenged further and they all needed some time and space to breathe before any greater demands were made upon them.

Once back at the farmhouse they sat on the veranda, each preoccupied with their own thoughts. It was late in the afternoon, but the sun was still bright and full with its own comfort for which they were grateful. Birds sang in the garden below, while sheep bleated high on the surrounding hills. They could hear children calling and laughing to one another on the nearby beach and the distant swell of the waves as they swept the sandy shoreline. Combined, these effects saturated their senses, coaxing their muscles to relax, despite the dread overshadowing them all.

But Phoebe wondered how life, in its daily rotation could continue, impervious to the sadness and drama darkening their own. It was as if everything was engaged in an uninterrupted march forward, with the exception of themselves, for whom time appeared to be suspended. However, she understood, they too must continue, moment by moment, hour by hour, day by day. Intuitively, she understood everything is in transition; there are no constants, no circuitous escape routes, life's traumas have to be faced before they can be overcome; however devastating the passage might be. For life continues despite these challenges and the forward march itself, in turn, becomes an integral part of the healing process. But, even this unconscious recognition brought little relief. She gently touched her bump and thought of Mason.

The hospital had been noisy, modern and clinical. The seats hard and unyielding; the nurses regularly bustled by but said little. The doctors in their long white coats looked harassed and serious. Everyone seemed to be at full stretch in an atmosphere which was cold and although professional, seemingly devoid of hope and well-being. Therefore, they'd all been glad to leave, welcoming any opportunity for respite. But respite was not to come. Their unspoken anxieties filled the atmosphere, isolating each within the dark recesses of their own fears. They sat in silence on the veranda, together yet alone.

Henry was the first to move; 'I'm going back.' He murmured heading for the car. Anna jumped up!

'I'll come with you!'.

'No!' As much as I'd like you to darling, I think it best I go alone.' Anna seemed disappointed; she'd travelled a long way to be with her husband and now, as usual, he was putting other people first. It was one of the things she both loved and hated about him; his capacity for empathy and compassion. She loved him but was jealous of his generous nature, which never turned away from the difficulties of others. It left her feeling she and their boys never came first with him; rather they were always having to share him, not with another woman, but rather with the whole world and its wife! A wave of indignation flooded her emotions. 'Henry! I

either come with you, or I go home! Which will it be?' Surprised he
turned to face her.

'Darling, you must be exhausted; do you really want to come and sit all
night in a hospital corridor, when you could go to bed and sleep?'

'I think I know my own mind; I'm coming with you!' Henry raised his
arms in a gesture of resignation. 'If that's what you really want.'

'It is!' She answered and inwardly Henry was relieved. He knew it was
going to be a bleak night ahead but facing it with Anna would be a
comfort.

In the emptiness of the house, Frances and Phoebe faced one another.
Phoebe had dark circles around her eyes and she looked worn and weary
at heart. Frances recognised that look of vulnerability and something
stirred within her. 'It's going to be alright Phoebe.' She said gently as if
answering an unspoken question.

'I don't know; I don't think Cynthia can go on like this for much longer.'

'I didn't mean Cynthia; I meant you and the baby.' Phoebe looked taken
aback.

'You've changed your tune, haven't you?'

'I was wrong. I saw how you were with that woman and baby yesterday.
You did well. I know you'll cope and...' Here she hesitated as if reluctant
to say more.

'And?' Phoebe prompted.

'And I'm going to help you! Financially, practically, anyway I can. I'm
comfortably situated, no one else to think about but myself. I'll be there
for you and the baby for as long as you need me.' She saw the
astonishment in Phoebe's eyes.

'Do you mean it?' Phoebe asked, with a hint of incredulity.

'Of course I mean it! Yes, I was in shock yesterday and I still don't think
you've been very wise, but you're my sister and I want to support you.'
These words did little to comfort Phoebe, who felt Frances was still
judging her and she had no right to do so.

The night was to be even bleaker than Henry had anticipated. Roger
was seated beside Cynthia's bed holding her hand as she lay still and
unconscious: her breathing irregular and rasping. He shook his head as
they entered, but was unable to speak. 'We'll just be outside if you need
us.' Said Henry and Roger nodded, his eyes never leaving Cynthia's face.

'She's your sister!' Anna exclaimed. 'You should be there too!' He squeezed her hand. 'Perhaps, but I feel Roger needs to be alone with her just now. Cynthia has been with us for the last few days and, in that sense, we've taken time away from them both, which she should have spent with him. We can't begrudge him these last few hours.'

'You think this is the end then?' He nodded but found himself unable to speak. Anna reached out to touch him and he felt her comfort, but inside grief had already claimed him.

The night had run its course, before Roger emerged, as grey as the dawn just breaking.

'You'd better come in the doctor says it won't be long now.' The doctor had been right. They'd hardly sat down when Cynthia breathed her last, with a long, low, whispering sigh. Nobody spoke: nobody moved in the stultifying presence of death.

Henry had to persuade Roger to come back to the farmhouse to rest before making the long journey home again. However, Roger argued he needed to get back, to break the news to the girls as well as all the arrangements which needed to be made. 'You've been up all night and you aren't in a fit state to drive. A few hours are not going to change anything.'

'I don't need you to tell me that!' He'd replied angrily; nevertheless, he allowed himself to be driven back. Nobody spoke for grief filled the car with unspoken anger, guilt, unbelief, regret, and excruciating sorrow, far beyond the reach of words. It seemed strange to each of them as they peered out of the car windows that, the daily business of living should continue as before. Children shrieking with excitement as they ran along the promenade. Serious pedestrians focused on their next objective, the rush of traffic in all directions; individuals isolated within the priorities of their own routine existence. As yet protected against the emotional bombshells exploding in the lives of others around them; oblivious to trauma, until it inevitably touched their own lives, with its indiscriminate but inevitable selection. Yet for Roger, Henry and Anna, encapsulated in a small car, the ignorance of the outside world concerning Cynthia's demise, descended on them individually as an experience both surreal and overwhelming; sealing each of them within the turmoil of their own grief.

The curtains were still drawn when they arrived. Frances and Phoebe had sat up together most of the night waiting for news, which never arrived. They'd taken this as a hopeful sign and had at last fallen asleep on the hard lounge sofas. They woke now cold and feeling stiff with discomfort, as they heard the others arrive. Phoebe was the first on her feet, her unspoken question answered by the look on all three faces. 'Oh no!' She whispered, her hands covering her face as if trying to catch the silent cry rising from deep within her. Frances too understood the unmentionable. 'You should have called us! We've sat up all night wondering, waiting, you could at least have prepared us with a text!' Phoebe broke the strained silence. 'Hush Frances, this is no time for recriminations. There is no right or wrong here; death and grief have their own rules and nobody can ever be sure, what they are or how they should be observed.'

'She's right! We all need to eat and sleep before we do or say anything else. Nobody is to blame.' Only Frances spoke, regretting her previous outburst. 'I'll make some breakfast.' Nobody answered as she left the room, but rather sat down heavily on the worn sofas in an all-enveloping silence; each with their own thoughts and memories, as well as a new self-awareness concerning their own mortality.

Everyone had also eaten in silence except Roger, who had left his plate untouched. He appeared not to hear the others in their attempts to encourage him; instead, he sat staring straight ahead as one mesmerized, until the table had been cleared when the sound of dishes clattering in the kitchen seemed to rouse him from his mourning. He stood and walked out to where Frances was washing the dishes. 'Did you tell her?' He was addressing Frances's back and she swung around knocking a glass off the draining board; it fell, splintering into shards as it hit the floor. Frances tried to remain calm. 'Tell her what?' She spoke quietly, but even so the nervousness in her voice betrayed her. 'You know what!' Roger's voice was angry and impatient.

'I don't know!' Frances spoke quietly as she bent to sweep up the glass, which lay scattered beneath their feet. But Roger seemed only intent on getting an answer and roughly drew her to her feet. 'D**n you! Tell me!' Frances felt unnerved; the others had disappeared thinking it best to leave Roger alone with his grief, which left Frances feeling vulnerable. She tried to still the beating of her heart, which seemed to have risen into her throat and she imagined the stress hormone cortisol coursing through her veins, as she struggled for breath. 'Of course I didn't tell her!' She whispered as she tried, unsuccessfully, to pull her arms from his grasp. He peered into her eyes. 'You didn't tell her we slept together?'

'Keep your voice down!' She hissed angrily. Her nervousness vanishing in a fit of panic.

Roger let go of her arms. 'Don't want your dirty washing on view in front of the family? A bit late for that now, isn't it? What would they think of good, solid, dependable Frances, if they really knew you as I do?' Something dark, disorientating, akin to shame made Frances recoil inwardly. It was as if she'd been publicly exposed by his words and the nakedness of their truth. 'Please Roger, let's go somewhere else to discuss this.' She reached out to touch his arm but he roughly pulled it away. 'Just tell me!'

'Not here Roger, please for the sake of decency, not here!'

'Decency? Decency? What would you know about decency?'

'That's not fair! You know that's not fair! Who was it who trailed after me, like a whipped dog with its tail between its legs, because life wasn't treating him as well as he imagined it should?' Red with anger he stepped closer to her, so close she could feel his angry breath warming her cheek. She was afraid. His anger had surprised her but she could understand the turmoil of his grief. He was still reeling from his loss and the family had taken his wife away from him in the very last days of her life. She understood his bitterness but had never known him to be this angry before. The goalposts of rationality had apparently moved and she didn't know where to aim. He was still close and had renewed his grip on her wrists and yet he spoke quietly now. 'Just tell me the truth!' Frances felt intimidated. The house was quiet and she wondered if the others had gone out, leaving her alone with this mad man, who she hardly recognised. She was conscious of her heart beating loudly and she tried to breathe deeply in the hope of calming it. 'No, I didn't!' She blurted out. 'I thought it was kinder not to, in the circumstances.' Suddenly, Roger crumpled inwardly like a string held puppet; he cradled his head in both hands, letting out a deep moan and looked like a man about to tear his hair out. 'Then she died not knowing how much I really loved her and believing me to be a liar!'

'I don't understand.' Said Frances, who seemed to find strength in his weakness.

'No! How could you ever understand the realities of love!' His words wounded her but she still couldn't understand his meaning. In withholding the truth Frances really believed she'd made the kindest gesture, the only one she'd felt able to make in the circumstances. 'I don't understand! Did you want me to tell her the truth? Did you want me to tell my dying sister, yes, I'd slept with her husband, but not to worry as it was only on one occasion, many years ago? Do you think it would have helped her to a peaceful grave?' Roger looked into her face, his expression desperate. 'Then she died believing me a liar! Worst still, doubting the love we'd shared for so long! Never knowing how much I really loved her!' Frances was confused, she couldn't understand his meaning. For a moment they both stood transfixed, unsure how to continue. It was Roger who eventually broke the silence between them. 'I had confessed all to Cynthia, many years ago. It was on my conscience, we'd been going through a difficult time in so many ways: we both longed for a fresh start. I wanted to pull down the barriers which seemed to separate us, wipe the slate clean and start again. It wasn't easy for either of us but we worked through it and I believed, at least until this moment, she'd forgiven me!'

Now it was Frances turn to crumble but only inwardly her exterior still appeared calm; she was reverting to the stereotype she knew everyone believed her to be. Performing on the stage of other's expectations, betraying herself, betraying her true emotions, betraying her humanity. 'I see!' she said, although in reality, she saw nothing, except an abyss of self-loathing opening before her. Nevertheless, when she fell into it she intended to be alone. She still had the self-control not to fall apart in the face of the enemy, as she now perceived Roger to be.

Roger left, leaving the others to pick up the pieces of their grief. Nevertheless, they were all exhausted and trying to come to terms with the events of the last twenty-four hours.

Henry suggested they all meet in the lounge for a family discussion. He and Anna felt they should cut short their holiday and leave; Frances agreed. The abyss of self-loathing still beckoned her ever closer towards its dark precipice and when she fell, she wanted to be alone.

However, it was Phoebe, who had spoken only a few words since Henry and Roger's return that morning, who now spoke; she felt all her efforts would be wasted if they left now. It was the memory of her mother and the need to, not just spread honey, but also to receive some herself, which prompted her. She spoke quickly and loudly a hint of desperation threading her tone. 'We still have three days left. I think it would be better if we stayed. What are families for? We need one another! The funeral won't take place for at least a week, but probably more like two, before Roger can make all the necessary arrangements. If we return now, Frances will be on her own and so will I. We don't have ready-made families waiting for us but; here together, we have each other, not just our grief and loss!' The look between Henry and Anna was not wasted on Frances and Phoebe. They could see the couple were longing to go home and spend some time alone together so Phoebe spoke hurriedly again. 'It is Cynthia, our sister who has died. Mum would want us to be together for a while, I know! Cynthia is our flesh and blood!' The agitation in her voice was heard by the others. Anna was yearning to be alone with Henry. There was so much she wanted to say to him, to help him understand what had made her make the decision to go away with a colleague instead of with him. It was true the last school year had been tough, cruel even and the concern for their sons' welfare even greater but there had been other reasons too, all related to her relationship with Henry. She'd been tired of sharing him. His relentless sense of duty had come between them. It wasn't just his overriding sense of responsibility as a headmaster but also the time and concern he regularly allotted to individuals; whether they were staff, pupils or parents. She felt she was always the last in the queue for his attention and she'd wanted to make him realise she wasn't always going to be available, just when he had the time to notice her. However, her time away had made her see him in a different light, as a man who genuinely cared about people; a man who recognised the plight of the human condition and one who was always trying to improve the quality of life for others. She knew her husband was a good man but she also wanted to know she was first in his life, not to own him but at the very least to know she owned his heart. Now she was being asked to put his sisters first again, just when her own need to be alone with him was so great. Her needs were expected to come last, yet again! Nevertheless, in that fleeting glance some unspoken understanding had passed between them, causing Henry to respond; 'Of course, if that's what you both want?' Phoebe looked at Frances and she nodded. Frances would have to live on the edge of her abyss a little longer and Anna would have to suppress her own need a little deeper. 'That's settled then! We'll see out our stay. It's what Mum would have wanted.' Said Phoebe and now the decision was made the strain between them eased a little, leaving Henry and Phoebe oblivious to the rising tension in both Anna and Frances.

Chapter 8

Frances wandered off into the orchard. The air was heavy with the warmth of May and the busy bumbling of bees. Some blossom still lingered on the sinewy boughs but most had now been replaced with tight buds of promise, which looked set to deliver an abundance of summer fruit.

Frances settled herself in the shade of an old apple tree, its bark gnarled and weathered. She felt an emotion akin to empathy with the tree's appearance. It looked as though it had withstood many turbulent storms, yet, judging by the number of burgeoning buds, was still capable of producing fruit.

Alone, at last, she looked into the dark threats of her own abyss. She felt tired, desperately tired. What fruit had her own life produced, she wondered? Was she no more than a barren tree incapable of producing anything which might be useful to others? Her doctor wanted her to stop taking the anti-depressants, but she depended on them and couldn't answer for what she might do without their support. Her future lay before her in darkness, without hope, without promise. It was at times like this the abyss yawned widely before her with its invitation to fall. It would be a relief to allow herself such a luxury, for too long she'd fought to resist the temptation. At first, following the intimate confrontation with Cynthia, she'd felt something akin to relief, seen some light breaking through the dark clouds which seemed to constantly overshadow her life. Nevertheless, with her sister's death the clouds had returned more menacingly than before. She hated what she'd done, but more than this, she hated herself for having given in to her chief weakness: her need to be needed.

This was her mood when she heard a man's voice close by. 'They told me up at the house I'd find you here.' Instantly, Frances recognised the Welsh lilt of Jones's accent and she looked up in surprise, annoyed at being interrupted in her dark thoughts.

'Yes!' She spoke angrily and knew she was being rude but couldn't help herself. Jones had been hesitant incoming and now found himself wishing he hadn't. 'I'm sorry, I heard the sad news of your sister's death and wanted to bring my condolences.' Frances remained silent, wondering how this man could possibly know. As if reading her thoughts, he continued. 'News travels quickly here, either on the village grapevine or the countryside web, whatever you might like to call it.'

'I see!' Replied Frances somewhat tersely, standing up and walking away. Jones was left turning his cap nervously in his hands. He felt stupid, unable to find the words he so desperately wanted to say. 'Can I walk with you?' He called after her, but Frances continued on her way, pretending not to have heard, her sights set on the high, rocky outcrop rising above the hills beyond.

Henry and Anna had retired to their room. 'Just to rest for a while.' Henry had told Phoebe. 'We'll be down later.' But rest was not to come. Alone at last, Anna released her criticisms and complaints; which like verbal missiles, hit their target, Henry's heart. He felt as though he'd no defence, against her accusations, which were true and rightly aimed at his character weaknesses, which in differing contexts, might also be considered his greatest strengths. He let her continue each bitter recrimination wounding him further. A bee, losing its way flew into the room; realising the window was open he turned to close it; noticing Phoebe below, walking away as he did so. She must have heard! Inwardly he dissolved. He'd tried to be all things to all people and now he was beginning to realise the futility of the task he'd set himself. He sat down on the end of the bed. Anna's diatribe ended as abruptly as it had begun and, to his surprise, she came and sat next to him. She leant into him; her closeness bringing him comfort, as well as a glimmer of hope. However, as exhaustion overcame them both the anger and bitterness of grief, gave way to sleep.

Phoebe felt perhaps she should rest too, but sleep wouldn't come; so, she made her way to the veranda, hoping Frances would soon return. She cradled the form of her unborn child; her hands moving in circular motions, as she gently caressed the round, blooming of her baby. Lazily, she allowed the sun to lull her into a doze, until the sound of raised voices broke into her consciousness waking her with a start. They were coming from the open window of Henry and Anna's room. Phoebe couldn't catch the words, but she recognised the angry tones of Anna's fury and the measured tones of Henry's responses. So even they have their differences she thought to herself, wondering if there was ever such a thing as a harmonious relationship. For Phoebe, Anna's anger at this time of family crisis felt like a betrayal, underlining the disunity which touched them all: fragmenting their relationships, fragmenting their lives. In disgust she stood, deciding her efforts were useless. Now, she too just wanted to be alone.

However, as she stood, she noticed Frances just leaving the orchard and so changing her mind decided to follow her, thinking she couldn't get too far ahead due to her ankle.

But Frances had taken a different route to the one Phoebe anticipated; her mind in turmoil she was heading for the rugged outcrop. Despair defeated her natural common sense and despite the pain radiating from her foot, she continued her struggle ever upwards.

Phoebe had taken to the grassy lower slopes of the hills behind the farmhouse, where most hikers headed to be rewarded with scenic views of the bay stretching across to Anglesey. Nevertheless, these were lost on Phoebe, whose thoughts stretched much further beyond the bay in search of Mason, currently tracing his father's footsteps into sheep farming somewhere in New Zealand. He'd never thought to tell her his address and she'd never felt the need to know, until after he'd left, then there had been no point, their baby still hidden in the beginnings of its being deep inside her, as was her love for Mason. She knew with a little effort she could probably discover his whereabouts but pride forbade her. But even so, she realised this wasn't just about her alone, rather it was about their child. Perhaps, I should give us both more time and wait until the baby is here, she told herself; after all, not every pregnancy ended in the birth of a new life. However, such an alternative was too painful to contemplate. She paused to rest on a fallen tree trunk, hoping the view which took in not just the beauty of the bay, but also of the surrounding countryside, might brighten her thoughts or at the very least bring some welcome distraction.

It was there, as she scanned the distant hills, she noticed two figures one much further ahead of the other. It looked as though these were both heading towards the craggy rocks to the far right of where she sat. The first figure was definitely a woman, who appeared to be dragging her right leg behind her, making slow progress up the bleak shale escarpment. She wore a red jacket similar to Frances's and as Phoebe raised a small pair of binoculars to her eyes, she realised with horror it was indeed her sister! With a sharp intake of breath, she stood up and refocused the lens on another figure. It was a man and he was a few hundred yards behind. He appeared to be running between the prickly gorse bushes, which dotted the outcrop, ducking down every time Frances glanced behind her. It was as if she knew she was being followed and was desperately trying to escape. Fear gripped Phoebe as she slowly grasped the truth; her sister was being stalked! Was this why Frances was struggling to reach such an unlikely place in an effort to find somewhere to hide, somewhere to escape?

Her mind befuddled with confusion and finding no rational explanation for what she'd just seen, Phoebe started running back to the farmhouse, if ever she needed Henry it was now!

Her ascent had been slow, leisurely even and as a result, the track hadn't threatened her foothold in any way; but now as she ran in blind panic, she didn't seem to notice the occasional rocks, which scattered the way, half-hidden in grassy tussocks or the roots of Ash trees, bent like old men, rooting the trail with their gnarled creepings. She was hot and her backpack heavy; breathless she stopped, throwing her baggage to the ground and quickly removing her jacket: leaving them both where they fell. She continued running her heart beating ever faster and more loudly in her ears. The perspiration trickled from her forehead dripping onto her cheeks, but still she kept running. Her head pounded and her right side ached, but still she ran driven by a terror too fearful to imagine. Inevitably, she tripped, falling with a thud, hitting the ground hard. For a brief moment, she lay stunned, but still conscious and willed herself to stand, her hands clutching her abdomen, aware of the pain within.

The farmhouse was in sight now and as she approached half-crying, half-moaning, she saw Henry and Anna on the veranda. Within moments she stood in front of them breathless and pointing to the far outcrop of rocks. They made her sit down and regain her breath, as they tried to make sense of her disjointed account. At last, they understood at least in part, and as Henry looked at Anna his glance full of enquiry, she nodded. 'I'll take care of Phoebe, you go!'

It was a desperate Henry who ran scrambling up the lower slopes of the mountain; the shifting shale causing him to slip and slide, slowing his ascent, leaving him wet with perspiration and breathless in his endeavours. He wondered how Frances, with her weak ankle, could maintain the steep climb. At times, he was reduced to climbing on all fours, his knuckles bleeding from the sharp stones cutting into his flesh. He thought of his sister and wondered whatever could have possessed her to have embarked on such a crazy exploit? He knew Roger had followed her into the kitchen and had heard some of the loud altercation, which followed. He and Anna had retired to their room when he'd realised, he'd left his mobile in the dining room and had returned to retrieve it. It wasn't in Henry's nature to eavesdrop, but he couldn't help overhearing part of their conversation and it had shocked him. For years he'd known there was a hidden family issue between Cynthia and Frances. However, he'd naturally assumed it was related to the one sister marrying the other's ex-fiancé, a difficult situation for anyone to cope with. However, it had never occurred to him as to the true nature of their obvious reluctance to be in one another's company. The revelation had truly rocked him. He would never have believed Frances capable of such a thing, until the moment he heard it from her own lips. It had been a hard truth to digest, just when he was about to face his own confrontation with Anna; when, for the first time in his married life, he'd decided to put his wife's needs first. Until, Phoebe had broken in breathless, panicking and injured.

He paused for breath and noticed movement above him. It was definitely the figure of a man following Frances but covertly. Moreover, Henry noticed whoever it was, they were fast running out of gorse bushes to hide behind; for the higher the ascent the more barren and rockier the terrain became. Did Frances realise she was being followed? He wondered; was this the reason for her bizarre behaviour or was it due to her confrontation with Roger? He felt the cold grip of fear within his gut and struggled to regain his self-control. For whatever reason Frances's state of mind was obviously unbalanced. He didn't have time to consider who the stranger might be or what his intentions were. All that filled his mind was his sister's safety and so he continued to struggle forward with his remaining strength. His breath breaking out in heavy gasps as the strain caused his chest to heave, beneath his thin shirt, wet with perspiration.

Anna and Phoebe were in the dark lounge, awaiting the doctor's arrival. Phoebe lay on the sofa, a blanket over her legs. She was cradling her now noticeable bump carefully in her hands, whilst murmuring something softly, repeatedly, as if soothing and caressing the child within. Anna had leaned in to try and catch her words, which sounded like, 'I'm so sorry!' It was this which had alerted her to the fact Phoebe must be pregnant. Since Henry had left, she'd been unable to get any sense out of her sister-in-law, who she believed to be in shock. She'd managed to make her comfortable on the sofa and had phoned the local GP; who she hoped would arrive soon. How much more would happen before the day was ended? This she wondered as she nervously sat, her fists clenched in a white-knuckle grasp, betraying her inner struggle. She understood Henry had responded in the only way he could and she wouldn't have respected him if he hadn't. Nevertheless, once again it had been at a cost to their own relationship and she couldn't help feeling resentful, despite her anxious thoughts concerning both Phoebe and Frances's plight.

Now, as she waited, she wondered if she'd been right if this really was an emergency or just a case of nervous shock. Henry had never mentioned Phoebe's condition and it was not until she'd settled on the sofa it had become apparent. Anna stood, walking to the window, wondering how long the doctor would be, but also hoping for any sign of Henry's return.

Frances wasn't aware she was being followed. She was driven by shame and guilt, which consumed her. She didn't feel able to face the aftermath of her disgrace or to be exposed for the hypocrite she felt herself to be. Her thoughts weren't rational but rather motivated by anger and humiliation. All she longed for was oblivion, anything rather than face her family. She believed Roger capable of betraying her and felt unable to cope with the disgrace, which would inevitably follow. How would she be able to manage the fallout, the rejection? How would she find the strength to continue?

She'd heard there was a crevice near the peak, where several walkers had lost their lives. Her sole aim was to find it and to lose hers also. To her unbalanced mind this seemed to be the only solution: so great was her despair. She was also driven by grief. Grief for Cynthia, grief for what might have been and now never would be. Grief for her family when they realised not only the death of the Frances they thought they knew but also the death of the real Frances, who they'd never known; simply because she'd always been too scared to reveal who she really was, especially to those closest to her.

Henry had been forced to take a five-minute break to still the rapid beating of his heart and to regain his breath, but it had been worth it and he now redoubled his efforts making faster progress. He was gaining on the unknown stalker, who was now scrambling in full view. It was now obvious, he was intent on following Frances, and to Henry that he had to reach his sister first, if he was to save her!

Frances struggled as the ascent grew steeper. Her strenuous output of energy began to have a calming effect on her mind and she began to regain something akin to her usual equilibrium. Yet, still she persisted in struggling ever upwards. During, these last few gruelling yards she hadn't bothered to look behind her, so intent had she been on reaching her dark destination, which unknown to her, now only lay a couple of hundred yards ahead. She was in no mood to admire the view, only to escape her humiliation.

Henry had made a good start after his rest, but as the incline grew and his pace slowed, he stumbled sliding backwards, rolling on the loose scree, cutting his face and hands whilst colliding with sharp rocks and large stones. He eventually stopped and made an ungainly stand. He wasn't seriously hurt, just a few scratches and cuts. Probably there would be a few bruises tomorrow, but nothing was broken. Nevertheless, as he rubbed the dirt and debris off his clothes, he realised he'd rolled for approximately a hundred yards. He held his hand over his eyes and scanned the hillside. Frances was near the summit and just a few yards behind her the unknown stalker. He groaned and began a rapid ascent once again, his weight of distress a heavier burden. His sister needed him and yet he was no longer a young man: neither was he a fit one. His chances of reaching her before her unknown follower were not only slim but impossible.

Phoebe's murmuring had turned to low moans. Anna crossed to her side and saw she was sleeping; noticing the minute pearls of perspiration on Phoebe's forehead, she removed the rug covering her; Phoebe looked flushed and Anna tried to remember in which cupboard she'd earlier noticed an electric fan. It was with relief she heard the screech of tyres draw to an abrupt halt outside; and looking out of the window she saw the doctor striding hurriedly towards the house. She arrived at the front door before him and to his surprise opened it before he had a chance to knock. She gave no greeting, but turned almost on heel expecting him to follow her down the narrow passage to the room beyond.

He was a man in his late fifties with thinning hair and a veneer of grey shadow spreading up from his chin to just below his cheekbones. It looked as though he hadn't shaved that morning and Anna found herself wondering why? He knelt beside the sofa and felt Phoebe's pulse. 'How long has she been like this?' His voice was kind and suddenly the tension within Anna relaxed and her fidgeting fingers stilled; transforming into the familiar, reassuring handclasp she assumed in the classroom, when looking over the shoulders of her students, examining their work. 'About an hour.' She replied, her voice controlled and clear. The doctor proceeded to take Phoebe's temperature, but still she slept on. 'Her temperature is just a little elevated; you say she fell?'
'Yes, I wasn't there, it was upon the hillside.'
'Could she walk?'
'Oh yes, she ran back! Something she'd seen startled her.'
'Hmm!' He gently pressed a place just below the side of Phoebe's temple and she woke, looking surprised. She sat up quickly and he gently pushed her back with one hand placing cushions behind her with the other. 'Now young lady why don't you and I have a chat. Perhaps a nice cup of hot, sweet tea might be in order.' He said, turning to Anna.
'Of course!' She was relieved to leave the room as well as her responsibility behind.

When she returned the doctor was about to leave. 'Nothing to worry about; a nasty shock and a bit of a tumble. I recommend the tea and rest. It is important she remains with her feet up for the rest of the day and possibly tomorrow too. However, if there is any change in your condition.' Here he turned towards Phoebe. 'You must contact me immediately do you understand?' Phoebe nodded and Anna noticed the fear in Phoebe's eyes. The doctor must have too, for he walked over to her and patted her hand. 'Just in case you understand. But to be truthful the only change I'm expecting is you will soon be on your feet again, doing whatever it is you young women do on holiday.' He smiled and so did Phoebe.

'Thank you!' Anna said, 'I'll show you out.

'No need: my memory is still quite good!' He turned to Phoebe again and winked, before picking up his bag and leaving.

'Well he was a patronising old so and so, wasn't he?' Said Anna, light-heartedly now her initial fears had been relieved.

'Oh, I don't know, sometimes it is quite nice to be patronised.' Said Phoebe, leaning back into the cushions and taking a long slake of the hot, deliciously sweet tea. Anna scrutinised her carefully. Phoebe appeared calm and composed. Had she forgotten the reason for her scare in the first place, she wondered?

Frances peered into the cavernous depths of the crevice, which had appeared starkly before her, wide like a gaping maw. Its shocking reality sobered her further and she found herself releasing a horrified gasp and stepping backwards. She stood one hand covering her mouth, as she contemplated the plight of her situation. That which only a little earlier appeared a viable solution to her dilemma, now to her more balanced mind looked more like an act of insane annihilation. What if she didn't die instantly, but lay perhaps even for days, alone in the cold, dank, dark, seared with pain, broken and battered? Surely, facing the fallout with her family wouldn't be anywhere near as catastrophic; also, with time, peoples' memories fade and more recent events take their place. People change, everyone makes mistakes in life, surely it was learning from them which was important? Would they allow her this one mistake, vile as she now felt it to be? These were the questions running through her mind as the rational, stoical Frances began to take up the reins of her self-possession once again. She stepped forward as if to peer into the outcome of her own folly once more. But, the terrifying reality of the dark abyss below her, forced her own abyss of self-loathing into perspective. She couldn't do it; she understood that now. This wasn't where she wanted her life to end. Her hopes were for a better life, a better place to end, following a life better lived. New hope seemed to momentarily surface. She searched her memory; she knew such a life crisis, if confronted and lived through, would strengthen rather than weaken her. She decided to turn back, but would first allow herself one last look into the outcome of her personal folly, as she now saw the gaping pit before her to be. She wanted to be able to remember it clearly, an indelible metaphor of her own foolishness, in more ways than one, which she hoped would serve to protect her in the future.

Frances stepped forward, not noticing the crumbling edge; suddenly she heard a movement behind her and turned to see Jones. He was red with exertion and out of breath, nevertheless, he extended his hand towards her, his voice thick with fear. 'Don't! Please don't!' Frances let out a scream, as she felt the cliff edge give way beneath her. Loose stones and rocks rumbled like near thunder breaking around her, as they tumbled into the depths below. Jones threw himself forward and caught her wrists, but only just in time, before the upper-part of her body followed the lower, over the edge. Her cries echoed deep, deep down reverberating into the depths of the ravine, echoing throughout the hills. Causing, even the sheep, to stop grazing and raise their woolly heads in fear. Henry heard and froze. Fear gripped his gut as he tried even harder to struggle forward, but his legs were like lead and he stumbled and fell again.

Once Frances had left the orchard, Jones had followed her. He wasn't sure why, but something he'd read in her eyes seemed familiar to him. It was something disturbing and when he saw her heading towards the Devil's Peak, as the locals called it, he'd felt his fears justified and made up his mind to follow her. Now, they were both in a predicament. For he too, in his present position, didn't have the leverage he needed to pull Frances clear and, of course, he couldn't let her go! He could feel the pull of gravity emerging from the depths of the ravine, gradually exercising its grip on her body and he felt engaged in a tug of war with death as his opponent. How long would he be able to hold on to her, he wondered?

Anna found herself pacing back and forth in front of the window. Henry had been gone a long time and she was becoming anxious. She'd cooked a light supper for herself and Phoebe and afterwards, they'd chatted. Phoebe seemed no worse for her fall only tired and had once again drifted off to sleep. Anna was tired too, but felt she couldn't allow herself the luxury of sleep, while so much was still unknown concerning Henry and Frances's safety. She wondered if she should call the police. She'd tried to phone Henry's mobile, but there had been no signal. Great if on a retreat, she thought, but dangerous in the face of an emergency! She was also worried about Phoebe, who although not showing any signs of a physical injury, hadn't alluded to the reason behind her accident; it was as if she'd no recollection of what she'd seen and Anna didn't think it wise to mention it. She sighed deeply and looked with envy at her sleeping sister-in-law, whose pallor had been replaced with a healthy glow as she slept. Anna thought how young she looked. Phoebe hadn't mentioned the baby and Anna didn't feel it was her place to ask. She'd enough to deal with as it was. Therefore, she continued to pace to and fro, hoping Henry and Frances would soon re-appear.

Frances's piercing screams had put new fear into Henry; a rush of "fight or flight" adrenalin helped him to make faster progress. Soon he was at the peak confounded by the scene before him. He tried to speak calmly and softly, so as not to startle either of them.

'Thank God!' He heard Jones mutter and with a rather desperate catch in her throat Frances whispered, 'Henry?'

'Don't panic, I'm here now.' He spoke gently sounding more confident than he felt. 'I'll soon get you both out of this.' He couldn't help wondering how it had all happened, but now definitely wasn't the time for questions, only for answers. 'Hurry up!' He heard Jones whisper.

Henry felt a rising panic. He ran his hands through his hair, he was distressed but trying to appear calm. He had no rope only his own hands and arms to relieve Jones who was showing his own signs of distress. His face was flushed and contorted with the strain of holding onto Frances, feeling as though his arms were being pulled out of their sockets. It was as though he was being stretched on some medieval rack: he felt faint with pain. At a glance, Henry had taken all this in and Frances's muffled sobs did little to reassure him.

Cautiously, he edged forward. His simple and only plan was to kneel beside Jones at the place where he and Frances held hands and taking one hand at a time from Jones into his own, to pull her to safety. Would he be strong enough though, he wondered? As if reading his thoughts, Jones said. 'Just take her left hand and with the other support her under her shoulder, then I'll be able to kneel and together we'll pull her up.'

'Are you sure?' Henry asked. 'Do you have muscle cramp?'

'Yes! But we can't run the risk of letting this go on for much longer; just do it!'

'Please hurry!' cried Frances, her voice frayed by fear.

There had been an anxious moment, when Jones had let go of her left hand and Frances had screamed pitifully, thinking she was about to plummet, but Henry held her securely and within seconds the men had dragged her free from the gaping darkness below. Once seated on solid rock, Frances collapsed both emotionally as well as physically. Momentarily, she blacked out and Henry in his nervous state, slapped her face. The sting left a red welt across her cheek; already grazed and cut. Henry felt bad, in his anxiety he hadn't noticed the injuries already on Frances's face. The slap had been an automatic response; this was not the time for her to lapse into unconsciousness, she needed to be alert. Slowly, she came to as if in a daze, before dissolving in a flood of tears borne from both relief and regret. Henry sat next to her and drew her in close. At first, the tension within her resisted; Frances felt she deserved neither comfort nor love; but Henry continued to hold her until at last, she found herself leaning into his reassuring presence, as Jones looked anxiously on. 'Thank you!' She said, her voice broken with grief. Jones, always a man of few words just nodded, whilst Henry managed a weary smile. Both men were exhausted! Jones too, tried to stand, but fell to his knees, moaning and rubbing his arms. 'Let's just all sit for a while and admire the view, shall we?' Said Henry. Both Frances and Jones looked at him in amazement, as if he was the only mad one in their midst.

As Anna watched the light fading, anxiety was great within her. Phoebe slept on, held in oblivion. Finally, Anna could wait no longer and rang 999 wondering why she'd left it so long, before doing so.

Half-an-hour later, like a rescuing angel, the air ambulance propelled into view. Henry stood waving Frances's red jacket frantically until they were spotted. Unfortunately, there was nowhere for the helicopter to land so it continued to hover above them creating a whirlwind of dust, as a paramedic descended a long rope ladder. He assessed the condition of the three, but it was only Frances who was eventually winched up on a stretcher and airlifted to hospital. Leaving Henry and Jones to make their own way down. It had been a race against the fading light and neither of them had spoken, each alone with their thoughts and the fatigue, which was so heavy upon them. They parted company back at the farmhouse, where following a warm handshake, an exhausted Henry stood watching Jones drive away. It was a thankful Anna who ran out to meet her husband and no words were necessary as he held her tightly.

It had been something in Frances's eyes, which had caused Jones to follow her. Something familiar resonated within him, disturbing his quiet, unsettling his newly found peace. What it was he didn't know, but he'd recognised its predatory nature and its ability to steal one's sanity by stealth. Intuitively, he understood Frances was a threat to her own well-being, just as he'd been to his own, only a few days before. He felt cold as the memory returned of the futile loss at his own hands, of his faithful dog, Bonnie.

His gratitude to Henry for saving his life could never find adequate expression; however, if in some way, he could offer protection to Frances in her time of need then, perhaps, he might repay his lifetime debt to Henry, at least in part. This had been his main objective in pursuing her.

However, Jones was no fool. He'd seen the disdain in Frances's expression that he should have presumed to interrupt the privacy of her grief, causing him to hesitate before following her. He understood he would have to keep out of her sight and knew such behaviour if noticed by others, could be misconstrued. For a matter of seconds, he'd considered what, if this should happen, it might mean for him. Nevertheless, he'd been willing to take the chance. Now, following recent events, he was glad he'd taken the risk. As a result, a change was slowly taking place within him: something akin to a sense of meaning and purpose had been ascribed to his existence; giving new birth to hope, vaguely defining an unforeseen future. He was still in considerable pain, nevertheless, he knew his body would heal, even as his mind had already begun to.

Frances had been kept in hospital overnight for observation only. She'd no serious injuries, although the duress to her ankle had been considerable and as a result, it was going to take longer to heal. Moreover, the injuries to her face were superficial. Nevertheless, for her, nothing could quell the relief and wonder of still being alive! For she'd already decided not to end her life when she'd slipped, lost her footing and fell. The terror she'd experienced in those few minutes when the ground had yawned cavernously beneath her, she felt sure would last a lifetime. However, in the aftermath almost like a revelation, she'd understood the extent of Henry's love for her and the tenacity of Jones's grip upon her life. This had also brought a new realisation, in discovering, she actually mattered to others, a fact most people take for granted, but one which led Frances, to a new understanding of her own worth.

The nurses had arrived at regular intervals through the night to make their observations, each time surprised to find her still awake after her long ordeal. However, their new patient was making her own observations and each swept over her in a wave of wonder and thankfulness. All her life she'd hidden who she really was, presenting an image of a strong, independent woman, who needed no one and who was content to lead a solitary and somewhat stoical life, complete in itself. However, today the real Frances in all her vulnerability had been exposed and it had taken a crisis to reveal to her, not only that she mattered, but the importance of living in a state of mutual interdependence with others. Frances had always known she needed others, but there had been very few close people in her adult life and now she realised it was not because no one wanted her, but rather her attitudes gave out false signals, which pushed others away. Consequently, as she lay on her hospital bed with its clean sheets and hard mattress, listening to the muffled snores of fellow patients cloaked in semi-darkness and the hushed chatter of busy night nurses, she smiled to herself. Much later and still awake, from some nearby corridor, she heard the clattering arrival of the tea trolley and the buzz of the fluorescent lights above. The dawning of a new day had arrived and cheerful nurses were propping sleepy patients up against pillows, whilst asking them if they would like a nice cup of tea. She thought of the day ahead and wondered how she would face the family after all that had happened. Frances knew she was going to need more than tea to get through the day ahead, not to mention all those still to come; delineated in terms of weeks and months, stretching into years ahead, which until today, she'd felt destined to face alone. Now, the onus was upon her to change. She smiled to herself, perhaps she could! For since yesterday and her almost miraculous escape from death. Frances had begun to believe that, sometimes the seemingly impossible might, actually just become possible.

Chapter 9

Phoebe had woken to find herself still on the sofa in the dark lounge. She threw back the blanket and stood feeling slightly dizzy and confused. Then she remembered! Frances struggling to reach the peak, followed by some unknown man. Herself running and falling, the face of a middle-aged man leaning over her and winking. She gasped and her hands flew to her bump; where as if in response she felt a strong flutter within. 'Oh! Thank God! You're still there!' She sat quietly as if held in a bubble so light, so spacious; she felt free to breathe, free to live, free to move forward once again. It was as if all the trauma of the last two days had fallen away from her; the waves which had so threatened to drown her fast receding. It was as if her brain had enforced a form of temporary amnesia to protect her from dark realities and the terror of even darker possibilities, but now she remembered, although, as yet, she still didn't know the outcome. Nevertheless, intuitively she felt it was not going to be as dreadful as anticipated. She heard movement above and then footsteps on the stairs. She wiped away her tears of relief, which had spilt despite her newfound hope, trying to compose herself before Henry walked in. 'You're awake; that's good! How are you feeling?' He sat beside her and put an arm around her. 'I'm okay, but what about Frances, what happened?'

'Frances is safe, they kept her in hospital overnight for observation. She'll probably be out today.'

'But who was following her and what happened?'

'It was Jones and a good thing he did otherwise things might have turned out very differently.'

'This is all my fault! Everything is my fault! If I hadn't suggested this awful holiday, none of this would have happened!'

Henry looked at her, his expression serious. 'You can't blame yourself; you planned the holiday with the best intentions; you know full well Phoebe you can't take responsibility for the decisions and actions of others. Neither are you able to control everything that happens. We're all imperfect people in an imperfect world, that's why we all need to...' Here Phoebe interrupted him: 'We all need to spread honey thickly like butter!'

For a brief moment, memories of their childhood united them. Anna walked in.

'I'm not so sure that's the best way to deal with life.' She said, walking over to the bookcase and running her finger along the titles. 'I'll take escapism anytime!' Then she selected a title and left them. Henry shrugged.

'She doesn't really mean it.' Phoebe wasn't so sure. She'd wondered why Anna had left for Spain without Henry. Had it been to avoid the painful realities she wanted to escape from? Then, having distanced herself for a while, had she found escapism didn't always deliver the expected results? People were different and found their way through life's rough places via differing routes. Such thoughts led her to consider her own situation and to wonder what route her own life was about to take.

Frances returned later that day in a hospital car. She looked exhausted. They'd all been there to greet her offering tea and comfort, for which she didn't feel ready. Henry had phoned earlier to offer her a lift, but she'd told him not to bother as a hospital car had already been booked. On arrival, she went straight upstairs to rest feeling embarrassed about all that had happened and wanting some time to be alone before facing the others.

However, she hesitated as she passed Cynthia's old room, remembering how things had ended between them. It had been good or so she'd believed. On impulse, she opened the door and stepped in. The curtains were drawn and she opened them letting in the bright sunlight, which touched her with the warmth of its comfort. She noticed several of Cynthia's things on the bedside table. There was a small pillbox, a pair of reading glasses and a book. She sat on the side of the bed and picked up the book. It must have been one Cynthia had found on the bookshelf downstairs. It was well-thumbed, a somewhat dog-eared, old Agatha Christie novel. She opened it flicking aimlessly through the pages; as she did so two envelopes fell out, one addressed to Roger and the other to her. She was astonished and quickly replaced both letters. She stood up and made a quick exit, hurrying to her own room, where she lay on the bed shivering, partly in shock, partly in fear. She remembered the last evening they were together and the warmth of Cynthia's embrace. It had been as genuine as her own had been sincere. They'd both just found one another again, before parting forever! Had Cynthia written the letter before they'd made up or after? What might it say? Would it be a rebuke from beyond the grave? Frances shivered.

Anna was brooding; she'd followed Henry downstairs and, just as she'd anticipated, found him engrossed in conversation with Phoebe. Disappointed she'd made some coffee and returned upstairs where she lay on the bed, first drawing the curtains against the light. She'd known Henry would make a beeline for Phoebe and there would be little opportunity for them to even eat breakfast alone. She felt weary and cross; weary with the demands' others seemed to make on Henry; cross because she always had to join a queue for her husband's attention, and finally cross with herself for being cross!

Before she'd married Henry, his compassionate nature had been part of his attraction. He was a man others respected and listened to. He was sought out for his understanding and wisdom; received for his sympathy and ability to empathise. He was indeed a very human, being! No one was more human than Henry! Paradoxically, it was his greatest strength, which created the greatest weakness in their relationship.

As she lay there Anna sighed and wondered if there was any hope for change. She remembered the days when they'd first met and the intoxication of their love. Then, she'd been the centre of his attention and the intensity of their love for one another seemed to enclose them in a world of their own. But of course, the real world had been waiting for their return. They were married and within the first year their sons arrived, pink, chubby, utterly gorgeous but nevertheless, exhausting! Their needs had taken most of Anna's time and attention. Of course, Henry had been there, taking his nightly turn as he paced the floors singing and whispering endearments to comfort those small bundles of humanity. However, the irony of their resulting intimacy, in the form of those two, tiny people, becoming the first of many separations between them, had always been felt by Anna. She would have liked more time alone with her husband, before the twins' arrival. Although, she was still able to recognise that, although their world had widened to include these two, tiny dependents; nevertheless, these new arrivals served only to expand, in a wider circle of inclusion, the love shared between them.

She thought of her friend's bereavement which, for the first time in their marriage, had provided her with an opportunity to holiday separately from Henry. She had answered affirmatively before telling Henry. All this happened before Phoebe had asked him to join them in a family reunion. Now she found herself wondering if he would still have come on this holiday without her? Would he have been willing to leave her alone at home? Probably not, but even so, she couldn't be sure; for both Henry's allegiance and decisions often left her perplexed. Therefore, she hoped on this occasion her decision would also leave him confused and uncertain of her true intentions. She'd thought a little uncertainty, a little less predictability in their marriage, might be a good thing. However, it was Anna who had been left feeling more vulnerable than ever. Laying on a hotel sun-lounger beside the pool, surrounded by anonymous couples, each engrossed with the other to the exclusion of all else, served only to highlight her own plight. Moreover, her friend was struggling with the first assault of the grieving process and was in no mood for the usual holiday pursuits; she read a lot and spent hours gazing out onto the vast expanse of blue stretched before them, lost somewhere in the labyrinth of her own memories. Consequently, Anna too had been left alone with her own inner world and to her surprise a deep longing to be with Henry. 'Why?' She'd asked herself was she here with someone who was lamenting the death of their husband and who appeared oblivious to her presence when her own husband was also apparently enjoying a holiday with his siblings and probably not missing her at all. Anna's plan hadn't worked to her advantage!

Lizzie, had at first, appeared indifferent to her departure, so deep had she fallen into the depths of her loss. Anna understood this, but even as she packed her suitcase, she thought of Henry and knew he wouldn't have abandoned his friend in a similar scenario; conversely, he would have been content to sit with them in undisturbed silence. But, Anna was not Henry and rather than support her friend in the loss of her husband, she felt the need to find her own. Perhaps, it might be possible to rediscover what they had both lost before it was too late. Nevertheless, her packing had seemed to rouse Lizzie from her grief; she decided to return with Anna and work through her sorrow at home; the place which held fond memories of better times.

However, unknown to Anna, her ploy had been more successful than she realised. For in her absence Henry's attention had indeed been turned towards her. Without her there, he'd felt incomplete. The demands of the vacation had taken their toll on him and even as he listened to Phoebe, gently teasing her in the way he had when they were still children, his mind was preoccupied with Anna. He'd heard her return upstairs and the swish of the curtains as they were drawn in a finality of disappointment and annoyance as if shutting out future possibilities and reducing them to obscurity. It seemed to be his fate to offer to others that, which through his own blindness, he withheld from his own. He loved Anna, of this there was no doubt in his mind; he needed her, more than she understood, but he'd taken the security, comfort, support, and love she so generously gave, for granted. He'd been such a fool!

Phoebe was talking, but Henry wasn't listening. To her surprise, he suddenly stood and walked out of the room. She heard his footsteps on the stairs, as gently she rubbed her bump addressing the new life within. 'That's not like Henry, is it? To walk away without saying anything; he could at least have waited until I'd finished!'

Henry and Anna were out walking; Phoebe had been about to ask if she could accompany them, but then thought better of it; there was something about Henry's determined expression which made her hesitate. Anna looked as though she'd been crying; her eyes were puffy and her expression weary. 'Well, that leaves just you and me, baby.' Phoebe silently spoke to her unborn child and a few minutes later took herself off in the opposite direction to Henry and Anna.

Frances heard them leave and made her way downstairs. She fixed herself some breakfast and took it out onto the veranda, where the morning sun was warming the roses, which had arrived that morning. They'd been for her, an unknown admirer, Henry had said with a smile. She'd seen the florist's van pull up outside and had wondered who the flowers might be for. She'd been surprised when Phoebe announced they were for her. Carefully, Frances had arranged them, noting the innate beauty of the delicate blooms. Afterwards, she'd carried the vase out onto the veranda where a gentle breeze sifted their faint fragrance. She inhaled deeply, noting the salty tang in the air. It was as if Mother Nature was silently offering her best gifts. Birds sang in the hedgerows as ewes called to their lambs from the hillside; she felt herself relax. Something akin to peace seemed to fill the morning. Frances felt glad to be alive.

She must have dozed momentarily as she was woken by a noisy car coming to an erratic halt in the driveway below; lowered voices were heading in her direction and she stood quickly smarting as the pain rose from her ankle. Her earlier composure disappeared as she saw Roger and his daughters approaching. She panicked in those few seconds, but realised there was no escape for her; she had to face this unpleasant task and something of the old Frances stirred within her; the stoic woman of common sense was coming to her rescue.

'Hello, Aunt Fran.' Their voices were watery with grief. She hadn't seen her nieces for many years and was amazed by these young women standing in front of her. She did a quick calculation they must be somewhere in their mid-twenties by now. Suzanne was older than Harriet by two years. She felt ashamed of herself for not remembering their exact ages, but of course, there had never been the opportunity to develop a closer relationship with them. Harriet shared her mother's beauty, but Suzanne favoured Roger, who stood between them, and Frances wondered if she should give the girls a hug, as both looked so morose and awkward. Instead, she heard herself say: 'If they'd known you were coming. I'm sure the others would have been here, but they're all out at the moment.'

'No matter!' Said Roger brusquely. 'We've just come to collect Cynthia's things.' Frances noted the tears brim in her nieces' eyes when their mother's name was mentioned. Roger cleared his throat, which had suddenly become gruff and continued. 'The girls wanted to see, where their mother had spent her last days.' Frances didn't know how to answer and decided one wasn't needed; she just nodded. 'I'll show the way she offered, but Roger coldly interjected. 'That won't be necessary, I know the way!'

'Of course! I'll make some coffee if you like?'

'No thanks! We've got a lot to do!'

'Oh, Dad!' The girls protested; 'We've been driving for hours; coffee and a snack would be great, thanks, Aunt Fran!'

'Suit yourselves! I'm off to sort Mum's things out.' Said Roger curtly. Suzanne came forward looking apologetically into her aunt's face.

'Don't take any notice, Aunt Fran, he's terribly upset and not himself at the moment.'

'We all are!' Said Frances as she led the way into the house.

However, it was only later as she sat with her nieces on the veranda, a plate of sandwiches piled high between them, she remembered the letters; had Roger found them, she wondered? Quickly she stood, almost knocking the rickety, bamboo table over, as she did so. 'Help yourselves! I won't be gone long.' She spoke trying to force a smile as she looked into the girls' surprised faces. They followed her retreating form with their eyes, before speaking. 'Mum's death has obviously hit her hard too!' Said Harriet.

'Of course! Why wouldn't it?' Her sister answered. Harriet just shrugged. 'I don't know, but don't you think it odd, we haven't seen Aunt Fran in years and Mum never spoke of her, the way she did about Uncle Henry and Aunt Phoebe. I mean, I hope Suze that we'll still be close when we marry.' Suzanne stopped eating mid-bite and turned to look at her sister. 'There aint anything gonna come between us two, honey! Certainly not any guys!' She'd spoken in an exaggerated American drawl and just for a moment they both giggled, then suddenly stopped, each feeling guilty. Neither realised how close Suzanne had come to the true reason, which had divided the affections of their mother and aunt. Moreover, neither would have believed their own father had been the cause of this rift. They looked around as if to check they hadn't been caught in, what they imagined to be, their betrayal of grief; but then relaxed when they saw they were still alone. However, both seemed to lose their appetite leaving, like some silent accuser, the large pile of sandwiches untouched between them.

Roger had been grateful to enter Cynthia's room alone. He'd tried to be strong for his girls, but his emotions were too near the surface and he dreaded them spilling over in a public display of grief. More than this, the few belongings which Cynthia had touched before her death, were almost sacred to him and he didn't want others handling them. He felt such intimate contact belonged to him alone and so was glad his daughters had stayed downstairs.

He felt apprehensive as he opened the wardrobe door and the familiar scent of Cynthia's perfume spilt over him, filling his senses with her absence. He reached out and felt the cold softness of her well-worn housecoat. He held it up to his face burying his tears in the lingering presence of her fragrance. Causing a tsunami of grief to well within him, leaving him feeling both shaken and lost. He tried to muffle his sobs, but all to no avail and soon his daughters were there, wrapping their arms around him as if they were the mothers of all comfort and he the child of their care. Soon they were all three weeping, yet even in their torrent of tears, they intuitively understood, in this moment of shared grief, they were all beginning the long process of coming to terms with death, the first step in their long journey towards healing.

Unknown to them Frances stood in the doorway. She had spent a few minutes in the orchard, trying to compose herself, before confronting Roger. Just, for a moment, when she'd heard the roses were for her, she'd wondered if he might have sent them. Now, she hated herself again, for having entertained such a thought, if only momentarily. She was about to retreat when her former self stepped into the room and took control. She waited for the sobs to subside and then spoke gently to the girls. 'Why don't you go downstairs and eat? I've made some fresh coffee and I'd rather not let those sandwiches go to waste.' Her timing was excellent and both Roger and the girls were grateful for her intervention; for neither of them knew what to say to one another, their emotions had spoken more eloquently and had articulated all that needed to be said on such an occasion. They'd drawn closer to one another and in doing so had made the bitterness of grief less grievous, understanding together they would find a way through. Cynthia would never leave them completely alone; for she'd given them one another and they would always carry her not only in their memories but also in their hearts; for they were beginning to realise the universal truth of love being stronger than death!

'Thank you!' Mumbled Roger, blowing his nose loudly and wishing Frances would leave. 'There is something I want you to see;' said Frances making her way over to where the book lay, enclosing the two letters. She lifted it and flicked the pages over gently until two envelopes slipped out. 'I noticed these yesterday, but didn't have the courage to open mine.' Roger looked uninterested; he just wanted to retrieve Cynthia's belongings and go. The thoughts of leaving his dead wife's things in the possession of strangers horrified him, trusting no one else to do the job

as thoroughly as himself. He wanted to complete his task, as quickly as possible, and leave. His memories of this place weren't good and he wanted to put them behind him. 'What is it?' He asked and Frances heard the irritation in his voice. She felt her own resentment begin to rise and hesitated before speaking. 'Well?' He repeated impatiently as he began taking Cynthia's clothes out of the wardrobe and laying them almost reverently on the bed; before folding them neatly in a case. Frances later remembered the gentleness with which he touched each garment and caressed each fold. It made her feel like some voyeur witnessing an intimacy, she had no right to. She felt uncomfortable. 'It can wait!'
'Is it anything to do with Cynthia?' He asked this almost absentmindedly as he continued to caress and fold her clothes. 'Of course!' she'd been about to add, 'Isn't everything between us about Cynthia?' But her self-possession and newly found dignity, would not allow her this indulgence. Instead, she said: 'It's a letter addressed to you. There is also one for me, which I haven't opened yet. Cynthia must have written them the night before she died.' She saw the pain in his eyes as he left his packing and almost snatched the letter from her hand. He looked, almost disdainfully into her eyes. 'I'd like to be alone now if you'll allow me to be?' Frances withdrew without speaking and made her way downstairs. Promising herself she wouldn't open the letter until she was alone. She felt it would be too great a risk to do so. For even though she longed to discover the contents, she also dreaded what they might say.

Henry and Anna walked in silence their tension, like some invisible link, keeping them in step. At last, when they reached the summit of a steep, grassy slope, Henry suggested they sit down and talk. 'We're unlikely to be interrupted here.' He said, spreading a rug for them both to sit on. Anna was the first to speak. 'Well, this is a treat having you all to myself, for once!' Her sarcasm hung in the air between them and Henry sighed deeply. 'I know we haven't had much free time together this year, but it was your decision to go off to Spain and leave me on my own.'
'You've hardly been on your own!' Henry sighed again. He knew it was pointless to rationalise with Anna when she was in this mood. She was hurting and therefore reasoning was negated by an all-consuming emotional pain. 'I'm sorry!'
'That's supposed to put everything right, is it?'

'You know it is a wider issue than that; we need to talk, make changes, look at our lifestyles, plan ahead a little more and build in protected times for ourselves.'

'Huh!' Anna was still hurting.

'Look, we have to work through this together, if anything is going to change between us; I'm not the only one who has been busy with other things!'

'People! You mean.'

'Be reasonable Anna, my work involves people!'

'But you don't know where to draw the boundary lines, do you?'

Then Henry was silent. He looked at the hills for inspiration and then at the grassy ground surrounding them. He began tugging at it and then pulling small handfuls out as if these were the weeds that needed uprooting from the barren ground of their current relationship. The garden of his marriage needed cultivating; this he understood, but they both needed to be willing to work at this, planting seeds from which to nurture new life. 'You know Anna I couldn't function if it wasn't for you.' This only served to inflame her indignation. She stood up glaring down at him. 'Is that how you see me? Just here so that you can comfortably get on with your life? Is that all my purpose is?' Henry stood too and reached out to hold her, but she stepped back out of his reach. 'Anna, I didn't mean it like that!'

'Then what did you mean? Have you forgotten I work full-time too? I'm also dealing with people every day. Yes, like you, children as well as their families, but still I'm there for you and the boys!' Henry held his hands out pleadingly. 'What do you want me to do. Anna? Tell me!' Anna bent to pick up her sun hat and started walking quickly away. Then without looking back she called out: 'Has it really come to this? I even have to tell you how to love me? I've had enough!' Henry sat down again, his head in his hands. If Anna had looked back, she might have felt some regret, but she didn't.

Frances saw Suzanne and Harriet were content to sit on the veranda as they gradually ate their way through the sandwiches she'd prepared. Evidently, their outburst of grief had renewed their appetites. Relieved temporarily of any duties she made her way to the kitchen and opened Cynthia's letter, which she read through on a roller-coaster of emotion.

Dearest Frances,

If you're reading this then it is both my time and my way to say goodbye!

You may think I have blamed you for all that has happened between us over the years, but that isn't true; rather, I have always blamed myself and have felt ashamed to face you.

You and Roger were engaged before I came on the scene. However, what happened between Roger and I, which I will confess began with sibling rivalry, deepened into the reality of love, the kind that lasts. I've tried to comfort myself with the thought I really saved you from a marriage, which probably was doomed to failure. For how could Roger have fallen for me, if he had been truly and deeply in love with you? However, I've always had a niggling conviction that, if I hadn't contrived to gain his affections, then he would have been content and ultimately fulfilled in his relationship with you. I feel guilty for cheating on you all those years ago and I now want to ask if you can find it in your heart to forgive me?

This was my reason for coming on this holiday of Phoebe's. I wanted to make my peace before I died.

However, after our conversation this evening, I've gained far more! For, I now realise the depth of love we share as sisters, despite our years of estrangement. You see Frances, I already knew you had slept with Roger for he confessed all, many years ago. This he did out of his love for me in an effort to restore our marriage, following his unfaithfulness: to wipe the slate clean as it were. More than this, wanting me to realise the true depth of his love and risking all to do so. I understood this and believed him; finding myself willing to give him a second chance. I forgave him and our relationship has been closer and more complete as a result.

However, I continued to bear a grudge towards you, until our time together this evening. You see, I came to understand it was out of your love for me, you lied and withheld the truth, which you believed I wouldn't be able to bear, due to my much-weakened condition. You will never know how much your thoughtful consideration and the realisation of your love for me, has made it possible to let go of my life in peace.

My dear Frances, thank you for your kindness. I take your act of love as a wonderful revelation of your true feelings towards me, as well as your forgiveness for my intervention in your engagement. If possible, will you always remember me with love, rather than the recriminations I deserve?

Your loving sister,
Cynthia. XXX

Frances felt herself shaking and sitting down at the small kitchen table, she wept for all that had been, for all that might have been and then for all that never would be, nor ever could be again!

Eventually, she dried her eyes. Although, she was far from calm. She was angry, remorseful, jealous, indignant her forgiveness should be taken for granted. For Cynthia, in the letter, admitted she'd knowingly made a play for Roger not despite, but because he was engaged to her sister. Until now she had always believed it had been Roger who had made the first move. She still remembered the transformation in his expression when Cynthia had entered the room all those years ago and especially how his eyes had followed her every move. But never had she suspected her sister of deliberately planning to ruin her engagement and ultimately her life. There had never been any serious relationship for her since Roger; there had of course, been the occasional night out making up a foursome with friends, from time to time, but there had never been anyone who stirred her emotions the way Roger had. He'd been her first and only love. Now, she was angry not only with Cynthia and herself for being such a fool but also with Roger. How dare he use her or speak to her the way he had! In that moment she loathed both him and Cynthia, but not as much as she loathed herself. Now, she still had to face her nieces. She tried not to think of the possibility that, if not for Cynthia's triumph these might have been her daughters. However, even as this uncomfortable thought surfaced in her consciousness, she struggled to banish it. She wanted to rise to her sister's magnanimous gesture, but found herself unable to do so; for unlike Cynthia she had to go on living with the reality of her wasted years and was left wondering if a futile future was to be the only legacy left to her by her sister. Suddenly her belief in the impossible, faded.

She heard her nieces talking and Roger's steps on the stairs; she splashed water on her face and smoothed her hair briefly in front of the mirror, before straightening her shoulders and walking out to meet them. They were already in the hallway about to leave. 'Oh, Aunt Fran, there you are! We wondered where you were?' They came forward to give her a hug, but Roger muttered he would take Cynthia's things down to the car. 'Won't you wait until the others return?' Asked Frances, but Roger was already walking out of the door. Harriet kissed her cheek. 'Dad isn't himself at the moment, I'm sure you understand it's nothing personal, Aunt Fran, don't you?'

'Of course.' She found herself answering automatically as she gave both nieces a hug. 'I understand completely.' She watched them walk down to the car, but found herself unable to wave them goodbye as they drove away. Not once had Roger glanced in her direction and if he had done so, she knew he would have seen nothing but fury blazing in her eyes.

Frances usually dealt with her stress by walking it off, but her ankle was too painful. Instead, she returned to the veranda and sat in the warm sunshine trying to regain her calm before the others returned. It was late May and the day was warm. Bees were buzzing busily between the apple blossoms in the orchard and somewhere in the distance, the sound of a lawnmower droned drowsily. Frances felt the tension in her limbs begin to fall away and despite everything, she found herself beginning to doze off; she almost succeeded until the sound of quick footsteps roused her. She looked up to see Anna entering the farmhouse. She called out to her, but apparently, Anna didn't hear. She was just about to drop off again when she heard the sound of a car pulling up below; it sounded its horn and Anna appeared at the front door carrying a suitcase. She slammed the door noisily behind her and made her way down to the taxi. Within moments she was gone without a word.

A few minutes later, Henry appeared. 'Was Anna in that taxi?' He was red in the face and perspiring. He looked as though he'd been running. 'Yes!' Replied Frances testily. 'Don't ask me where she was going because I haven't a clue!' Without a word, he disappeared inside and soon emerged with his luggage.
'I'm sorry Fran to take off like this, but I'm afraid I have to go. I'll be in touch though.' Then, without waiting for an answer he too drove away. Frances felt drained; too many emotions had sapped her energy in one morning.

Phoebe was still recovering from the surprise of Henry and Anna's hasty departure. She'd returned from her walk expecting to be able to continue the earlier conversation Henry had abruptly ended; it was out of character and it left her feeling rejected, although she hadn't been able to admit this to herself until now.

During her walk, she'd been thinking of her brother not just as a reliable confidante or someone she could rely upon for emotional support, but more as a close friend; one who loved her and who would always be there for her. Therefore, it was a surprise to hear both he and Anna had left, without saying goodbye; as well as a further shock to hear they'd left separately. However, she hadn't forgotten the raised voices raining down on her from the open window, which had been the reason for taking herself off in the first place to shut out the unpleasant presence of conflict, which always seemed to permeate her life in various ways.

Phoebe hated confrontation of any kind and always took measures to avoid it where possible. She felt that a similar distaste for this unpalatable aspect of life, was what motivated Henry to get involved in the problems of others; always offering a listening ear, taking time to find practical remedies on their behalf and always, yes always, putting their welfare before his own! This was what hurt her the most. He was her brother, not a colleague, therapist, or even a friend, but family! They shared the same flesh and blood. He'd always been there for her, always taking her part in any dispute and yet he'd walked away when she most needed his support. Of course, with her head, she understood his relationship with his wife must take priority over their own, but her heart didn't seem able to agree. For as Blaise Pascal had once written: "The heart has its reasons that the reason doesn't understand." At least she thought it went something like that and in this moment, she would have to agree. How could Henry walk away from her at this time, without even so much as a goodbye?

The next morning, to their surprise, Jones arrived. Both Frances and Phoebe were together in the parking area, arguing. Phoebe was insisting Frances couldn't possibly drive with her ankle as it was and she should leave the car and have a lift home with her. However, Frances wanted neither the inconvenience of having to make the return journey or the expense of having her car delivered.

Jones had taken the opportunity to walk up to the farmhouse to say goodbye to Henry to whom he felt he still owed a debt, which he would never be able to repay.

He'd overheard Phoebe's pleading with Frances and the reasonable persuasion she used. He also heard Frances's determined protests and her reasons for wanting to drive herself home. He stepped in graciously doffing his cap to the two women, like some grateful peasant to the landed gentry, as later described by Frances; although Phoebe had disagreed interpreting it as a gesture more in line with a polite Victorian gentleman, passing the time of day. However, neither of them was right; Jones simply felt uncomfortable, nervous even at what he was about to suggest. He wasn't an eloquent man and far from articulate, but he had a kind and generous heart and mainly, in response for that which Henry had done for him, he offered to drive Frances home.

Part Two: Chapter 1

Two years had passed and Frances was once again behind the wheel driving to North Wales. She was trying to remember the spot where, due to the heavy rainstorm, she'd pulled off the road and watched the lightning strike the outbuildings of Jones's farm. On that occasion, she'd been no more than a detached observer, vaguely wondering how the ensuing fire might impact the owner's life and having no awareness as to how it was about to impact her own. However, she did remember the sense of foreboding that had settled upon her at the time; and found herself wondering how different her life might have been if she'd intuitively given in to her instinct and returned home, as she'd felt the need to do.

She wanted time to reflect and so pulled in at the next grassy verge from where she could see the outline of Jones's farm, stretching in the distance. Only then did Frances realise she'd returned to the same spot of refuge as before, without recognising it. She remembered how she'd previously been tempted, in this very place, to swing the car around and head for home. It had been a feeling very much the same, as she now felt descending upon her.

Gazing, she took in the work of the new tenants; they'd already rebuilt the outbuildings, which she'd previously watched lighting up the sky, as they were consumed by hungry flames, razing them to the ground. Now they stood proud, their design modern and pragmatic, fire-resistant no doubt; yet echoing the aesthetic functionalism, found in current farming practices. She could just discern the field, which had been allotted as a campsite, but as yet there were no caravans or tents to be seen. She already knew what their particular choice of farming was to be and wondered, if in the longer-term they would make a better success of it than Jones had done? She sincerely hoped they would.

Her thoughts anxiously turned to Roger and the possibility of meeting him again. How would she greet him? She truly hoped he was a closed chapter in her life, as she was now able to think of him more objectively; nevertheless, she hadn't seen him since the last holiday and she could not be sure if being in his company again would leave her untouched. She shivered slightly; her love for Roger had begun many years ago in a time of innocence and trust. However, it had ended in guilt and self-loathing. Because of this Frances promised herself, she would never leave herself open to such exploitation again. Her defences were up and she was ready to ensure they were not violated in any way. Would the girls accompany him or would he come alone? She told herself it would make no difference to her whether or not he came, but then why did it cause her distress to think he might? Was it him or herself, who she was unable to trust? She had to find out but dreaded doing so! Despite this apprehension, she hoped the girls would be there; they'd visited her on several occasions over the last two years and she'd enjoyed their company, always looking forward to their next visit. She wondered if their motives were linked with their need for a maternal reference point and she had simply been the nearest. People had always commented on the vague likeness between herself and Cynthia; something she'd never been able to discern for herself. Nevertheless, she knew she could not replace their mother; neither did she wish to try. However, her need to be needed had surprised her yet again, with the newfound happiness in her nieces' company. At first, she'd been bewildered, wary even, of being sought out by them, but she'd gradually grown used to their visits and now looked forward to their times together. They were great company and padded her life around with increasing warmth and comfort, like some cosy jacket. The company of her nieces, a safe and familiar place in which to relax.

Henry and the boys had promised to be there too, but even at this late hour, she still didn't know if Anna would come. Henry and Anna had built a marriage, home and family between them and although it had been partially demolished, for some time now, she hoped it could be rebuilt, despite the fact they'd separated following the holiday two years ago.
Frances could not understand how people who had given so much to one another, could just walk away from it all. To her, it was like leaving a building only partly built and without the protective roof it needed, or abandoning a masterpiece of art still in the making. For Frances believed whatever you started in life you should finish, not trusting to leave loose ends untied. To her way of thinking, Henry and Anna should have resolved their differences by now. It was all too messy! She preferred ordered symmetry, as was reflected in her immaculate home, where not

a cushion was out of place. However, it escaped Frances that her own relationships had also at times left loose ends untied, when a little more understanding and even forgiveness, might have established these on a firmer footing. Some, also considered her blinkered to the onerous reality that, one could not always account for one's own mistakes, usually unpremeditated; or the responses of others to them. These, often seemed to bolt, like small animals jumping out of a cage, in which the door has been inadvertently left open. Rather, Frances preferred to keep her doors locked and to ignore those things she couldn't control. Others recognised this aspect of her character, thinking her intolerant. Whilst Frances herself was completely oblivious to it; not realising the judgements she made of others were, in turn, also made of her. Consequently, such attitudes had left many loose ends untied in her life; thereby, leaving them in danger of unravelling at any time!

Her thoughts turned to Phoebe and her infant daughter, Lucy; now a toddler, who brought a warm flush of emotion to Frances, as she pictured Lucy's cherubic face and the wonderful, silky softness of her skin; as on the last occasion when she'd carried her little niece, warm from her cot, downstairs. Now, she was looking forward to holding her again and motivated by this thought Frances eagerly turned back on to the road, her need for refuge temporarily postponed.

The holiday farmhouse appeared unchanged, except it looked brighter in the sunlight than before. This time she took care not to trip on the high step, noticing as she opened the door, that just as before, she was again the first to arrive. Momentarily, she felt a pang of regret, yet mixed with relief knowing Cynthia would not be joining them and immediately hated herself for such a thought. For even though their peace had been made before Cynthia's death; due to the nature of it, Frances still felt a great sense of injustice and as a result a lack of closure. This was one of the reasons she'd suggested their return this year. She was haunted by unwanted recollections of their last holiday there, which she hoped to replace with better ones; thereby exorcising the old. Moreover, she also suspected the others had their own difficult memories to expel.

She had just set her luggage down in the dark kitchen with its spacious slate floor when she heard a car pull into the rough parking area below. She peered out of the window, dusty and in need of a clean, to see Anna arrive in a red sports car. The driver, a man perhaps in his early fifties, jumped out and hurried to open the door for her. He bowed in mock chivalry as she stepped out, which made Anna laugh. 'Don't be an idiot Charles!' He stepped back in jest, his hand on his heart; 'Fair Lady, have you no need of a knight in shining armour?' Anna chuckled. 'Not today Sir Galahad!' He pretended to be heartbroken and turned slowly away, just as Anna reached into the back seat for her bag. Her back was turned away from him as he spun around and taking hold of her waist he lifted her in mid-air, twirling her around like a dancing dervish; 'Idiot!' She said laughing loudly; while Frances looking on, gained the impression that Anna had quite enjoyed the experience. She was about to turn away when she saw Charles plant a kiss on Anna's cheek. Again, Anna pushed him away laughing. 'Am I permitted to carry your bag up to the house? I'm dying for a cuppa!'

'No, best not, somebody might get the wrong idea.' He put his head on one side questioningly. 'Oh, and would you mind, if they did Anna darling?' Suddenly his voice was serious and Anna, momentarily, seemed to be at a loss for words. Still, he waited and the weight of his question bore down heavily on them both. 'I'm still a married woman, Charles.' He shrugged.

'In name only!'

'No, it is more than that.' Again, he shrugged.

'If you were my wife, I'd definitely make sure we didn't live apart for almost two years! What sort of a husband puts up with that?'

'Please Charles, don't. This is neither the time nor place to bring this up again.' He climbed back into the car and revved the engine, calling over his shoulder loudly as he left. 'Well, perhaps one day you'll let me know when and where that is!' Anna looked after him as he left, before bending to pick up her suitcase. Frances moved away from the window, but not before Anna had noticed her there. Both women felt awkward.

'I've just put the kettle on!' Called Frances as she heard the door open and Anna setting her case down in the hall. 'Oh good! Just what I need.' Anna, smiled, walking into the kitchen and giving Frances a hug. They both felt embarrassed and for a while neither spoke. Eventually, sitting opposite one another, either side of the huge oak table, Anna spoke. 'It's not what you think.'

'Isn't it?'

'Goodness no! Charles is just a colleague and a good friend. He has family in these parts and when he heard I was coming this way, he offered me a lift, that's all!'

'I see.'

'I hope you really do see, Frances? Because I wouldn't want Henry to get hold of the wrong end of the stick.'

'It's really none of my business.'

'No, it isn't! So, you won't mention it to Henry, will you?' Frances set down her cup, rather noisily.

'No, I won't!'

'Good! "Because people, who live in glass houses, shouldn't throw stones."'

'What do you mean by that?'

'I think you know what I mean.' And with that parting comment, Anna walked out of the room. This was not the beginning Frances had anticipated for the holiday and with a heavy heart she picked up the tea-stained cups, leaving them unwashed in the sink.

Anna did not reappear immediately and so, wanting some time to herself before the others arrived, Frances wandered out onto the veranda and down the stone steps to the orchard. Anna's words had stung her and even here, among the fruit trees, she felt taunted by memories of the past when she was last here, gazing into her abyss of self-loathing. It had been on that occasion when the unwelcome presence of Jones had almost literally tipped her over the edge. Nevertheless, he'd also saved her from certain death. She shuddered at the memory of the precipice, which had almost claimed her life. Since then she'd promised herself, she would never again fall into the same pit of despair. Her life was precious and she wanted to make it count. Her aim in organising this holiday had been to finally put to death both the traumas and the oppression of her past experiences and yet here they were rising up and confronting her at the bidding of Anna's spiteful speech. But within her, she knew it was not Anna who was her worst enemy, rather it was herself. Frances still had not been able to forgive herself for sleeping with Roger. She had wholly taken the blame and had lived with the consequences ever since. Was there to be no end to this torment, which like some sleeping Furie rose up occasionally to goad and torment her?

She thought of Roger; he'd sought her out not the other way around. Why, she wondered for the millionth time, had he done so? Had it really been due to the crisis in his life at the time when Cynthia was ill and unable to give him the support he needed? Or was it due to their broken engagement, from which she'd never really recovered? Because of this did Roger think he'd a rightful claim on both sisters? Even perhaps a debt to be repaid? Momentarily, she bridled inwardly at his arrogance as the Furie within again woke with a roar. She felt her heart rate increase and her head begin to pound. So, sitting down, on a wooden bench sequestered within a dry-stonewall and placing her hand on her heart. She tried to calm it by breathing deeply and focusing on the bees buzzing, busily amidst the blossom, but to no avail. She knew she couldn't place all the blame on Roger for she was just as culpable. Had she not wanted retaliation for the blow Cynthia had dealt her? Had she not wanted Roger as a woman wants a man? Hungry for both the fulfilment and completion love yearns for, which until then she'd been denied? Yes, she admitted to herself; I'm guilty as charged! But! For Frances, this was a very big but; for she felt just as she'd found revenge in sleeping with Cynthia's husband, had she not also vindicated her guilt by protecting Cynthia with her final lie. In her head these thoughts seemed to be a workable equation, but in her heart one which just didn't add up. For no matter how many times she tried to balance the books in her favour; Frances was still left with a large deficit of guilt, which she felt unable to clear. Because, far from the sweetness, she longed to savour, revenge had only brought her bitterness and regret.

Frances's self-persecution was interrupted by the arrival of another car. The car park was on the same level as the orchard and walking towards the iron gate linking them, she saw Henry pulling his suitcase out of the boot. She was genuinely sorry not to see the boys with him; she'd hoped their presence might be a helpful tool of reconciliation between their parents. Nevertheless, as usual she managed to hide her true feelings, disguising her inner turmoil and hiding her disappointment as she strode out to greet him smiling and effusive. Frances the stoic was once again in control.

'Anyone else arrived yet?' He asked, setting down his case and giving her an affectionate hug. Frances intuitively knew he was asking if Anna was there. 'Yes, Anna arrived about an hour ago. She was still unpacking when I came down here.'

'Good!' His reply was curt as he started for the house, walking quickly. Frances had to almost run to keep up with him. 'The boys couldn't make it then?' He didn't appear to hear her and continued towards the house not slackening his pace. Frances repeated her question as he continued walking. 'What? Did you say something?' With a sigh, Frances asked again. 'I don't actually know Fran, as I haven't seen them for a while.'

'So, do you think they may still be coming?'

'I really haven't a clue and to be honest, I really don't care!' Frances was shocked. These were not the words of the loving father she knew Henry to be. He must have seen the effect of his words upon her as stopping he turned towards her in way of an apology. 'Look, I'm sorry Fran; they aren't boys any longer, but young men. They're not very forthcoming these days, but just getting on with their own lives; maybe they will turn up, I really don't know.'

'Oh well!' Frances shrugged. Henry was still walking at a fast pace towards the house; he'd seen Anna appear on the veranda and so had Frances, who decided to turn back retreating beneath the soft fragrance of the orchard's blossom.

Chapter 2

Anna had settled herself on a sun-lounger, her eyes shielded by tinted sunglasses. Henry came and stood beside her, but she didn't move or acknowledge him in any way. 'Hello Anna.' His tone was as soft as a caress and she turned towards him, removing her glasses as if to see him more clearly. 'Hello Henry.' Her tone was not upbeat, neither was it welcoming and it left Henry without any certainty of the reconciliation for which he both hoped and longed. He would have liked to talk there and then, but Anna replaced her glasses before resettling herself in cushioned comfort, dismissing him, not with words, but with her body language. Henry understood and moved on. He'd not anticipated this encounter being easy but similarly had not expected the scenario of the last few seconds, which was worse than he'd hoped for. Perhaps Jack and Jake had been right. He didn't deserve Anna and had lost her completely due to his own foolishness! He'd been shocked to hear his sons speak to him in this way. How dare they interfere! He was angry with them, but not as angry as he was with his own lack of sensitivity, blinding him to the warning signs; causing him to lose Anna.

The lazy drone of the bees had soothed Frances's nerves; she hoped Phoebe would soon arrive with lovely Lucy. The child always drew happiness in her wake and had given Frances so much joy over the last fifteen months; she sat half-dozing in the warmth of the sun and thinking back over this time. She'd kept her word to Phoebe and had supported her both financially and emotionally throughout the pregnancy and after. Frances was present at Lucy's birth, helping Phoebe to remember her breathing exercises, cooling her face with a wet flannel, rubbing her back and holding her hand as each contraction squeezed the tiny life within her closer to the light of day. She'd groaned with Phoebe, pushed with Phoebe and finally wept with her as the little girl, after taking her time and exhausting them both, suddenly rushed into the world with a cry of protest. Phoebe had fallen asleep almost immediately and so the nurse handed Lucy to Frances. For all of two minutes she'd gently held the bundle of pink loveliness close; feeling as though nothing in her life had ever touched her heart as deeply as this tiny scrap of humanity, lying so peacefully in her arms.

Phoebe had moved in with her for the first three months and she'd been there, another pair of arms to share the demands of maternal care; it had been a learning curve for them both, an experience Frances would always remember. Until Lucy's birth, Frances had always thought she was not the maternal type, but now, too late, she realised this had been no more than a self-defence mechanism. After all, what was the point of yearning for what one could never hope to attain; Lucy was not her own but nevertheless had expanded both her life and experience into dimensions she'd been incapable of imagining before the baby's birth. Lucy's infant loveliness enabled her to experience not only new birth, but had also touched her life in new ways, augmenting her essence, rearranging her priorities, creating a more rounded character and a more complete Frances. In many ways, Lucy had provided her with a taste of motherhood, which she'd never thought to enjoy. Consequently, Lucy would always be more to her than just a niece.

It had been hard for her when Phoebe, after those first three months, had insisted on returning to her small London apartment. She still had several months maternity leave left and wanted to establish a routine with her baby. 'I have to do this Frances; I'm grateful for all your support, but I have to be able to cope alone.'

Frances wondered if Phoebe realised how attached to Lucy she was growing and might have felt threatened in some way. She'd felt a pang, akin to jealousy as if having just found a reason to look forward to a brighter future; it was to be cruelly snatched away. Nevertheless, she understood such thoughts were unreasonable and Phoebe's instincts were right; Lucy was her child and ultimately her responsibility, but to her annoyance her heart could not agree with her head. Frances, was still blind to her own need to be needed a trait which, if better understood, could be managed more as a strength, rather than a weakness. Phoebe had gone to great lengths to explain, Frances would always be involved with their lives and this had initially helped, but then fate had taken another turn and Frances could not then be sure of her own standing in the future.

At that same moment, Phoebe was bathing Lucy. The child chuckled and splashed in the soapy water, which spilt over the side and continued dripping onto the floor. Phoebe laughed and lifted Lucy out, reaching for a warm towel, which she wrapped snugly around the toddler, as she wriggled and chattered in her baby tongue. Phoebe gave a sigh of contentment as she thought back over the last few months whilst drying the child and wondered at all that had happened in so short a time. The outcome had been totally unexpected.

Out of the blue, Mason had returned unannounced! He turned up at Phoebe's office one day hoping to surprise her and take her out to lunch. Of course, he'd been shocked to learn she was on maternity leave, but nevertheless asked if she was still living at the same address. Her colleague, Emma, who was also a friend of Phoebe's, knew who Mason was and so willingly and hopefully informed him, she did! She'd seen the dismay and unasked questions in his eyes and had told herself, it was no more than he deserved. She was not going to be the one to tell him all he longed to know. So, perplexed and anxious he'd hurried away, without even thanking her. Once outside he'd hailed a cab, garbling the address and throwing his case in first. The driver had turned in his seat, sliding the small window separating them to one side. 'Hey! I can see you're in a hurry, but we'll arrive faster if I know the address.' He'd smiled good-naturedly; as impatiently Mason repeated it, at the same time asking him to 'Step on it!'

Twenty minutes later it had been a dumbstruck Phoebe, carrying her baby, who opened the door to him. Mason looked from the bundle in her arms into Phoebe's eyes. 'Is it mine?' For moments she neither moved nor spoke. A helter-skelter of emotion sent her spiralling down, dizzy with confusion, shock, unasked questions and a fair amount of anger at his audacity in just turning up unannounced like this. She nodded, standing back for him to enter. But it was his turn to be stunned and he stood immobilised staring at the child. 'What is it?' He asked. Phoebe had begun to recover and with an edge of agitation, laced with more than a thread of resentment murmured. 'This is Lucy; she is three and a half months old.' Mason, rather awkwardly, but also with extreme tenderness lifted the child out of her arms. He unfolded the shawl and noting her tiny hands and feet, caressed her soft rounded cheek with his finger. A slight fragrance of baby lotion and breast milk, emanated from her tiny form, as she screwed her face into a red ball and began to yell. Quickly, he handed her back to a cross and angry Phoebe who held her protectively, wrapping her close again in the shawl. At last Lucy's cries subsided, as she fell asleep in her mother's arms.

'Why didn't you tell me?' It was Mason's turn to feel angry.

'What makes you think you had any right to know? You were the one who walked out of our lives, remember!'

'That's not true.' He protested. His eyes were glassy and his face red with emotion.

'Oh! Denial now is it? Then where have you been for the last nine months?'

'You know where I've been and I didn't know you were expecting when I left!'

'Would it have made any difference, if you had?' He ran his fingers through his hair and moved self-consciously. 'Of course it would have! Don't you know me Phoebe?' She felt close to tears.

'How dare you come back here and try to put all the blame on me. You left with no promise to return, without leaving a forwarding address, with no contact not even a text during all these months and you turn up unannounced and expect...' Here her words faltered falling unspoken from her lips and it was her turn to shift uncomfortably. She'd imagined his return, so many times, but in her imagination, it had never been like this. She'd always thought they would be overwhelmed with the emotions, which had driven their brief affair, but now as she looked at him, she felt he was no more than a stranger and she resented his proprietorial attitude towards both her and Lucy. He'd no understanding, no insight into what she'd been through, both before as well as after the birth. The mountain of inexperience and abandonment she'd tried to climb alone. If it had not been for Frances's support, she didn't know how she would have coped. Leaving Frances's home and care had been a wrench, but something she knew it had been right to do. She had to learn to manage on her own if she was to succeed. Nevertheless, looking after her baby single-handed had left her exhausted and concerned for the future. She knew Frances was waiting in the wings to step in when needed, but felt it was not fair to either her sister or Lucy, to put what she perceived to be her sole responsibility on another. At least this was how she had justified her actions to herself, not realising how badly she had misread the situation. However, although she would never admit it,

Phoebe knew within herself, she was jealous. Frances was mature, organised and self-sufficient. She'd money to spend and time to give, which Phoebe hadn't; therefore, she fretted that when she returned to work, the bond between Frances and Lucy might grow into a barrier, which excluded her. To Phoebe, Lucy was the most precious individual in her life and her affection was non-negotiable. Phoebe remembered these things now as she looked with hostility into Mason's face. It was not all his fault; she understood she was just as culpable. However, despite this, she still blamed most of her suffering, anxiety and concern, for the future of their child, on him. 'I think you should leave! The one thing you're very good at!' She realised she was shouting and Lucy woke with a cry. 'No! This time I'm going nowhere.' Mason said as he sat down on the sofa looking defiant and resolute.

Suddenly, Phoebe felt weak and shaken. The last few months had taken their toll on both her energy and confidence. She sat on the sofa beside him suddenly deflated, as a strange wave comprising a mixture of resentment and relief washed over her, causing Lucy to tremble and howl. Tentatively, Mason held out his arms. 'Let me take a turn.' His voice had been gentle but insistent. Without a word and yet reluctantly, Phoebe surrendered their daughter into her father's arms. 'Why don't you try and get some sleep, Phoebe? You look exhausted!' The softness of his tone swept over her like a cool breeze bringing relief in the heat of summer. He saw her hesitate. 'It's alright, Lucy and I will still be here when you wake, because this time I'm here to stay!'

Frances hoped Phoebe would soon arrive with Lucy; she missed their company and would rather have someone else here than be alone with Henry and Anna. She'd heard nothing from either of them since their arrival, when each had gone to their separate rooms. She felt herself alone but content to be so, for it provided her with the opportunity to daydream and remember.

Chapter 3

The bees were again bumbling lazily; their honey labours a stark contrast to the languorous mood, which seemed to gradually sweep over Frances in the heat of the day. Her thoughts returning to their last holiday here and how Jones had so unexpectedly offered to drive her home. At the time, his generous proposal had surprised her; nevertheless, despite the fact he'd saved her life, she hardly knew him and the thoughts of being held captive in his company for five uninterrupted hours, had filled her with alarm. She'd politely refused, pointing out the inconveniences such a gesture would incur on him. However, these he'd easily dismissed. Frances felt cornered and like a cat with its back to the wall, her hackles had risen. She'd been about to point out that, she'd no intention of being in his debt; before suddenly remembering how much she already owed to him. However, Frances had no wish to increase the debt and desperately wondered how she could avoid his offer and yet retain her dignity. However, the vision of herself hanging, screaming from the cliff face brought the embarrassing realisation, her sense of propriety had already been compromised. Neither, did it occur to her that, for Jones, the circumstances were also regrettable. Therefore, she'd resorted to rudeness, naming the proposal as impossible, for her only intention was to drive home with her sister. 'No help needed, thank you!' She'd said with all the assertion she could muster as she turned to Phoebe, appealing for her support.

Unexpectedly, Phoebe had sided with Jones, reasoning it was a good solution. So, although reluctantly, Frances eventually agreed. She knew if she went with Phoebe it would take her sister miles out of her way and in her condition that would be an extra drain on her energy. Moreover, she'd seen the tired hope in Phoebe's eyes and understood she was desperate for her to say, yes. Therefore, she decided to trample on her pride, for as well as Phoebe's needs, she also had her own to consider. The pain in her ankle had been great and she knew to drive alone would be a hazard. Therefore, she accepted, but with one proviso, to which Jones had eventually agreed. Frances would pay him for his trouble and also for his return train fare as well as any intermediate accommodation needed. Once decided, the relief on Phoebe's face was undisguised and strengthened Frances for her ordeal ahead; knowing she'd at least spared Phoebe any further distress. That settled, with her usual stoical nature, she resigned herself to an awkward and uncomfortable few hours ahead.

And so, the first hour of that memorable journey had begun with both of them sitting somewhat stiffly as well as silently, just staring ahead as the road unfolded before them. Frances was thinking about Jones's erratic driving when he'd given her and Phoebe a lift back to the farmhouse and she was anxious. However, to her relief, he seemed to be in a more measured frame of mind, his driving skills competent and careful. 'Do you mind if I switch on the radio?' She'd asked. He gave an almost imperceptible shrug. 'It's your car! I'm just the driver.' He hadn't even turned to look at her, but just kept his eyes on the road.

'It won't distract you?'

'What do you think I am then? A maniac of the roads, is it?' She was startled.

'No, of course not!' She was now also embarrassed, until glancing sideways she saw him smile.

'Just my way of speaking like.' He said turning towards her and grinning. Frances had never seen him smile before and noticed how it transformed his face; until now always so serious, always so sorrowful, as if the footprints of living had trampled all over it, disfiguring the real man behind a tragic mask.

She began to relax. 'Any preference?'

'No, you put on your choice.' Again, his eyes were on the road. She'd hesitated wondering if her choice would be acceptable, trying to guess what his might be, if any. But she'd been unable to and so resorted to Classic FM, which at the very least, was usually soothing and calm. The perfect antidote to the fast-flowing traffic weaving in and out of the four lanes and the likely congestion they would be bound to endure at some stage of the journey.

The first tune had been mellifluous, flowing in soft melodies, saturating the atmosphere between them, with a new sense of light-heartedness; screening the noisy rush of passing traffic. Frances had lain back in the seat closing her eyes; she must have been more tired than she'd realised, for she'd fallen asleep, not waking until they'd pulled into a service station. She'd sat up quickly trying to hide her embarrassment, feeling awkward. Wondering if she'd slept with her mouth open: snored even. She wiped the damp drool from her cheek, confirming her worst fears. The radio still played and without thinking she turned it off. 'Cup of tea, is it?' He asked and not for the first time Frances felt irritated by his manner. 'I insist on buying then.' She'd answered reaching for her handbag. 'What would you like Mr Jones?' Again, he surprised her by sitting back in the seat, lifting his cap and scratching his head. 'My name is Davyd.'

'What would you like Davyd?' She'd tried to hide her discomfort, but nevertheless, it fell from her faltering lips heavy with resentment. He noticed. 'I mean no offence Madam.' Again, she felt embarrassed.

'None taken.' There had been a moment of silence, as if an invisible curtain was being drawn between them; one which screened them both from any understanding of the other. She'd felt its unseen presence and so after a while, reluctantly added. 'Call me Frances.' Again, he'd surprised her by turning and saying.

'Well Frances, now we're on first name terms, perhaps we should go in together? I could do with stretching my legs.'

Again, she felt compromised, but as she couldn't think of any reasonable objection they'd entered the services together. Jones headed for the coffee bar and she followed. Reaching the counter before her he ordered two teas. 'I was going to have coffee!' Jones heard the anger in her tone, but his expression remained inscrutable. 'The teas are for me! Thirsty I am, you see?' Her face turned a crimson hue, a mixture of embarrassment and self-righteousness. Jones paid for his teas and went to sit at one of the small laminated tables. After paying for her coffee, she considered sitting at another, but thought this wouldn't be very helpful with at least three enforced hours in one another's company, still stretching before them. Therefore, fuming inwardly; she'd joined him, wondering if he would have behaved in this way, if Henry had been with them. Then she remembered; Henry had saved this man's life and in turn, he'd saved hers. Why then did he irritate her so much? Finally, she decided it was the way he ended most of his answers with a question. As if on cue he spoke again. 'I see you liked the roses then, didn't you?' Frances looked confused.

'Sorry?' She asked questioningly.

'The roses, I noticed you've brought them with you. You like them, don't you?'

'They were from you?' Frances's voice echoed both her surprise and obvious disappointment.

'Indeed, they were!' He grinned with a new bashfulness, which again surprised her.

'I see!' She answered, but in reality, she didn't. For she'd wondered if they might have been from Roger, offered as an apology, perhaps. Jones smiled. He didn't seem offended at not being thanked. Just pleased that Frances knew.

They drank in silence and this continued until they were again seated in the car. Then Jones turned to her. 'Look, Frances, I know you'd rather be driving yourself home, but I'm here and I'm asking, can we make the best of it?' She turned to face him, her eyes flashing with anger at his directness, 'I understand you're doing this for Henry; I know you feel in his debt. But this is not about you or Henry this is about me. I'm not a child and I certainly do not want to be patronised!' He pushed his cap back and scratched his head again, which inflamed her fury further. 'Do you have to keep doing that?' For at least a minute he sat holding the steering wheel and gazing ahead. It was as if he was engaged in some sort of inner struggle. Finally, he spoke, his voice bewildered. 'Do you really think I'm driving you home for my own benefit or Henry's?' His face was incredulous as he turned again to face her. 'Frances, the only reason I'm doing this is for you!' She opened her mouth to speak, but before she could he continued. 'That day, following Cynthia's death, when I found you in the orchard;' here he paused and she wondered what was coming next. 'I saw something in your eyes, not the anger I can see at this moment, but something, which I identified with because I'd felt the same way when my wife died. Guilty, responsible, desperate as though I'd messed up both my life and hers. A failure, I felt, as well as a fool! I hated myself and I'd had enough of living. I just wanted out! And that's what I saw, just as though you'd rubbed a face cream, which spelt defeated, all over your face!' Frances was taken aback. She'd never given Jones any credit for emotional discernment. She saw him as some barbarian to be tolerated in small doses, or at the very least as some socially deprived land worker, with little conversation and even fewer manners. But never had she caught a glimpse of this man, the one sitting beside her, speaking in soft, sensitive tones. 'It's the only reason I followed you and glad it is that I did. I understand you see, the mask you put on for your family. I see what they don't see, a woman who is pretending.' Here she bristled again, but only slightly this time. 'What I'm trying to say is; I see someone pretending not to be torn apart with pain when they can barely breathe for the hurt inside. A hurt buried so deeply because they are trying to hide it not only from others, but also from themselves. I know this because I've been there and I've come to understand one can't go on living in this way. You were meant for more. Life is meant for more! If I hadn't learnt this, I would have no right to speak to you in this way, would I? But I have and I want to help you learn it too, I want to be a friend to you Frances; I really do! Will you let me?' She suddenly felt the need to blow her nose loudly. 'You really are an infuriating man! Why do you always end your questions as well as your answers, with another question?' Her words revealed her irritation, but nevertheless the anger had melted from her tone. He'd turned away from her, but before he switched on the ignition, she caught the smile on his face in the driving mirror and as they drove off, she heard him mumble: 'Seems I'm not the only one who ends their sentences with a question, isn't it?' Frances smiled. His words seemed to lift the curtain of tension between them, enabling them to see, as through a window, straight into the other's soul; beginning for them both a new chapter in their lives.

Frances was abruptly interrupted in her reverie, by voices below. Roger and the girls had arrived. Now they were here, she was happy to see them and called out a welcome. The girls waved and Roger nodded as they pulled their luggage out of the boot. Frances went down to lend the girls a hand and laughing the three of them struggled, up the steep path, with their ungainly load. Roger followed silently, his face grim and taciturn. 'Glad you could make it.' She said after the girls had noisily disappeared upstairs, leaving them alone in the lounge. The farmhouse had been built in the seventeenth century and its walls were thick, pierced by two tiny windows, which let in little light. 'Hmm!' He said setting his case down and looking around with distaste. 'Can't say I'm pleased to be back here! I only came for the girls' sake. Whatever possessed you to call us all back here? Couldn't you have found better accommodation?' She looked at him, no longer ashamed to meet his gaze. 'We all need to move on Roger and in order to do so we need to exorcise the ghosts of memory, which still haunt us and replace them with better ones, if we are ever to have closure.' He cleared his throat and seemed to find it difficult to answer. Nevertheless, he continued, his voice taut with tension. 'I owe you an apology, Frances.'

'Oh really?' This was unexpected and she wondered what he was about to say. 'I read Cynthia's letter!'

'Ah!' She said, folding her arms defensively across her chest. 'And what did she say?'

'That she understood why we'd both told her different versions about what happened between us and you weren't to blame and...' Here he lowered his voice. 'Neither was I!' Frances's hands moved from her chest to her hips. 'I know, my letter said much the same thing. However, because Cynthia forgave us both, it doesn't mean I've also forgiven you or that I ever will!' He looked taken aback, this obviously was not the reply he'd anticipated. 'I loved Cynthia and I never meant to hurt you, Frances.'

'So that makes everything alright then, does it?' He turned to the small window, there were two dead flies on the sill and for a moment he stared at them, before turning back to face her. 'Look, I know this is not going to sound good, but the time we met at the motel, I was in a bad way and you were there.' She was looking at him directly, but he couldn't meet her eyes. 'So, you used me!'

'No! Not in the way you infer.' He protested.

'Which way then?' Her arms were folded once again, and her words were like liquid acid burning into his conscience. 'You don't understand Frances. I needed someone and you were there! I never meant to hurt you or Cynthia.'

'But you did! You hurt us both for your own selfish ends.' He held his arms out, almost in the gesture of a plea. 'Look, I thought you wanted closure? But it seems to me you're determined to stir up the past and not in a good way!'

'You're wrong Roger. I've moved on and I've brought us all here to help us all move on.'

'Well, it seems a strange way to go about doing so.'

'To the detriment of us all, we've hidden the past for too long; now we need to bring it out into the open.'

'But you can't forgive me?' He spoke like a little boy, who after stealing another child's book and scribbling over every page, tries to hand it back; it appears to still be in one piece, but nevertheless ruined. 'Saying one didn't mean to hurt another, doesn't bring healing, just as saying 'sorry' can't repair the damage which has been done. I need to see you are really sorry, but I haven't seen any sign of it, so far!' Roger still couldn't look at her, as she stared relentlessly into his face. 'You've changed Frances; you're a different woman to the one I used to know!'

'Yes, I am! Thank goodness! But no thanks to you!' He didn't look back as he slowly walked out of the room, reminding Frances of a dog chastised for some misdemeanour that slopes off with its tail between its legs. Just for a moment, she wanted to call out to him to come back, sit down and talk with her! She felt annoyed with herself for her lack of patience, understanding and even forgiveness. What was the matter with her, she wondered? Was not this the reason she'd called them all back here in the hope they might move on to a better place? Yet here she was refusing the olive branch held out to her!

Chapter 4

'Hurry up won't you! We'll be late!' Phoebe was trying to put Lucy's shoes on her and the child was making a game of it her chubby, little legs kicking as she chuckled aloud. Phoebe sighed, but smiled as she lifted Lucy onto her knee and strapped those fat little feet into their canvas shoes. 'Now Lucy, be good! Today we're going to meet all the family; well most of them anyway and mummy wants Lucy to be well-behaved.' The child looked into her face with toddler intensity, before laughing and jumping off to focus on her toy farm. She sat contentedly lifting each plastic animal and trying to imitate the noise it should make. Phoebe watched, her eyes alight with love, close to adoration. This was contentment she thought, a state which only fifteen months earlier she would never have thought possible. The wheel of fortune had turned in her favour, or so her friends told her; but Phoebe believed her contentment was borne of love the invisible Spirit, which manifested its presence in and through so many situations, incidents, coincidences and of course: people. For her, Mason and Lucy both embodied and generated the love, which suffused her being, generating the energy with which she now embraced life. For Phoebe, love was not just an ineffable emotion, but one which could be practically expressed and experienced in this material world.

Mason's return had been a shock, accompanied by mixed emotions and a great deal of resentment. However, he'd patiently and stubbornly borne her avalanche of icy rebuffs and gradually her heart had begun to melt. His return had been solely to find Phoebe, without any knowledge of Lucy's existence and as he professed, if he'd known about his little daughter's imminent arrival, then he would have returned much sooner. He regretted the time he'd missed; the anticipation of planning, preparing and wondering, which surrounds every birth. He was sorry Phoebe had carried all the responsibility alone and in quiet moments he admitted to himself he was also slightly jealous of the joy, excitement and experience of bearing and birthing new life, which had been hers alone. However, he wasn't stupid and understood the trauma, anxiety, doubt, and confusion, such circumstances had placed firmly on her young shoulders and at times he wondered, if he would ever truly be able to forget all the worry his unthinking attitudes and actions had caused. He tried to appease his conscience by acknowledging his ignorance of the true nature of her predicament; after all he reasoned, Phoebe could have got in touch, but in doing so he failed to perceive the pride and dignity of her decision. Only gradually, over the months following his return, did the full realisation of her lonely journey begin to dawn upon him and he vowed never to leave her again. In doing so he extinguished his youthful flame of self-assurance and selfishness forever; replacing it with a newfound humility and faithfulness, which expanding through his heart embraced both Phoebe and Lucy, as an extension of himself.

Originally, he'd returned to New Zealand, simply to fulfil a promise made to his father, to spend some time on the farm, before finally deciding where his strengths lay. He had left unaware of his true feelings for Phoebe and had been surprised and then stricken by an emotion akin to bereavement, which had engulfed him, threatening to overwhelm him within the first month of his return.

At first, there had been a wonderful sense of homecoming; the return to all that was familiar. The pleasure he saw on his parents' faces as they greeted him, with such an effusion of love each morning, when he appeared at the breakfast table. Each would speak to him alone of their sadness during his absence, the way this had hung between them, unspoken, but nevertheless present every morning, every mealtime and evening. They reminded him of the ewes who called out over long hours and into the nights when their lambs were first separated from them. But his parents were not sheep and he was no longer their lamb, but a man who needed his mate. He now realised, no one and no brilliant prospect or promise, could fulfil the need he felt for Phoebe; the proximity of her body, her laughter that gilded her sense of fun, the security of being together, knowing at the beginning and end of every day she would be there, making sense of their time and experience, adding purpose, motivation and meaning to his life. His grief and sense of loss had grown beyond his control, unable to focus, unable to concentrate, he'd withdrawn into himself. He became taciturn and uncommunicative spending much of his time alone, torn between loyalty to his father and his struggle to forget Phoebe. His parents had been concerned at this unknown malady, which seemed to be changing their son into a stranger they no longer recognised. Consequently, they'd finally broached the subject with him and he'd told them about Phoebe. 'Go and bring her back with you son!' They'd said with relief; having been plagued with concerns Mason might have been trying to hide some terminal disease from them; he'd lost so much weight, which had only reinforced their worries. 'She may not want to come back;' he'd said, remembering the almost flippant leave he'd taken.

Phoebe remembered driving him to the airport and watching as he'd disappeared through the departure gate; he'd turned and waved before disappearing and she'd felt as if her heart had disappeared with him. At the airport they'd discussed their times spent together, the fun they'd found in one another's company. Mason had taken her hands in his, stroking them gently with his thumbs. 'It's been so good; thank you Phoebe! I wouldn't have missed the last few months for anything!' He'd seemed so nonchalant in his body language and yet the intonation in his voice was sincere. Phoebe was left puzzled over this seemingly bitter-sweet contradiction; an oxymoron in terms of behaviour. A term which comprised two opposites to express one meaning, just as two differing lives had united as one to express a new dimension of themselves, to which the necessity of the other became paramount. Conversely, Mason's departure had seemed to reduce their relationship; hyphenating it to no more than a holiday romance, comprising the integrity of their union. But, for her it had been different. Already, she'd felt her life intertwined with his. She'd given him her soul as well as her body and he'd taken both so lightly, almost as his due, not treating them carefully, handing them back to her at the departure gate, like unwanted goods, for which he took no responsibility.

She'd struggled with her tears as he'd receded into the distance with just a casual last wave and friendly grin, taking her heart with him and also her hopes.

Months later he'd returned professing his love, the inability to live without her and asking her to return with him to New Zealand. Something, she found herself unable to do.

Many texts and phone calls had crossed the world, between parents and son, until a surprise offer was made. Mason's father had been thinking of expanding his farm. However, now his only son had decided to stay in the UK; he offered to set up a second farm there, if Mason was willing to run it for him.

Mason had been brought up with sheep farming and knew as much as his father. Since a young child, he'd helped with lambing and shearing. He understood the ailments as well as the necessary treatments, having accompanied every vet on each of their visits to the flock, since his boyhood. Neither was he afraid of the hard work involved or the demands such care required. He'd discussed the idea with Phoebe, tentatively at first, unsure of her response. To his delight, she'd responded positively, later remembering that Jones's farm was still on the market. Together they'd looked over it and discussed possible changes and improvements. His parents had come over to look at it and to meet their new daughter-in-law to be, as well as their first granddaughter. They were both as smitten as their son. Phoebe had found them easy to relate to, not the unapproachable in-laws' scenario at all, and it filled her heart with a sad joy to see Lucy so at home in their arms. She was grateful their little girl would at least have one set of grandparents to indulge her as she grew.

They had bought the farm and work had taken place over the last few months. They were also going to run a camping site overlooking the bay. It was on the furthest outlying field and commanded a wonderful view. They had built shower-blocks and toilets. There was running water and electric hook-ups. It was a great place for families to come and so strategically placed for much of the North Wales coastline and attractions. They were now due to open in a month and had already taken fifty bookings! Tyrone and Megan's finances had been ploughed into the farming side of the industry; whilst Mason and Phoebe had taken out loans to support the camping venture. They knew between farming and camping they would be at full-stretch and would have to take on staff at some point. However, they were young, in love and felt invincible in their small family unit. First though, they had the wedding to celebrate and their guests had begun to arrive; even though the ceremony was not until tomorrow. Nevertheless, Phoebe felt, they should have been there to meet them. 'Hurry up Mason! We need to leave now!' Shouted Phoebe as she carried a struggling Lucy out to the car, trying to strap her wriggling form into the baby seat.

Frances had arranged for them all to eat at the White Swan. The table had been booked and the time set; Jones had been invited to join them; Frances and Phoebe having agreed, in the circumstances, it would have been churlish not to. Jones had sold them the farm at a very reasonable price, so eager was he to leave and begin a new chapter in his own life; even as Mason and Phoebe were also longing for a new beginning in theirs. Moreover, he'd saved Frances's life, even as Henry had saved his and these significant events had created a bond of commitment between them or at the very least, a strong sense of gratitude and friendship, which leant towards familial inclusiveness.

Anna had emerged from her room, just as Henry was passing. He waited as he heard her door opening; she suspected him of lurking, but his expression was one of uncertain hope and for a moment her guard was lowered. 'Henry?' Her tone was questioning, but at the same time accepting his presence without conflict. 'Anna!' His voice almost trembled so strong were his emotions and he tried to rein them in as if they were dogs on a leash straining to run free. Except, Henry didn't want his freedom; two whole years without her had created a yearning to once again be close to her. Lying closely at night and walking and talking closely by day. He'd never wanted to run away, but apparently Anna had and still continued to do so, pulling relentlessly at the marriage bond, which still held their relationship together. She faced him silently and yet her eyes were full of questions. 'Anna, could we meet later and talk, perhaps after the meal?' Momentarily, she hesitated, but it was noticed by Henry; anxiety rose within him as did the fear of continuing rejection. 'Please!' He heard himself whispering aloud. If he'd any pride left, he might have felt embarrassed, he was pleading for a few words with his wife, but Henry felt no shame, only a kind of desperate desire. Anna noted all this with mixed emotions. She still loved Henry and hated herself for reducing him to this; he'd always been so strong, so confident, so robust, but nevertheless, he'd hurt her and she refused to let herself be so placed in such a relationship again. Nonetheless, she thought what harm could a short conversation do? They had to talk sometime, as there were both practical and legal matters to be discussed. 'Alright, after the meal we could meet on the veranda for a while, but not for too long I'm tired after the journey.'

'Thank you!' His words rushed at her as he leant forward and took her hand in his. The warmth of his touch ran through her with the familiarity of remembered tenderness, something she'd almost forgotten. She withdrew her hand quickly as if she'd been burnt and looked into his eyes, so earnest, so full of unconcealed love and sadness, causing her to hate herself even more. At that moment, she could almost have wished for the return of the old Henry she knew. The one who was so decisive, so focused, so task and people orientated that, she always found herself the last in the queue for his attention. Silently, she heard her inner voice questioning her: 'What have you done Anna? What have you done?' He was still looking at her intently as if trying to read behind the mask of her features, which gazed back at him inscrutably. Anna's guard was once again raised and determined to dutifully resist any advances he might be ready to make. Suddenly, Frances called out, her voice echoing through the house. 'Phoebe and Mason are here everybody! Let's go!' Her summons broke the emotional standoff between them and without another word they walked briskly downstairs.

Jones was already waiting for them at the White Swan and both Henry and Frances were pleased to see he was chatting with a group of locals. His move to a smaller house on the edge of the village had been a good move. He no longer had the worry of the farm and its failures, hanging over him like the sword of Damocles. He was now in a position to choose when and where he would work. The local farmers, who had known many struggles themselves, didn't blame him for his misfortunes, but rather respected his hard labour and perseverance. Consequently, they often called on him for help and advice, as well as offerings of part-time work, which furnished him with a frequent income, which more than covered his needs. Jones had also begun to learn the art of relaxation for the first time in his life. He would walk the hills for miles, enjoying both the beauty and wildlife of the Welsh mountains. At times, he wondered why he'd never really appreciated or even noticed the area of outstanding natural beauty in which he'd lived for so many decades. A new contentment seemed to have settled on him as if the landscape had imbued his frame with both their sense of permanence as well as peace. He now lived life at a slower pace, but free from anxiety, as if surrounded by a protective circle of stability and security. Jones was a changed man!

He walked over to them as they entered, a broad grin on his face, and shook hands warmly with both Henry and Frances, before leading the family over to the table already prepared for them. 'Lovely, it is to see you all again!' Henry nodded as he pulled out a chair beside him for Anna, who moved on choosing instead to sit next to Phoebe. Henry tried to hide his embarrassment by offering it to Frances, but Jones was already steering her over to sit beside him. 'Next to me you are then Frances, isn't it?' Phoebe looked across at her elder sister and noticed a slight, pink flush suffuse her cheeks. She could only wonder at her sister's thoughts in response to this new, confident man who now seemed to possess the body of Jones. Was her heightened colour the result of annoyance or pleasure? It was difficult to discern for Frances remained silent, but, nevertheless, smiled graciously as Jones positioned her chair, before sitting down beside her with almost proprietorial aplomb. Henry noticed, as did Roger, who sitting opposite had watched this scenario with a look of querying annoyance.

Harriet and Suzanna were discussing the menu across him, both leaning forward and pointing out various delicacies. However, he leant back in his chair and stared at Frances, now deep in conversation with Jones. He knew he felt uncomfortable, but couldn't fathom why. He felt nothing for Frances of this he was sure. Nevertheless, he didn't enjoy the sight of her, laughing and chatting in the way she was with this stranger. For Cynthia's sake, he would have to look out for her. 'Dad!' Suzanne was waving the menu in front of him, trying to get his attention. 'What are you going to order?'

Anna had also been preoccupied. She'd hoped, even now at this late hour, Jack and Jake might have put in an appearance. She'd noticed the tenderness between Mason, Phoebe and little Lucy and it had triggered memories of the time when her own boys were still toddlers; more than this, it had reminded her of the love she and Henry had once shared. What had happened to diminish it so? Of course, she blamed Henry, but that didn't alleviate her pain, if anything, it only added to it. For, apart from the earlier moment of self-questioning, Anna had never thought herself to blame for the breakdown in their marriage. Although, now she wondered if she should have made different choices or responses at certain times; but her unhappiness had grown over many years and it was easier to blame Henry for it, as she still felt herself to be the injured party. Anna sighed inwardly; what was the point of turning old memories both good and sad in her mind, when they'd reached a point of no return. She still loved Henry; the moment on the landing when he'd held her hand in his, had stirred emotions long suppressed. But now, Anna felt it would be foolish to return to a partnership, which had already dramatically failed. Surely, such a turning would only bring future pain and open old wounds, just when she was beginning to heal. Raising her eyes to look across at him, sitting so silently and alone; her eyes met his. Again, this unsettled her, so quickly she picked up the menu to hide her discomfort. Then hearing Jones address Henry, Anna took the opportunity to again look up. Now, she could scrutinise him more closely. He looked older and had lost weight; his forehead was furrowed and his hair greying, causing him to look much more serious and tense, than he used to. Anna had to admit to herself their parting had obviously taken its toll, more on Henry than her. However, this insight far from vindicating her actions gave her no satisfaction or comfort. Conversely, she felt a growing conviction of mistaken judgement. Her thoughts were interrupted by Phoebe asking what she would like to drink. So, with a huge effort, to stave off unwelcome memories, Anna turned her attention to the wine list.

Phoebe looked around the table wondering what her mother would have thought if she'd been there. Contented or concerned? Probably a mixture of both she thought, turning her attention to Lucy who was trying to escape from her highchair. She looked at Mason his head bent, scanning the menu and felt a flood of affection.

Tomorrow would be their wedding day and her nerves were already beginning to distract her. Not because she'd any serious doubts about the marriage, only a slight niggle, which frequently occurred in the dark early hours, while he slept soundly beside her, his breathing soft and rhythmic. At those times she was given to wonder, if Lucy and his guilty absence, in the first few months of her life, had not been facts; would he still have wanted to marry her or eventually have returned to New Zealand anyway? This wasn't something Phoebe felt she could ask, but the question pursued her throughout the days as the ceremony drew ever nearer; but, she lacked the courage to broach the subject. However, as their wedding drew ever closer, she felt this was something they should both do before it was too late. Nevertheless, even at this late hour she still lacked the will to do so.

They were to be married in a small chapel, which abutted a meadow on the periphery of the village. It was a beautiful location with panoramic views of the surrounding hills and bay. Sheep grazed the surrounding fields and the bleating of ewes and lambs seemed to combine into a chorus of praise, boding well for the future success of their new farming venture.

It was to be a small wedding, just family; they were still awaiting the arrival of Mason's parents. They'd arrived in Wales two weeks earlier and after spending a week with them, getting to know their new daughter-in-law and granddaughter, had decided to spend a week travelling. Today, they were travelling down from Scotland and had been delayed by an accident on the M6. 'Unfortunate, but at least they will be here in time for the big day.' Mason had told Phoebe, trying to calm her nerves, by reaching for her hand, under the table and holding it tightly. 'Hopefully before!' She replied, yet more for Mason's sake than her own. After all, her family were already here, but she wanted everything to be perfect for them both.

The soft lighting of the inn, the warm burr of conversation, occasionally broken by the slight chink of cutlery on plates, seemed to hug them all in a relaxing embrace of goodwill and contentment. Even Anna began to unwind and little Lucy fell asleep in her father's arms. They were lingering over coffee, all reluctant to make the first move out into the chill darkness. When the door opened noisily and three people entered. Anna suddenly froze; she was facing the door and had been the first to see Charles with his elderly aunt and a woman, probably of a similar age to himself, who accurately fitted the description of his step-sister, who he'd once unkindly described to her as his joke material! Now, reluctantly, Anna could see why. For she not only looked formidable, but was dressed in a strange assortment of scarves and shawls, wrapped haphazardly around her and worn over an ankle-length dress, which rippled in crumpled waves to flow over her furry boots, which seemed to peep out from beneath, like timid rodents with each step she took. Conversely, the aunt was dressed with meticulous care, yet incongruously a long, pearl necklace hung from her thin neck and fell over her chest with barely a contour. Indeed, one might have mistaken her as the ageing dowager portrayed, so brilliantly, by Maggie Smith in the TV series: Downton Abbey.

Anna looked down at her plate, not wanting to be seen, but too late! Charles had spotted her and was now ambling over to their table, his face beaming with delight. 'Anna darling! What a delightful surprise!' Anna looked at the two women, whom he'd left standing just inside the doorway. Their faces conveyed irritation as they seated themselves at the nearest table and remained frowning in her direction. They were not the only ones frowning; at first, everyone had looked up to view the newcomers, only to quickly lose interest, until only Henry focused his attention on this intrusive and irritating man who appeared to be on such friendly terms with his wife. He sat glancing from one to the other with open hostility. Anna spoke and her embarrassment was obvious to all. 'Charles! This is unexpected!'

'Likewise, darling, likewise! How could I have known we would meet again so soon?' His speech was affected and the humour in his eyes, conveyed perfectly to Anna, his intention had certainly been to find her. She was aware Henry was staring at her and so tried to appear cold and distant towards Charles, but his audacity amused her, as it always did. Therefore, despite biting her lip, a smile escaped which quickly bubbled up into a laugh. 'Charles you're incorrigible!' Now, he laughed too but soon became serious again.

'Look, now I've found you, could you spare me a few minutes, to go over the timetable for the new term?' She looked at him in disbelief, but also with admiration for his total lack of discretion. 'Charles we're on holiday. Can't this wait?'

'Anna we both know how demanding the new term is going to be. We really do need to plan for those lessons we'll be sharing.' She leaned forward, lowering her voice. 'I thought we'd covered all that. Charles! This is family time.' However, he just gave her a knowing grin. 'We've not covered all of it! There are still some final points we need to consider.'

Anna could feel Henry's eyes burning into her; she wanted to end her embarrassment; for now, the others were watching her too. 'Alright, when?' She found herself asking.

'Well, look darling, I'll drive my aunt and Rose home in a few minutes and I'll come back and drive you home, if you like? Then we can talk on the way.' Now Anna just wanted to be rid of him and so found herself agreeing. She'd seen Henry begin to make a move and was worried what the outcome might be. Satisfied, at last, Charles apologised to the others for his interruption and returned, with something of a swagger, to his two frowning ladies, who consequently were forced to down the quickest tipples ever! Before finding themselves unceremoniously ushered outside.

Anna felt mortified and refused to look in Henry's direction. She found herself apologising to Phoebe and Mason for the intrusion, but they had found it amusing, as did the others; with the exception of Frances and Henry. The latter looked across at her, but she refused to meet his gaze; nevertheless, she heard him say for all to hear. 'Should be time enough for such planning in school hours!' To which Anna angrily replied. 'Of course, Henry you're well qualified to lecture me on the subject of professional as well as personal time management, aren't you?' Everyone stopped talking and looked towards her. Phoebe also looked anxiously from one to the other and broke the awkwardness of the moment. 'Well, I guess it is time we all made a move; big day tomorrow!' Like children released from a stuffy classroom on a sunny afternoon, they all rose in unison, scraping their chairs noisily as they stood. Then left with hurried kisses and goodbyes, but Henry hesitated, leaning towards Anna across the table. 'Are you sure you want to do this?'

'Absolutely!' She replied, raising her glass and draining the last dregs. 'So be it!' He replied, angrily picking up his coat and leaving.

Anna was in turmoil. It was true she enjoyed Charles's company; he made her laugh and her mood always lifted when she was with him. Nonetheless, she knew he could be bombastic as well as conceited; yet he was also generous and enjoyed life, always ready to meet new challenges. However, she now feared, she herself had become one of these and this was the problem. Charles wanted more than she was able to give. He was a good listener and had been there for her on those days when being alone had become unbearable. They had occasionally been to the theatre together or out for a meal. They belonged to the same golf club and had covered many miles as well as topics of conversation together. He was interested in so many things and Anna was never bored in his company. Yet it was only company she wanted, not love. Her heart still belonged to Henry, even though she believed their temperaments were incompatible. Anna, knew she'd been unfair to Charles, although companionship had always been her only motive. Anna still considered herself Henry's wife and had taken great pains to make this clear. However, true to form, Charles still continued to hope. Now, her loneliness had led them both to this impossible impasse. She knew a confrontation lay ahead and wasn't looking forward to it. Anna was not unkind, she didn't want to hurt Charles, but neither did she want his delusions to continue. So deep had she been in thought, Anna was suddenly surprised to see Charles striding towards her, grinning foolishly in a way which seemed to ask her. Can you ever forgive me? 'You idiot!' She said, standing to leave.

'Look I thought we could have a drink first, better talking here rather than in the car.' Anna understood this was a ploy to detain her, but nevertheless agreed. He looked triumphant as he returned with a bottle of Burgundy and two glasses. But as he leaned in closer to pour some into her glass, she placed her hand over the top. 'No thanks! I've had more than enough for one night.' He shrugged his shoulders and filled his own large glass to the brim. Then leant on his elbows leaning across the small table, his fleshy face almost touching hers. She could smell his breath, which betrayed his earlier drinking and she leant back to try and avoid its taint. She was tired and her patience wearing thin. 'Look Charles, I'm dead beat! What are these burning issues which can't wait until we're back in the classroom?' He began to laugh loudly, his nose blue-veined, his faced inflamed by over-indulgence. Anna noted the jaundiced white of his eyes and the tiny broken veins, which appeared in spreading patterns like fine red filigree. With his sleeve, he wiped the tears from his eyes and looked at her once again with a foolish grin. 'Oh, Anna dear! Surely you didn't fall for that old ruse, did you? Don't you remember darling, you mentioned you'd be dining here tonight with your family and I truly believed you only did so, because you hoped I would come and rescue you. Did I misunderstand?' He leant back in his chair, raising his glass, spilling red tears of liquor onto the polished table. Anna was furious! In her anger, she stood pushing the table aside and causing the bottle to overturn. It momentarily spun like a broken compass, spilling its contents in all directions. Anna was quick to grab her coat off the chair, but not so Charles who continued to sit foolishly grinning as the wine rippled into his lap, staining his trousers and causing him to stand awkwardly and ask, in a fleeting moment of sobriety; 'Anna have I perhaps misjudged you?'

'You certainly have!' She said, walking swiftly towards the door.

The pub had become silent, for everyone was watching with unveiled relish as this mini-drama unfolded. Anna's cheeks burned, as she walked doggedly passed the questioning stares, straining to subdue her emotions. A gentle gust of cold, night air greeted her like an old friend, as she stepped outside. She gulped it in gratefully, her anger and embarrassment beginning to subside. Unfortunately, her reprieve was short-lived as within seconds Charles was standing astride, in front of her, arms and legs akimbo, blocking her way. She tried to step to one side, but as she did so, he reached out and pulled her close, pushing her arms behind her. Panic rose within her as heart racing, she tried to struggle from his grasp. She wasn't a weakling, but his grip was vice-like in its intensity. She tried to speak calmly. 'Please let go Charles; you're drunk and you're going to regret this once you're sober again.' He tightened his grip. Through slurred lips, he spoke, his voice vindictive and full of resentment. 'You've led me on! You can't deny that!' Anna's nerves were taut, her patience stretched, but she knew better than to give in to them, after all, she was the only sober one in this conversation, despite the fact she'd drunk more than usual. 'Charles, you know I've always enjoyed your company and you're a friend as well as a colleague, but I've been honest with you on many occasions; I'm still Henry's wife and…' Here she hesitated, for even to escape this conflict, it was hard to say the words her heart knew to be true. 'I love Henry! I always will; for me…' Here her voice dropped. 'No other man could ever take his place.' At this point a sober Charles would have let her go; but he wasn't sober and pushed her arms further behind her back, pulling her closer to him. She could feel the heat of his body and the taint of his breath on her cheeks. 'Liar!' He said, his voice soft as velvet and as potent as the alcohol which filled his veins as well as his delusions. 'I know you want me, just as much as I want you!' His lips were wet and bruising as he pressed them against her mouth. Anna struggled to call out, but he was too heavy, too strong. Frantically, she wondered if it would be safer not to resist, but to pretend and humour him in his delusion, as he was obviously beyond reason. Then suddenly she felt Charles being pulled off her and thrown to the ground. She opened her eyes to thank her rescuer, to see Henry bending over the still, torpid body of her colleague, his fists clenched. 'Get up you apology for a man and give me the pleasure of applying my fist to your face!' She ran and held onto him.

'Henry don't he's drunk!' Henry turned towards her.

'You want to protect him after what he's just put you through?'

'No! But I want to protect you; it wouldn't be the right thing to do. Look at him, he's pathetic! You won't forgive yourself if you harm him in this state. I know you Henry, perhaps better than you know yourself.' She was exhausted. 'Take me back to the farmhouse, please?'

Henry heard the appeal in her plea and after a lapse of several seconds, he reluctantly agreed. He was experiencing a Jekyll and Hyde moment his fists still clenched ready, if necessary, to knock Charles to the ground again. Then slowly, reason began to return and he unclenched his fists. 'I suppose you're right, but first.' Here he paused, rubbing his chin, searching for Anna's eyes in the light escaping through the pub's open doorway, through which a crowd of curious faces apparently hoping for a fight, peered out. 'We need to find out if anyone knows where he's staying. We can't leave him here like this.' She sighed, rubbing her bruised arms wearily. Henry, had reverted to form and this time she was glad he had. In her mind, she searched for excuses both for herself as well as Charles, but with a growing sense of shame, she could find none.

They drove in silence as Charles snored loudly on the back seat; until they arrived at the small cottage, where he was staying. They waited patiently for a few minutes before the women reluctantly opened the door. They didn't take kindly to being disturbed at such a late hour and looked with disdain at Anna. Frowning impatiently at Henry they signalled to him to help Charles to the sofa, where he collapsed in pathetic style. With a brief nod to the indifferent relatives, who had not uttered a word either of surprise or thanks, Anna and Henry gratefully left. As they did so the door was unceremoniously slammed on their heels. Anna blessed the cold, fresh air, which soothed her frayed nerves and irritability. Neither spoke until they arrived back at the farmhouse. The warm, dark interior of the car and the hum of the engine had isolated each behind the warm curtain of their thoughts, each leaving the other out in the cold.

As Henry pulled off the narrow lane and began the ascent to the farmhouse his thoughts were racing. He'd so wanted to have a civilised talk with Anna, who he'd watched for most of the evening with growing anxiety, trying to assess her mood and thinking of the right words to choose; words which might serve to heal and restore all that was broken between them. However, these attempts had been rudely foiled by Charles. Now, he felt annoyed resentful even. He'd waited outside the White Swan, shaded in the shadows, intending to follow them after they'd left, just in case Anna might need him. His protective instinct had been right and not misplaced. Nevertheless, instead of being grateful, Anna appeared angry with him and he realised the intimate conversation he'd hoped for was not going to happen tonight. However, he'd heard Anna say she still loved him and to this lifeline, he decided to cling.

The house was in darkness when they pulled in and as there were no outside lights. Henry spoke. 'Here take my arm.' He said and was rewarded as Anna linked arms with him. Encouraged by this, he spoke. 'I heard what you said about still loving me.' There was an awkward pause and Anna felt her throat close on the words she longed to speak. Henry's gentle protection in contrast to Charles's odious presumptions had softened her heart further towards her husband. Yet still, she could not bring herself to reveal her true feelings for him. It would only give him false hope and create future tensions between them; better therefore to leave such truths unspoken, hidden deep within her own heart and understanding. Therefore, instead with an inward gasp of silent pain, as yet again she suppressed her true feelings, she answered. 'It was just my way of trying to keep Charles at arm's length.' The little flame of hope, which had begun to flicker in Henry, was quickly extinguished. 'I see!' Was all he said as together they entered the inner darkness, only to separate, each to their own rooms.

Chapter 5

The small chapel was almost filled to capacity, not only with family, but also with a few curious, yet nevertheless, faithful members of the congregation, who had squeezed into the back pews.

As she walked down the aisle, her hand gently resting on Henry's arm, Phoebe looked stunning in her simple wedding dress. She was no beauty, yet comfortably wore her attractiveness offset in a minimalist style, which she always managed to create. Today, she'd excelled in this ability and a murmur of appreciation flowed over the congregation as she entered, dressed in the vintage satin of her mother's wedding dress; this slightly yellowed by the years, nevertheless, appeared iridescent as rainbow shafts of light, filtering through the stained-glass windows, created a kaleidoscope of shimmering colour, which crisscrossed the satin sheen, with every movement she made. Her dark hair, swept up and held in a simple tiara became her crowning glory. She was carrying a small spray of white blooms, and just a few steps behind Suzanne and Harriet followed; their pale blue costumes, of a more contemporary cut.

Mason turned to watch his bride as she drew ever closer to him. She walked smiling and nodding at first one and then another who in turn, whispered words of encouragement and compliment to her as she passed. He wondered, and not for the first time, why the realisation of his love for her had evaded him until his return to New Zealand. Now, he gazed with something akin to awe towards this, slowly advancing, image of loveliness, willing to gift her life to him, wrapped in a promise of love. At that moment he also promised himself, he would never leave her again.

Momentarily, his gaze wandered across the aisle to Lucy; this wonderful, energetic bundle of life: the result of their love. She was dressed in pink cotton, chuckling and wriggling in Frances's arms; she wanted to throw the confetti as she saw her mother approaching, whilst Frances struggled to curb her little niece's enthusiasm. Everyone smiled; for joy always followed in Lucy's wake! Mason felt the place in his heart, which belonged only to her, swell with pride as it opened in a paternal flowering of love. If only his parents had arrived on time the day would be perfect. He'd heard nothing from them since the night before and wondered what could have happened.

Anna too, still found herself hoping, Jack and Jake might put in an appearance and so kept turning anxiously towards the door, willing them to appear.

The ceremony began well, peaceful and orderly as befitted the occasion. It was only the chatter and chuckles of Lucy, which accompanied the solemnity of the ceremony. However, these served only to add to the celebration of the day and nobody seemed to mind. All were focused on the eternal mystery of love, which threads each generation in many guises. Some were remembering their own wedding day or the loss of their beloved one. There were tears, smiles and sighs from many sides and even one or two of the locals were seen to raise their handkerchiefs towards their eyes; blaming the sun, streaming through the windows, for their tears.

However, it was while the happy couple were exchanging rings the spell was broken, by voices outside and the creaking of the thick, wooden door opening. Everyone turned, including Mason, hoping it might be the late arrival of his parents. Instead, he was greeted by the broad grins of Jack and Jake. Anna's heart leapt as she raised her hand in a self-conscious wave, indicating the two spaces she'd reserved for them on the pew beside her. Unabashed, they nodded to Mason and made their way cheerfully to Anna's side, causing some frowns from those who were made to stand at this important stage of the ceremony. The minister cleared his throat, a gesture designed to recall order, but the awe of the moment had been broken and Mason couldn't help wondering what might have happened to his parents. There were a few whispers and some tutt-tutting amongst the family. Jones, who was sitting next to Frances, whispered to her. 'Frances, a shame this interruption is, but no real harm has been done.' She smiled at him receiving his reassurance and enjoying the soft, Welsh intonation of her name. He understood her, knew she wanted only the best for Phoebe today. After all, she thought even in an imperfect world, one hopes, for a perfect wedding day. Almost against her will Frances glanced across at Roger and blushed as she met his gaze. She wondered if he shared her thoughts. For many years ago, she'd imagined them both in a similar setting to this, exchanging rings, exchanging their vows. Then, despite trying not to, she found herself compelled to look at him again, but he'd turned away and for some reason, she felt betrayed all over again.

A few photos were taken outside the chapel and Phoebe insisted some be taken of the local people who had come to wish them well. These were delighted to be included, but at first protested they were not really dressed for the occasion; however, on Phoebe's insistence, they followed the photographer's instructions, their faces beaming as if something of the young couples' happiness had reached out to touch their lives too.

Phoebe and Mason's delight was obvious to all who looked on. But if they had been able to look into their minds, they would have seen a shadow of anxiety flitting from one to another. Mason's parents had still not arrived and there had been no contact from them either. Mason had at least expected a telegram. Therefore, as soon as they arrived at the hotel, where the reception was to take place, he tried to contact them, for the umpteenth time that day, but to no avail. He continued to smile broadly though, as he heartily shook hands with everyone before they all sat down to the wedding breakfast.

Jones being the family's only guest, they all sat at one table. Jones was seated next to Frances, due to Phoebe's seating arrangements, which did not go unnoticed by the rest of the family including Roger, who seemed to be the only one enduring rather than enjoying the occasion.

Roger was struggling; last night he'd witnessed what others had also noticed; the growing chemistry between Frances and this unlikely character. He was annoyed with himself for caring and tried to reason why he should. He was convinced it was on Cynthia's behalf. He wanted to protect Frances against what he thought to be, a potentially disastrous liaison. He imagined himself as being more of a brother to her than an in-law. Forgetting, in his inner conflict, he'd never behaved like a brother towards her, in any previous context. Forgetting also, she already had a brother. He sat, surreptitiously scrutinising their every move. Trying to listen in on their conversation and to read their body language. He felt irritated with Suzanne and Harriet, who once again sat protectively either side of him, but who insisted on leaning forward and chatting across him. A distraction meant to eliminate the absence of their mother, but which, instead of comforting him added to his annoyance, which had begun to steadily increase since his arrival.

However, if we had been able to look into his unconscious mind, we would have understood his self-denial in these matters. For Roger had always thought of Frances as his own. Someone who would be available when needed to listen, soothe his worries and comfort him in his troubles, as she once had many years previously. For him, it was as if those intervening years had never run their course. Despite their broken engagement and his marriage to Cynthia, despite the birth of his two daughters, despite his past affair with Frances, which had ended in acrimony causing pain to her as well as pain to Cynthia throughout the remainder of their marriage. Despite all these things, Roger still saw Frances as his possession, a woman ready to be recognised and possibly repossessed when his need arose. Of course, he would have denied all such thoughts even to himself; for self-deception is blind and has the ability to hold one in ignorance, clouding one's own motivations. For, just as the ego is capable of camouflage, hiding the base aspirations of the Id, beneath a cloak of apparently worthy intentions: so, it was with Roger.

He was not the only tormented soul suffering during that happy celebration. For, Anna too was flanked by her two children, who were enjoying the family gathering and showing their goodwill towards the young couple, by consuming huge portions of food, washed down by copious amounts of alcohol. Knowing their past tendency to addiction, she frequently looked across at Henry, willing him to intervene; but although he was delighted to see his sons, memories of the previous evening harassed him still. Anna's denial of her love for him, even though he'd suspected this to be the truth for a long time, had burnt into his heart, branding his expectation, which had so quickly risen at her words to Charles. Now, with something akin to despair, her denial, had reduced his hopes of ever rebuilding their marriage: to ashes. Consequently, he deprived himself of the pleasure of looking towards his wife and sons. To do so would only turn an unseen dagger in the already gaping wound of his loss. The whole context of the occasion seemed to mock him, but true to character, he continued to smile, made a beautiful speech and proposed several toasts to the happy couple, but never once did he look in Anna's direction; thereby, leaving her distress to grow unnoticed.

At this very moment, Megan and Tyrone, Mason's parents, were laying in a deep sleep, the dim light of their motel accommodation, crisscrossing their room with a stratum of shadows. Megan, was the first to wake and gazed anxiously at her husband's grey complexion. She'd tried to persuade him not to make this trip, despite her own desire to be present at the wedding of their only child. Even the doctor had advised him against it, but true to form, his stubbornness had prevailed.

Since they'd landed in the UK she'd continued to plead with him, to slow down, to stay put in Wales and to enjoy this time with his son and granddaughter, but he'd insisted this was his only opportunity to see a little more of the world, as this was only the second time he'd left New Zealand; the first having been only a few months before when they'd arrived to assess the viability of Jones's farm. Moreover, on that occasion, as he'd pointed out to Megan, all their time had been spent in Wales. Whilst back in New Zealand he'd always been tied to the land by the multiple demands of his farm. 'It's now or never, my love! Besides, the youngsters don't want us two old biddies hanging about. They've enough to do, with the wedding looming and getting the farm sorted. We'll only be in the way.' With these words he'd persuaded her to make this journey north; he knew his wife and that the thoughts of being a burden to Mason, would be an anathema to her. She was delighted with both Lucy and Phoebe and would have appreciated the opportunity to get to know them both a bit better, but she also knew the time she and Tyrone had left together was limited. Now, she turned to look at the bedside clock, which they'd set for an early start at 6:00 a.m. With a cry, she sat up in bed with a start. 'Tyrone get up! We're very late!' How they'd managed to oversleep for so long, she didn't know. However, they'd travelled a great distance, cramming in many sites and places of interest. Tyrone had loved it all, but it had taken its toll on both of them and they'd arrived at the motel late the previous evening having broken down on the motorway and lost several hours in waiting, not only at the roadside but also in the garage, until they'd organised yet another hire car to complete their journey. Except, they'd both been exhausted and unable to drive any further. Megan had been particularly concerned about the sudden pallor, which had drained Tyrone's colour, as well as the slight confusion he'd begun to demonstrate, whilst they were still at the garage. As a result, she'd insisted on driving to the motel, while he dozed. On arrival he'd almost fallen into bed, barely undressing. Likewise, she'd been grateful to turn out the light and fall into the welcome oblivion of sleep. Now, glancing at the clock, she realised they'd seriously overslept and she wondered how they were going to get to the wedding on time. It seemed impossible. Nevertheless, jumping out of bed, she called her husband, but no response. So, she decided to have a shower and give him a few extra minutes lie in: he looked exhausted.

Megan was not a stupid woman, but often our expectancy can blind us to the reality of circumstances, tingeing the truth with what we anticipate, rather than what actually is. Therefore, she called out to him again with no sense of foreboding. 'Five minutes lay in, only; we need to be on the road!' She'd not expected a reply and emerged from the shower, anticipating he would be up and about, but he still lay still and silent. Impatiently, she strode towards him. 'Tyrone! Wake up! Mason's getting married today!' It was only then something cold and fearful gripped her heart as she leant close to his face. There was no sound, no soft warmth of his breath on her cheek; she touched his forehead; it was cold and with a sound both primaeval and piercing she drew back in shock. The realisation he was dead drowning her in a tsunami of grief.

Traumatised, she sat for several hours on one of those uncomfortable chairs motels always seem to provide. At first, she cradled her middle, rocking to and fro trying like a child, to seek comfort, from the rhythm of her movements, trying to assuage her tears and the juddering sobs, which rose from deep within her. When these eventually faded, the shock of her loss descended on her: numbing her senses and clouding her mind. For the first time in many years, she felt alone and unsure of what to do. She sat like this remembering the years they'd shared and how the repetition of their daily routine had drawn them ever closer in their comfortable, loving marriage. Theirs had not been a passionate love affair, but one which had begun with friendship and gradually developed into young love, which had matured with the years, binding them ever closer in understanding as well as an intimate dependency. Together, they'd experienced, the hills and valleys of Life's multifarious highways. Their hearts drawn ever closer, through the rhythm of the journey, until they'd begun to beat as one, think as one and even live as one!

Now, Megan held tightly onto her husband's cold hand. As if the contact would transmit his thoughts to light the way forward for her; however, no thoughts came, only more numbness. They'd discussed death, prepared for death, but today death had overtaken all their plans, leaving Megan overwhelmed and unprepared. She shifted on her chair letting go of Tyrone's hand. The same hand which had been a source of strength and love to her on so many occasions; a strong yet tender hand, warm and gentle, ready to soothe; a hand ever ready to caress and bring comfort, but one which now lay cold and inert on the duvet.

She stood and picked up her mobile. She thought of phoning Mason, but couldn't bring herself to do so. After all, it was his wedding day! As if by telepathy, Tyrone's phone began to vibrate on the bedside cabinet. She knew without looking it would be Mason and she resisted the urge to run and pick it up. She willed herself not to answer and waited for her own phone to ring in turn, which it did. She hurled it away from her and it hit the wall, continuing to ring with her favourite melody, a sweet nostalgic melody, which today was not welcome. Megan covered her ears to shut out its sound, but it continued, piercing her heart creating more pain. In an effort to escape its relentless strains, she ran into the bathroom bolting the door behind her, as if she could turn the clock back a few hours, before the veil of widowhood had descended, shrouding her in darkness. But now, the full realisation of her status had found its way into her consciousness and as the reality of her situation closed in upon her, Megan sank down onto the hard tiles and wept bitterly.

Impatiently, Mason strode the length of the hotel's terrace. He was concerned, but not anxious, only restless as he listened to the relentless drone of his mobile trying to connect with his parents. 'Pick up! Why don't you?' he spoke aloud; his words evaporating in the ether. He turned, looking back at the hotel wondering what the family must be thinking. He noticed Phoebe peering questioningly through the French windows and waved, smiling, trying to appear more relaxed than he felt. This was his wedding day and his parents had flown from the other side of the world to celebrate it with him, yet they remained conspicuous by their absence. He couldn't make any sense of the situation. They should be here by now. He'd thought, because they'd been delayed and missed the ceremony, they would at least have made it to the wedding breakfast and to think this too, was drawing to an end, caused annoyance and unease to converge, disturbing his equilibrium. Both their phones had rung and yet neither of them had answered and he was at a loss to imagine why? Such behaviour was unlike them. He decided to try one more time, but as he keyed in their number, Phoebe appeared. 'Mason darling, they're waiting for us to take to the floor.' He looked at her questioningly; her face, so radiant, yet flushed with an almost girlish self-consciousness. 'We're supposed to start the dancing, to begin our married life on the right footing, a happy one, filled with music and joy!' She explained. He slipped his phone back inside his jacket and put his arm around her waist. 'You look beautiful Phoebe!' She looked up into his face and smiled. 'I love you, Mason!' He drew her in close and kissed her long and lovingly, as a raucous cheer and loud clapping erupted behind them. Everyone had spilt out onto the terrace and was watching them. They both laughed and joining hands ran up the steps towards them. For the time being at least, Mason had forgotten about his parents. It was his wedding day after all!

The couple were due to leave. They'd planned just two nights away. There was still much work to be done on the farm before they could open, for the holiday season. They'd decided to manage the work themselves to reduce costs and Frances and Mason's parents were supposed to be looking after Lucy, while they stole these days to be alone. Therefore, it was in a shower of confetti and rice, with their car covered in foam messages of goodwill and trailing a tail of clattering cans behind; they pulled out of the hotel driveway, the best wishes of everyone carrying them ever forward to their brief honeymoon escape.

It was the chambermaid who discovered Tyrone's body. She was used to finding unpleasant reminders, which thoughtless guests were content to leave behind them. Nevertheless, this was the first macabre experience to start her day. At first, she thought she'd intruded on somebody still sleeping. Many folks forgot to place the 'Do Not Disturb' sign outside their door, this was not unusual and she was about to withdraw when she heard a sort of wailing emanating from behind the bathroom door. She was alarmed and at first thought, she should call the manager rather than investigate herself, but as she listened, she sensed the sobbing was not threatening, but rather an expression of profound grief and desolation. This prompted her to put down her armful of bedding and towels on the nearest chair and walk timidly towards the bed. It was evident the occupant was dead and she looked towards the bathroom door, where somebody on the other side sounded still very much alive. She tiptoed across the room as if it might have been possible to wake the dead man from his eternal rest and cautiously tapped on the bathroom door. 'Hello, it's Julia, your chambermaid. I want to help!' Momentarily, there was a brief respite in the crying and sounds of slow movement. Then the lock clicked back and a dishevelled Megan, her eyes red and swollen, her face drawn and pale, stared at the young woman in front of her. Julia moved towards her and put an arm around her waist. 'Come and sit down, I'll make some tea.' Later Megan would remember these words, so normal, so mundane, in the face of such devastating abnormality and, thinking to herself; for these English, the brewing of tea remains a universal panacea even in the presence of death! Nevertheless, she was grateful for the hot sweet liquid and the warmth it brought to her frozen limbs. While she sat and drank, the maid phoned the manager and soon both the police and medics were on the scene.

The wedding breakfast over, it was time for Frances to take Lucy back home. She'd been looking forward to this as well as the opportunity to get to know Phoebe's in-laws a bit better, but now she was concerned at their non-appearance. She wondered what might have happened; it must be something serious to have kept them from their own son's wedding and this left her with a sense of disquiet. The thoughts of having Lucy to herself were comforting, but she wondered what news the next few hours might bring; her intuition caused her to shiver and Jones noticed. 'Cold you are, is it Frances?' Despite her anxiety, Frances could not help smiling. Just a few months ago, such a question would have infuriated her, but now she'd grown used to Jones's figures of speech, his unique syntax, and his expressions of concern for her well-being, from which she derived a hidden sense of comfort. It was as if, because he'd saved her life, he'd also taken upon himself the responsibility for her welfare; almost as if he'd earned the right to do so and she wasn't sure how she felt about this. 'I'm fine thanks! Just wondering what could have happened to Megan and Tyrone? They're supposed to be helping me look after Lucy for the next couple of days. I can't think what has happened to them? I mean not turning up for the wedding is strange, but not letting anyone know, is stranger still.' Jones looked concerned and seemed to hesitate before suggesting,

'I could help with Lucy, couldn't I?' Frances looked at him in surprise.

'Well I suppose you could, but I can manage fine on my own.' Jones seemed to want to say more but was uncertain how to say it. He scratched his head in the way which had become so familiar, endearing even. Frances waited, wondering what he would say next. 'You know Frances: it might be as well for you to have a man about the house and who better than myself? I know the farm, after all I used to live there, didn't I?' Frances tried to restrain her smile and look grateful. 'That's very good of you Jones, but I'll be fine, really. Besides a lot of changes have been made since you lived there. It is hardly the same house.' He scratched his head. 'Indeed, to goodness, I know you're right! But just suppose something went wrong, what would you do?' Frances wanted to laugh; his expression was so serious.

'Like what for example?' Jones thought for a moment.

'Well, I know there is new plumbing and drainage as well as the electrics and there is many a time these new installations break down, isn't it?'

'Most of the new installations are based on technology, rather than just mechanics, Jones. I'm not ungrateful for your offer, but I'm sure I'll manage.' He looked directly at her and she noticed the sadness in his eyes. 'Just wanting to be with you Frances; that's it, do you see?' His directness took her by surprise and for a moment she was unsure how to answer. She was aware of something both beautiful and awesome beginning to blossom inside her; it was unfamiliar, yet filled her with emotions, which she'd once known before, but had long forgotten. 'Well,' she said. 'I do have a presentiment of sorts I might well be the recipient of bad news and if that should be the case, then it would be good to have somebody else there too.' He smiled, rubbing his hands together. 'That's it then Frances, settled between us it is! I'll be there with you, won't I?' Frances laughed; something akin to a bubble of joy rose in her mouth and floated out into the air. 'It is, Jones! It definitely is, isn't it?' If he'd understood the gentle mocking of her reply, he gave no sign.

Rather he'd understood the fun in her tone and laughed too. Mocking, from anyone else but Frances, he would not have tolerated. However, he knew her reply, reflecting her sense of humour, had filled the moment with something which was to bring them closer than any genteel eloquence ever could.

Chapter 6

It was the first morning of their married life and Mason, resting on one elbow, looked lovingly at Phoebe sleeping peacefully beside him. A tendril of hair had fallen across her eyes and he brushed it gently away, tracing the line of her cheekbone with his finger, but still she slept on. He wanted to wake her to share his anxiety, but knew this was something he couldn't do: not on their honeymoon. This was supposed to be all about them and their new life together: not about his parents. Even the marriage ceremony had spoken about leaving and cleaving. However, it was difficult for him not to think about Tyrone and Megan; he knew it was completely out of character for them not to have contacted him before now. Moreover, as he watched each hour turn in time, concern grew within him. He tried to convince himself all was really well and there would be some simple explanation. They would apologise profusely and feel disappointed for a time, but then, eventually, make some joke about the whole scenario and laugh together. It would be a story to tell their grandchildren. Briefly, he imagined himself and Phoebe bouncing grandchildren on their knees, at some time in the distant future, each looking remarkably like Lucy.

Phoebe stirred beside him and stretched lazily as she opened her eyes. Her smile met his and they drew close, covering one another in light kisses. They relaxed into the pleasure of their love, for a while suffocating Mason's gnawing anxiety beneath the duvet. Later though, at breakfast, Phoebe saw the trepidation in his eyes, noticed the slight quaver in his voice and asked if he'd heard from them. He shook his head and took her hand in his. 'There's probably some simple explanation. We'll find out tomorrow darling; let's keep today to ourselves.' Phoebe wanted to be generous and offer him the opportunity to either go back or to spend the day making phone calls, but she too thought there would be some rational explanation. It would be a shame to ruin their brief time together, all to no purpose. Furthermore, she was reluctant to share her husband with anyone else at this time. Surely, they were entitled to these two days of seclusion. So, she said nothing, but wrapped her arms around him and nestled into the warmth of his body. Mason, held her tightly resting his head on hers as if this would create an impermeable barrier of love, with which to ward off all bad news.

Frances and Jones entered the house each with the self-conscious anticipation of beginning a new stage in their relationship. They were both aware, they were about to cross from the threshold of friendship to something deeper, but as yet each was unsure of the other and so they treated one another with coy deference, becoming both hesitant and diffident in their attitudes. It was Lucy who bridged the gap between them with her childhood innocence and toddler charms, filling it with chuckles of glee and shrieks of sheer fun. They were both grateful for this and it helped them to relax into one another's company.

Jones asked if Frances would show him over the farmhouse and the irony was not lost on either of them. However, with Lucy in her arms, Frances, happily led the way, pointing out the changes and commenting on the new installations, with pride, which might have caused a stranger to think these had all been her own idea. She was pleased to see the admiration on Jones's face and to hear his noises of approval as she brought each minutia of change to his attention. 'In deed to goodness, beautiful it is! Truly wonderful what modernisation has done for the old home, isn't it?' Frances knew he wasn't really waiting for an answer and just smiled at his bemused expressions. 'Well, I would never have recognised the house if I hadn't already known, it had once been mine, would I?' He said as they mounted the staircase, still steep, but now covered in thick brightly coloured carpet, which brought an air of freshness, even to this dark enclosed area. Lucy led him by the hand into her bedroom, one of the lightest rooms in the house, yet brightly coloured. A painted rainbow formed an arch on the wall, above her small bed. Over which a mobile of colourful butterflies hovered, dancing in circles of light. Her toys and books decorated the shelves and a tiny white wardrobe housed her clothes. There were bright scattered rugs and cushions for her to sit on and Jones stood smiling at the charm of it all. Gently, he bent down to Lucy's level. She'd not paused in her chatter since they'd entered the house; but now as Jones took her tiny hands in his and looked into her eyes, she returned his gaze expectantly, smiling with toddler charm, anticipating his appreciation. 'Lovely it is! Fit for a princess, just like you, isn't it?' She laughed and ran off to return with a plastic tiara set askew on her head. He smiled, tousling her hair as he stood to meet Frances's eyes full of light and pleasure. He took her hands in his and leaning forward kissed her cheek. It was the kiss of a friend, not a lover, nevertheless it left Frances unsure how to respond. She suddenly wanted to cry, not understanding quite why and struggled to suppress her tears, which she didn't want to fall in front of the child. Nonetheless, Jones had noticed. 'Why the tears now? Is it because of the clumsy oaf, I am?' Frances shook her head, unable to explain the emotion, which had risen in her as she watched him bend to the child. Was it because this was the domestic scene she'd always imagined, but been denied; lent to her for a brief moment, in somebody else's house, with somebody else's child? With a man who was not her husband or even her lover. Was fate always to treat her so cruelly? 'It's nothing!' She said wiping away her tears before Lucy noticed. 'I've just been a bit stressed with the build-up to the wedding, family tensions, you know.' Jones didn't know, but nevertheless, without a word, he drew her in close and she did not resist, laying her head against his shoulder. She remembered thinking he smelt of fresh mountain air and pine forests. Then Lucy was there, reaching up her tiny arms. 'Lucy hug too!' She cried and together Frances and Jones stooped to raise her up to their face level, each laughing for reasons known only to themselves, but which touched them all.

Back at the holiday let, Henry and Anna were conscious that, apart from Roger, noticeable by his absence, they were together as a family for the first time in years. For, Suzanne and Harriet had already left. Largely, due to the drunken behaviour of Jack and Jake; who having both thrown up on the lounge carpet, had further managed to disgrace themselves, by ridiculing the girls for their lack of spontaneity and fun, as they so perceived their cousins' refusal to join in with their partying. Their language had bordered on the abusive, but had fortunately been overheard by Henry, who intervened with a vehemence of his own; infuriated by his sons' over-indulgence and their lack of family respect. He'd made them apologise and this they'd reluctantly done, but with evident contempt for both their father and cousins. Henry, after apologising himself to his nieces, had helped his sons, somewhat roughly, upstairs to sleep off their shame.

Anna had seen the disgust in the girls' eyes, increasing the inner pain, she already felt. Nevertheless, she'd tried to persuade them to stay, but they made excuses, saying they'd always planned to leave that evening anyway, which Anna knew to be an excuse covering their embarrassment. However, to save them any further humiliation, she said nothing only expressing her sadness, by shaking her head as she helped them to pack. Later, she stood waving from the terrace, until their taxi was out of sight. With a sigh, she returned inside to clear the mess in the lounge and opening the windows wide to let in some fresh air. She'd found disinfectant and some cleaning liquid, hidden away under the sink and now gazed with a heavy heart at the dark patches on the carpet, where she'd soaked and scrubbed. A metaphor of their family life she thought: stained and sickly. Would it ever be healthy and clean again, she wondered, or was the damage beyond repair? It was true she blamed Henry, but only in part, for she blamed herself more. She was the one who had left the family home. Anna, knew she still loved her husband but found living with him difficult. She also understood Jack and Jake blamed Henry entirely for the breakdown in their relationships. For like herself, they too felt he always put the needs of others, before the needs of family life. Like her, both felt they did not come within his immediate radar. Rather, they were second best, if that, in terms of his attention and they felt both unloved and unneeded. Their memories had become selective, due to their biased perspective and they'd forgotten the good times, the special times, which had been planned by both parents for their benefit and enjoyment. Conversely, they saw themselves as victims of a loveless marriage and a workaholic father. Consequently, they were immature, angry, bitter, unwilling to take responsibility for their actions, critical of their childhood, unable to see with any understanding, beyond their own pain. Of course, being twins they discussed these things, each adding some further fictional dimensions to their collective memories, reinforcing their sense of injury, through a somewhat distorted lens. If they had been a little older, they might have appreciated some of the demands which both Anna and Henry faced in their working lives, but nothing in their experience so far, had equipped them with this depth of comprehension. Therefore, they continued to rant and rave, rejecting and despising love in all its various forms, breaking both their parents' hearts in the process.

The air still smelt sickly and so Anna went out to the veranda, where she stood her arms folded across her chest, gazing out over the peaceful bay, aware of the heaviness in her own heart as well as her lack of peace. It was here Henry joined her and together they stood in silence, each alone with their thoughts and inner unrest. They both felt the weight of their childrens' addictive habits and each accepted what they considered to be their past failures. However, these were hard to admit, even to themselves, let alone to one another or their sons. As they stood in silence, watching the last of the sun disappear over the horizon, Anna shivered. Henry reached out to put his arm around her shoulders, but she pulled away, shaking him off as if she was being bothered by some unwanted pest. He turned and walked away, heavy in heart and confused in his mind. Leaving Anna alone in the gathering gloom.

During the wedding ceremony, as he observed Phoebe and Mason making their promises to love and cherish one another, Roger found himself remembering the time when he and Frances were first engaged. He was appalled at himself for doing this and wondered why it was not Cynthia, filling his thoughts and mind with a deep sense of loss. He'd loved Cynthia, had chosen her over Frances. Why then was it Frances who now filled his thoughts with a longing, which had lain dormant for decades. He chided himself for his fickleness but continued to feed his obsession with frequent glances in her direction. He was annoyed to see Jones at her side and irritated when he saw him whisper something into her ear, suggesting a deeper intimacy between them than he'd realised. This he resented and decided to put a stop to it at the earliest opportunity, which was not long in coming. For he was later to overhear Jones offering to spend the night at the farmhouse with both Frances and Lucy, which caused his indignation to boil. As her one-time fiancé and now brother-in-law, he felt such a position of care should be his: after all, he was family! Who was this unknown, failed farmer, who was no more than a stranger? Whatever could have possessed Frances to be open to such a suggestion? What would people think in such a small community?

Roger failed to consider, folk would probably not notice or even if they did, why should they care? Neither did he appreciate the high esteem

Jones was held in by the locals, respected for his perseverance in the face of adversity and his willingness to undertake hard manual labour to support his neighbouring farmers, when they in turn had needed help. No mud would stick to Jones, at least not metaphorically. Also, Frances was her own woman and only holidaying in the area, yet none of these possibilities registered with Roger, who ignoring his own lack of chivalry towards Frances in the past; continued to boil inwardly with a quasi-self-righteousness as he watched every move the couple made. He convinced himself Frances needed his protection and Jones was no more than some unknown, predatory male, ready to take advantage of her. It didn't occur to him he'd once done the same, or that Frances was quite capable of making her own decisions. Neither, did he reason Jones's intentions might be those purely of a friend, ready to assist in an emergency. Rather, he'd convinced himself the worst scenario was about to take place and it was solely up to him to make sure it didn't. Therefore, the very same evening the couple together with Lucy, were wrapped in their spontaneous, innocent group hug. Roger was driving towards the farm, his foot heavy on the accelerator.

Neither Henry nor Anna wanted to eat and found themselves thrown back on their own company. They sat in the kitchen, on opposite sides of the huge oak table on hard, uncomfortable chairs. Each with a glass of green tea, having first made sure every bottle of alcohol, had been safely locked away in the boot of Henry's car.

They both sat holding the glasses cupped between their hands whilst looking abstractly into the murky depths of the tea as if they might find some inspiration there. It appeared they did, for looking up in unison they both began to speak at the same time. They smiled, amused, and it broke the tension between them. 'You first.' Said, Henry. His face had once again put on its inscrutable mask, which caused Anna to hesitate. Was this really the right time for them to speak honestly to one another? Would she be able to speak calmly and rationally? Finally, she decided things could not get any worse, so what else had she to lose? 'Look, I'm sorry! I know this is probably a little too late, but I truly *am* sorry!' Henry wondered what was coming next and felt his gut tighten. Was she about to ask for a divorce? He'd been expecting this for a long time. He became aware he was holding his breath and let it out in a silent sigh of resignation. He braced himself and waited for the long-suspended sword of Damocles to fall.

Anna, began to speak. At first, he found it difficult to hear her words clearly, such was his apprehension. Then, slowly, he realised Anna was not asking him for a divorce, rather she was asking him if he could forgive her and could they try again to make their marriage work? He looked at her, his expression incredulous. Had he really heard correctly or was it just wishful thinking on his part? 'I'm sorry, could you repeat that please?' Anna coloured, she felt embarrassed, she'd taken a risk and now it was about to humiliate her. After all that had happened between them, why would Henry be prepared to put himself through another, goodness knows how many, more years of potential anguish, all over again? 'I think you heard what I said; just say if you're willing to try again? If you feel that you can't then I'll understand.' Henry, looked at her his face revealing the doubt he still felt. 'Do you mean it?' Anna nodded. If he'd been younger he might have pushed the table aside and leapt across the black, slate floor to face her; but as it was, he walked quickly around to her side, taking hold of her hands and raising her up, pulling her in close, smothering her face with light, delicate kisses and softly whispering. 'Of course I'm willing, how could you think otherwise? You and the boys are everything to me and I'm determined to show you this is the truth. The question is darling, how can you ever forgive me for my insane blindness?' Anna raised a finger to his lips. 'Hush! Henry, can't you see I already have?'

So, lost were they in one another, neither of them noticed Jack and Jake as they tiptoed passed the kitchen door. Neither, did they hear the front door click loudly as it closed behind them. Giggling and running without shoes over the damp grass, the twins fell awkwardly into the old banger they shared. Jake took the wheel, driving haphazardly along the narrow lane, he sounded the horn at a pheasant and they both laughed with delight as, in a flurry of feathers, it flew over the hedge, flapping and calling as it went. They rounded a sharp bend, just as they were approaching a mobile home park, where the car careered onto a side bank, almost overturning. They both laughed again as if tickled by their own recklessness and the relief of leaving all parental control behind.

Frances was just pulling away from their trio hug, to allow Lucy to return to her toys, when Jones's eyes met hers in a silent understanding. The child had bridged the distance between them and they found themselves equals in a spacious place of new mutual comprehension, just waiting to be explored. However, their intimate moment was suddenly broken by a loud knock at the door. Frances's heart missed a beat. This must be the harbinger of bad news, which she'd anticipated. Glancing, nervously at Jones she opened the door surprised to see Roger, who without waiting for an invitation, stepped quickly over the threshold closing the door behind him. 'What is it?' Asked Frances, who wasn't happy to see him. Roger had removed his coat and thrown it over the stand in the hall, without saying a word. Now, he rubbed his hands together and nodded at Jones, forcing himself to smile. 'Well, I've come to relieve Jones, of course! At times like this, families should stick together.'

'What are you talking about? I don't understand?' Replied Frances.

'Well, I'm staying the night, of course! This wouldn't be the first time you and I have spent a night under the same roof, would it?' Frances coloured, partly due to his crassness, but largely due to anger. Roger, noticed and turning to Jones tried to put a different spin on his words. 'What I mean is, as my sister-in-law Frances sometimes stayed with Cynthia, me and the girls.' Frances couldn't believe his audacity; she'd never stayed with them not even for one night, in all the years of their marriage. Nevertheless, she was grateful he at least tried to put their relationship in a better light; however, the intended inference had already been made, as well as understood by Jones, who was now looking from one to the other trying to read the situation. So, far from allaying his suspicions concerning a previous relationship between the two, Roger's attempt to cover his intentional slip, only served to confirm Jones's earlier thoughts. Frances, tried to take control. 'Look, Roger, there is no need, thanks. Jones has offered to stay, just in case he might be needed, but I'm sure Lucy and I will be fine. I think you should return to the farmhouse with the others.' It was Roger's turn to feel humiliated. 'Look, Frances the girls have gone home and Henry, Anna and the boys are there together. To be honest I feel I'd be in the way and I know you have some spare rooms here.' Turning to Frances, Jones spoke. 'Perhaps it would be better if I went home and caught up with you tomorrow, isn't it?'

'No, not at all! I invited you to stay and so you will. You can have my room and Roger can have the spare one. We'd better leave Megan and Tyrone's bedroom empty, in case they turn up tonight and I'll use Phoebe and Mason's room. Neither, of the men was happy with these arrangements, nevertheless thought it better to agree. Jones, would now rather have gone home, he'd never felt comfortable in Roger's presence and had noticed his sly glances in their direction, throughout the day, weighing their movements, scowling with disapproval. He wondered again, if there had ever been anything between the two, now suspecting that there probably had been. However, he reminded himself it was none of his business; even though now, it really mattered to him. For, he felt the last few hours had brought both him and Frances closer and he'd begun to think, just possibly, they might have a future together. However, in the last few minutes, it had become clear to him, Roger was not just another family member, but also his rival!

Frances called both men into the kitchen asking them to prepare a simple salad for tea, while she gave Lucy hers and got her ready for bed.

They worked in silence, each ignoring the other as an atmosphere of mutual dislike, sullied the air, staining their moods and straining their nerves.

Frances, was grateful for the child's endless chatter and chuckles, which relieved her tension and made her smile. For, she too was uncomfortable with Roger and wondered why he'd decided to turn up unannounced. Was it really because of his discomfort at being left alone with Henry's family or did he have some ulterior motive? She felt it was the latter, but couldn't think what it might be.

However, the scene at the holiday let could not have been more different. Henry and Anna were also in the kitchen, but it was as if the floodgates of hope and planning, which had been so long closed, were at last open. They talked incessantly, at times over one another, each laughing and giving way occasionally as they gazed almost with reverence into the other's face, not hearing their words, but each marvelling at the sudden transformation in their relationship. They decided to eat alone and let the boys sleep off their stupor. It was good to be together again and each of them vowed they would never look back, but rather work to rebuild, both their marriage and family life. Each making the other promises, which only time would either keep or break.

At the farm, their conversation had been intermittent and sparse, the evening long and strained. Jones had suggested a game of cards, which they all settled to play, but without enthusiasm or concentration, each absorbed with their own thoughts. Anyone, peering through the window, would simply have seen three adults whiling away the evening in a somewhat boring pastime, held against their will in a vortex of tedium. However, if they'd been able to look into their minds, they would have seen a frenetic buzz of scheming, planning and plotting to their own advantages. The two men were determined to out-sit one another in Frances's company, whilst Frances was torn between the desire to go to bed early and escape the awkwardness of the situation, but felt she ought to stay up, just in case Megan and Tyrone should arrive. She hoped they would and so continued to wait, wishing for the advent of morning and Roger's departure.

However, as the hall clock struck eleven and the couple had still failed to appear, so Frances announced she was going to bed. Immediately, both men stood agreeing it was time for them to do the same. Frances longed for the seclusion of her own room, so left the men to their own resources. She sighed with relief as she felt the cool sheets greet her tired body and stretched luxuriously enjoying her solitude, for the first time that day. Her thoughts were with the young couple and their happiness. Nevertheless, such thoughts were not totally detached from her own regrets and so combined to lull her into a restless sleep, from which she was rudely awakened only an hour later, to hear her name being called in a loud whisper and to see Roger, standing beside the bed, in his pyjamas. She sat up, pulling the bedclothes over her upper body. 'What is the matter? Is it Lucy? Have Mason's parents turned up at last?' He put a finger to his lips to silence her.

'No, hush, I wanted to talk to you.' She scowled at him.

'You have the audacity to wake me up at this hour, after the day we've had, to tell me you want to talk to me? Well I'm tired and all I want is to sleep, so go away!'

'No, you don't understand, I want to talk about us and I never seem to find you alone. We need to talk Frances.' She looked at his face, pale in the moonlight, which also highlighted the first traces of grey in his hair. 'There is no us Roger; nor will there ever be. Again, go away!' This wasn't the response he'd anticipated; within his heart, Roger had always imagined Frances still loved him, still needed him and this delusion had enabled him to despise her and to self-righteously reject her. Therefore, it was hard for him to understand Frances meant what she said; conversely, he thought if only he could hold her, then all her resistance would melt away. As a result, he decided to try cajoling her. 'Look Frances I'm freezing, can I just get in beside you for a minute, while I explain.'

'No is no! Go back to your own bed to keep warm.' With that Frances turned away, pulling the bedclothes around her shoulders, signalling an end to this unwanted intrusion. But, deluded Roger, was still unwilling to take no for an answer and pulling back the covers climbed in beside her. She, turned both alarmed and furious, trying to push him out, but he caught hold of her arms, encircling them in his own. He tried to kiss her and she struggled, shouting out in her fury. Suddenly, the door opened and there silhouetted in the doorway stood Jones. 'I heard shouting, are you okay Frances?' Shame silenced her; she hoped he would just turn and leave, if he thought her asleep, but rather he snapped on the light and mistakenly registered what he saw. Momentarily, he stood like one stunned, but then quickly apologised, switching off the light and walking out, closing the door behind him. 'Get out!' Frances shouted, struggling to free herself from Roger's grasp and eventually managing to scramble out of her side of the bed. A vase holding the spray of white flowers, which had been Phoebe's; gleamed in the silver light and she grabbed it in her panic threatening to break it over Roger's head. 'Alright! I can see you're upset and I haven't handled this well. We'll talk tomorrow.'

'No, we won't! You'll leave now or I'll call the police.'

'Don't be ridiculous Frances, it would only be your word against mine and you have totally misconstrued my intentions. I told you I only wanted to talk.' Frances, was still holding the vase high ready to aim, she felt sick with loathing. 'Get out!' He looked at her in disbelief; his pleasant dream exposed for the nightmare it really was. Humiliated, he held his hands out towards her almost as a silent plea; but Frances raised the vase higher, as if about to take aim, and he ducked, covering his head with his hands as he left. Shaking, Frances replaced the vase and dragged a bedside cabinet over to the door, attempting to build a barricade in the absence of any locks. But, she needn't have bothered as both men, unknown to her, had left the house. She crumpled into bed, ashamed, humiliated and wondering if she would ever be able to explain the truth to Jones. She was sick at heart but also exhausted, her nerves frayed; nevertheless, despite her grief she unexpectedly, sank into the welcome arms of sleep.

The evening had been very different for Henry and Anna, who chatted late into the night, speaking of their regrets and making plans for the future. They had decided not to disturb the boys and so hadn't as yet, discovered their absence, when exhaustion at last, compelled them to climb the stairs.

Henry, hesitated outside Anna's door, feeling somewhat bashful in the light of their newly renewed relationship. He felt perhaps after all that had happened, they should take things slowly, rather than falling into bed together, like the married couple of twenty-five years they really were. He felt diffident, unsure of Anna's expectations and not wanting to take the recent progress they'd made for granted, by expecting too much too soon. So, ignoring his bodily sensations, he kissed her lightly on the cheek as he whispered goodnight. Therefore, he was unprepared when Anna hungrily turned her mouth to his, her arms pulling his body closer. They fell back against the bedroom door and Anna, her arm behind her felt for the latch; as it lifted, so she found herself lifted in Henry's arms, as like a young bride and groom with passion aroused, he carried her over the threshold, laying her with long stifled urgency upon the bed, where he was in a hurry to join her. 'Darling! close the door first.' She whispered, her voice taut with desire. And so, as Henry swiftly and obediently did so, we leave them to the privacy of their love as it peaks and plateaus in the heights and valleys of fulfilment.

However, any similar honeymoon contentment failed to accompany Phoebe and Mason. Their location was idyllic, their accommodation perfect, but despite their best efforts their minds were preoccupied; Mason's with his parents' absence and Phoebe's with concern for her husband. She was aware of the effort he was making to hide his anxiety and understood; nevertheless, she noted the distant gaze in his eyes, the way he seemed to look beyond her, during what should have been those shared moments of intimacy, when she longed for his undivided attention, yet felt herself alone.

Mason tried to rein in his concerns, to focus on his bride; with all his heart he longed to make their brief time away, one of tender memories and yet his mind was full of questions, bewilderment, and hurt, that his parents had missed the wedding. Why had they not contacted him? How could they have failed him on such a momentous occasion? He was their only child! His imagination spiralled, yet left his questions unanswered and him floundering in a restless void.

Eventually, Phoebe could take no more. 'Let's go back to the farm; you'll feel better there and be on hand for any news of their progress.' She added the last three words hurriedly trying to play down the negative implication of the previous ones. Although, in her heart, she knew as well as Mason something serious must have happened. He looked at her, his expression a mixture of gratitude and regret. 'We could always get away later in the year, couldn't we?' His tone had an edge of appeal, but they both knew his words were full of empty hope, for the year ahead had already been planned, each day long and full of bookings! This was one of the reasons they'd only allowed themselves these two nights away and now even this was to be cut short. She nodded, trying to restrain her rising resentment and turned away to pack her belongings. For Mason, it was as if the sun had emerged from behind the clouds, filling the hotel suite with the sudden hope everything was going to be alright. He felt energised; ready to meet any challenge and Phoebe recognised this. She tried to suppress the emotions rising within her, for she felt it was as if their newly made vows, spoken only yesterday, were already under strain and about to be broken.

From somewhere in the depths of her sleep, Frances could hear a child calling. She tried to break through the fog of fatigue, confused and disorientated; she thought she was only dreaming and turned over allowing the comfort of oblivion to claim her once more, but there it was again, breaking the hold of sleep and causing her to sit up feeling anxious and disturbed. She switched on the bedside lamp, as memories of the previous night fell into her consciousness. She buried her face in her hands and groaned at the thoughts of the trial awaiting her. The calling had stopped and she wondered if she'd only been dreaming. It was still dark and she was about to turn over and go back to sleep when she heard it again. Suddenly, she was wide awake, almost falling out of bed as she scrambled to get up, pulling on her dressing gown and dragging aside her barricade, made the night before. She hurried across the landing to Lucy's room. The child was sitting in a muddled swirl of blankets rubbing her eyes and crying; when Frances appeared, Lucy cried all the more loudly. 'I want my mummy!' Frances cradled her, lifting her tiny form, warm from sleep; trying to comfort the child, who was struggling in her arms and crying more loudly still. For a brief moment, Frances felt like crying herself, thoughts of the previous night and the day ahead pressing in on her. She felt almost as inconsolable as Lucy but true to her character, she drew on her inner reserves and knew herself to be more than equal, to whatever the day might bring. Hugging the child tightly and whispering endearments she carried her downstairs managing to calm her. Thankfully, she noticed there was no sign of Roger or Jones and wondered why Lucy's cries hadn't woken them, not realising both had already left the house, several hours before.

Lucy soon quietened as those first moments of waking confusion dissipated, leaving her aware of her hunger. She now sat contentedly in her highchair attempting to spoon porridge into her mouth, but most of it missed, tumbling in soggy splodges onto her bib. Frances tried to help, but Lucy, who was just exploring the possibilities of her independence, would have none of it. Watching the child seemed to mesmerise Frances and she found herself smiling when their newfound peace was suddenly broken by the sound of a car arriving, followed by a loud knock at the door. Frances started and glancing towards the window saw a taxi disappearing down the drive. Lucy turned towards the door as yet another helping of porridge slithered off her spoon and onto the floor. 'Mummy!' she called expectantly. But it was Megan rather than Phoebe, who was standing on the doorstep looking pale and strained. Frances noticed the deep shadows beneath her eyes as she tried to smile a welcome, looking tentatively over Megan's shoulder to see if Tyrone was following and with rising foreboding realised, he wasn't. Megan stood as if in a daze, which not even the sweet image of Lucy seemed able to rouse her from. 'Come and sit down and I'll make you some breakfast;' said Frances, guiding her towards the table. Lucy banged her spoon on the highchair, sending porridge splaying in all directions and chuckling to herself, but even this did not manage to rouse Megan from her stupor. Frances returned with tea and toast, it was as if Megan was locked in, held a prisoner by her thoughts. She still hadn't taken off her coat or uttered a word. In her mind she was back in the motel room, reliving the horrors of the last forty-eight hours. Such flashbacks were constantly replaying in her mind, numbing her emotions, disorientating her and leaving her out of touch with reality. Frances, felt out of her depth but realised something unthinkable must have happened. She wondered if Jones might be able to help and so knocked timidly on the door of his room; there was no answer so she opened the door slightly, before pushing it fully open, realising the room was empty and the bed had not been slept in. She closed the door again, before leaning against it, trying to avoid the crushing realisation of her loss and feeling more alone than ever.

Jones sat alone in his living room, gazing at the flames as they leapt and swirled behind the glass of the log burner. It was as if they provided the only light and warmth in his life, through what had been a very long night. He'd been looking forward to spending the evening with Frances and had visualised himself as some kind of shield, there to protect her against any distress, but rather he'd been the one to cause her distress. If only he hadn't entered her room; if only he hadn't switched on her light! His concern had been genuine and yet he couldn't deny there were other more personal reasons too. During the time he'd known her he'd become emotionally involved, this he knew, but it had only been more recently, during this holiday period that, he'd begun to think perhaps they might have a future together. Last night when he and Roger had gone their separate ways, he'd felt too awake to sleep and had sat wondering if Frances really felt the same or if he'd misinterpreted her changing attitudes towards him. He'd felt so sure he'd every reason to hope for what he most desired. More than this, he believed Frances felt the same way. Until Roger had turned up. Now he sat recalling how intently Roger had watched them both throughout the wedding and he began to wonder, if his previous thoughts concerning the two, had some foundation. Could it be possible they'd once been lovers? His mind dwelt on the situation and burdened him with humiliation. How could he have so misread the signals? He'd convinced himself almost inexorably, fate was drawing them both closer together and Frances returned his feelings. Until last night, when he'd found them in bed together. But surely, he'd not mistaken the tenderness in her eyes, when they'd met earlier or the pleasure she'd shown when he'd offered to accompany her back to the farm. But then Roger had appeared, and he could no longer deny the evidence he'd witnessed with his own eyes. Worse still, Frances yelling at him, to: 'get out!' following his intrusion. Which, still resonated in his ears, causing him to berate himself for his stupidity. How could she ever forgive him now? Perhaps, worse still, how could he ever forgive himself for being such a fool! He promised himself he would never make the same mistake again!

Frances was worried. Megan sat in an almost catatonic pose. She neither spoke nor moved: ate or drank. She seemed almost in a trance, unaware of her surroundings, causing Frances to wonder what she ought to do. She felt agitated since this was not what she'd anticipated! Instead, having imagined a pleasant two days with Lucy, and when Jones had offered to stay over and provide support if needed, she'd been grateful. As she too had begun to feel an affection for him; she'd seen through the mask he wore publicly, just as he'd seen through hers. They were very different characters, but it was almost as if through their seeming incompatibility, they completed one another! But now, she feared her hopes of a better future together with him, were obliterated by last night's events. Her anger towards Roger simmered dangerously beneath the veneer of her calm exterior. He'd been a blight upon her life ever since her youth, and even now in late middle age, he continued to persecute her, disrupting her hopes and plans. The bitterness in her heart would have erupted in uncontrolled anger, if it had not been for the sweet innocence of Lucy's presence combined with the desolate disposition of Megan. As usual, the needs of others drew on Frances's stoic reserves. For when needed, she always rose to the occasion, suppressing her own needs even as she did so. Looking again at Megan's expressionless face, she wondered if she should call a doctor. But at that same moment, there was the screech of tyres, as another car carelessly braked outside. Before, she could get to the window, the door burst open as Phoebe stepped breathlessly over the threshold. 'Mummy!' screeched Lucy, from her highchair, holding her arms high to be lifted. Phoebe made a beeline for her, swinging her around before hugging her tight. Frances smiled, she was relieved to see her and even more so to see Mason as he entered carrying their cases. She nodded towards his mother, placing a finger over her lips to signal caution, for Megan had failed to flinch, despite the noisy displays of affection surrounding her.

Mason spoke gently, his tone questioning. 'Mum?' At first it was as if she hadn't heard, but when he repeated himself, she slowly turned to look at him. It was as if that intimate term had filtered through deeper layers of consciousness to touch her heart. Mason drew up a chair to sit opposite her and took her hands in his, noting how cold they were. 'Mum, what has happened? Where is Dad?' She slowly shook her head and a tear rolled down her cheek; it was tiny, glistening as it fell, but it might have been a crack in the wall of a dam, for suddenly a reservoir of tears broke, dripping onto their joined hands and spilling over into their laps, soaking her coat and his jeans. He held her as groans and sobs rose from within her, racking and heart-breaking. Frances signalled to Phoebe to take Lucy out of the room, quickly following in their wake. Leaving mother and son alone with their grief.

When Henry and Anna woke, they were still holding one another. Henry was the first to wake and gazed almost with a sense of awe at Anna nestled in his arms. It was as if he couldn't believe she was real, but rather a figment of his imagination. But then with a warm sense of satisfaction and delight, he recalled the ecstasy and energy of their lovemaking the previous night and sighed with long denied satisfaction, now fulfilled. She opened her eyes and smiled at him. 'Even better than our honeymoon!' She whispered, tracing the line of his cheekbone with her finger. In response, he kissed her tenderly, as if remembering all the months he'd been unable to do so. Gently, Anna pushed him away. 'The boys weren't with us then, but they are now and we're not alone. Time to get up!' Reluctantly, they both stirred and made their way down to breakfast; still not realising they were alone. Anna began to lay the table, while Henry, who was feeling much better than he had in months, was cooking a hearty breakfast for them all. Both he and Anna were hoping, today would be a fresh start for them all, in the long journey back to a functioning family life.

The smell of fried bacon filled the farmhouse and Henry called loudly: 'Come and get it!' The boys never could resist a full English breakfast and he was sure the aroma of bacon, must have reached their nostrils by now. However, his voice seemed to echo in the empty recesses of the staircase. There were no pounding feet on the stairs, as he'd anticipated, or slamming of doors and whoops of joy, only an empty stillness, which seemed to threaten the healing of the day. 'I'll go and wake them.' Said Anna.

'Tell them to hurry up, before it gets cold!' Replied Henry, serving generous portions of meat and eggs onto each plate. He was placing these on the table when Anna called down the stairs. 'They're not here! Their beds haven't been slept in!' Henry ran upstairs as if in doubt of what he'd heard and together they looked in on the empty room. This was not the start to the day that either of them had anticipated. They looked at one another, as if searching for an answer, then back into the room. It felt almost to them both that, if they gazed long enough at the empty beds, then their sons would materialise before their eyes. Anna eventually broke the silence. 'They didn't even take their shoes!'

The reality of what had happened descended on Mason in an avalanche of emotion a mixture of grief, guilt and regret. Irrationally he blamed himself for his father's death. He reasoned, if his parents had not made the long trip for his wedding, then his father might still have been alive. Tyrone's heart condition had been unknown to him and he resented the fact this information had been withheld. It would have made a difference to their plans. They could have married in New Zealand; he would have loved to introduce Phoebe to his childhood home and the environment he'd grown up in. In turn, she would have enjoyed the experience. They'd already spoken of making the trip, in a year or two, when their business would be better established and the temporary management could be handed over to others. He felt guilty at his anger in their absence. Also, of his sense of rejection believing himself to be secondary to their desire to see more of the UK. Moreover, their failure to appear on his wedding day had ultimately compounded his sense of injury. Now he felt remorse for these emotions; which like frozen snow, when trodden underfoot, compacted his grief.

Frances was relieved to see the couple return. The strain of the previous night was heavy upon her and she was pleased to be able to take herself off and leave the family alone with their grief. This was not the normal, stoical behaviour of the woman she really was, but a transformation had occurred overnight, reducing her natural resilience. Her first thought had been to head back to the holiday let, but then she remembered Henry's family would still be there and, for all she knew, Roger might have returned there and she'd no wish to confront him. She needed to walk and so headed towards the village, oblivious to the beauty of her surroundings and the birdsong that threaded the hedgerows.

Eventually, she found a tearoom just opening its doors and gratefully sat down at a window table. She gave her order to a robust, matronly woman wearing a red and white checked apron and then turned her attention to those passing by outside. However, she'd not seen Jones passing the window, as she gave her order, but he'd noticed her and so she was both surprised and embarrassed to find him standing by her side, asking if he could join her. Her first response was to refuse, telling him she wished to be alone, but he sat down anyway. Annoyed, she stood to leave, but he reached over and held her arm, his expression pleading. 'Please Frances, we have to talk. I was on my way to the farm when I saw you here. I won't stay long, will I? But I need to ask you some questions, I do, I really do!' The soft lilting tones of his accent and his gentle expression calmed her nerves, as they always did. The waitress returned with her order and asked Jones for his. He mumbled: 'A coffee will do, won't it?' And she gave him a quizzical look as she turned away. Frances found herself smiling. She loved the idiosyncratic way Jones spoke. She found it endearing and his presence soothing. He noticed the melting in her and smiled. 'That's more like it, isn't it?' He said smiling broadly. He'd been about to say: 'That's more like my girl, isn't it?' But had stopped himself just in time. The matronly figure returned with his coffee. 'Will that be all?'

'It will. Thank you!' He replied rather peremptorily. She raised her chin, folding her arms to show her disapproval, before turning and walking away. Frances felt herself relent as she smiled. Jones looked at her smiling broadly. 'Was it something I said?'

Frances was grateful for his presence but apprehensive as to where their conversation would lead. How could she explain last night? Then to her surprise, Jones took the initiative. 'Look, Frances, I just want you to be honest with me, isn't it? Is there any hope for me? Or is Roger the man you want to be with? I will accept whatever you say, won't I?' His directness surprised her, but it should not have as everything about Jones was direct and open, and in her heart, she knew this and loved him for it. For a while she was silent, suspended in time, somewhere between last night and this moment. How could she explain? Jones spoke again. 'I left as soon as you told me to, "get out!"' Then, he paused, as if trying to find the right words. Frances looked at him, distraught that he'd misunderstood, wondering what he was about to say. He seemed to be as tongue-tied as herself. But Jones had more courage and continued. 'But then I started to think about it and wondered, if perhaps, just perhaps mind, it was actually Roger, you were telling to "get out." Who was it, Frances, Roger or me?' A mixture of relief and anxiety flooded her. Relief Jones had taken the hard part upon himself, but anxiety at having to explain her past. As always, Jones read her like nobody else ever had. 'Look, Frances, I'm not asking you about your past. I just want you to answer my question, don't I; was it me or Roger you told to "get out!"?' Frances lowered her head. 'It was Roger, not you.' Jones leaned in closer, he'd missed her words. 'Sorry I am, but I didn't catch that, did I?' Again, her head still lowered, but louder this time, she replied. 'It was Roger!' Suddenly, she felt his large, warm hands reach across the table and take hold of hers. She lifted her face to look into his and saw the joy and pure delight of love, smiling at her. In the relief of the moment, she felt her anguish, dissolving in the tenderness of his gaze as the joy of unconditional acceptance, rose within her, breaking down her barriers of guilt and shame. 'I love you my darling, don't I?' He said, gently rubbing her hands in his. His palms were large and leathery and Frances's, slender fingers, cold yet soft, were lost in them. But neither of them seemed to notice, as Frances replied. 'I love you too Jones!'

'Davyd! My name is Davyd, isn't it?' So captivated were they by the significance of their words, that neither noticed the waitress in the red and white checked apron, standing behind the counter, rolling her eyes to the ceiling and then quickly disappearing into the kitchen. Leaving the door to bang loudly behind her.

Roger had not returned to the holiday let. Rather, like a fox caught raiding the hen-coop, he'd sloped away, a metaphorical blunderbuss blasting his arrogance with anger at his misjudgement and what he understood to also be Frances's. How she could prefer such a man as Jones to himself was beyond him. Nevertheless, he now knew it to be true and he'd decided to leave and lick his wounds in private, yet still hoping Frances would eventually come to her senses, as he understood them to be.

Consequently, Henry and Anna were alone. They sat in silence, the atmosphere between them as congealed as the uneaten breakfasts, lying cold between them. Finally, Anna spoke. 'It's our fault! All of this is our fault!' Henry thought differently and reminded her of the drug problems the boys had at university. Anna looked at him, almost in disbelief. 'Can't you see that was our fault too? If you'd been at home more, there when you were needed, instead of getting so involved with the lives of other families, ours might have stayed together!' He winced at her words. Patiently pointing out it was when they were away from home the problems had started. She shook her head angrily, 'No! The problems started long before; you weren't there for them! You missed so many important dates in their calendar because you were attending the events of other peoples' children!' He knew she had a point but was reluctant to take all the blame. The first bliss of the morning had evaporated like early mist, leaving them both angry, upset and exposed. The only place Henry could hide was behind his profession. He tried to reason; 'You know it was because of my work. As headmaster, the buck always stopped with me. I had to attend all those occasions; it was my duty! Anyway, you're exaggerating again. I didn't miss all their parents' evenings or performances or sports days! I distinctly remember attending some and the problems I had getting others to stand in for me!' His words were like petrol thrown onto an open fire. Anna stood; her face inflamed with anger. 'And I distinctly remember all those occasions I attended on my own! You came to so few; you weren't there for our boys! I was their mainstay and it wasn't always easy for me either! I may not have been the head teacher, but I was the head of my department and also had to take responsibility for others.' Henry still felt her accusations were unjust; he'd worked hard for them all as a family and they had all benefitted from his efforts. He felt there was no comparison between his responsibilities and those that Anna had in her school. Exasperated, he replied. 'So, if you were their mainstay, where have you been for the last two years? Perhaps you've forgotten you were the one who walked out of the family home!'

'Oh! you just had to bring that up, didn't you? I suppose you're never going to let me forget it, are you? That's very neat making our failures all my fault!' Even as she shouted, Anna realised the implication of her words, it was really their failures in part and also the boys, who no longer were children, but adults. They'd all had a part to play in the breakdown of their family life. Suddenly, she stopped shouting and sat down, holding her head in her hands. Then she said. 'Look, none of this apportioning blame is going to help, if we're going to find the way forward as a family.' Henry sat beside her and placed an arm across her shoulders.

'I know. I'm sorry!'

'I'm sorry too! We're both worried and throwing accusations about isn't going to solve anything.' At that moment the doorbell rang and they looked at one another in surprise. They weren't expecting anyone and wondered if Roger might have lost his key. However, when they opened the door it was to see a policeman standing there with a rather subdued Jack and Jake by his side. 'I believe you know these two young men.' He said: it was more of a statement than a question. 'Of course, we do!' Said Anna impatiently, relieved at seeing her sons apparently safe and in one piece, despite simultaneously feeling angry at the grief between her and Henry their unexpected absence had caused. 'What's happened, officer?' Henry noticed the faces of his sons. He understood their expressions, which the presence of the policeman confirmed. Something had happened, placing them on the wrong side of the law and his mind was racing with various possibilities. The policeman, portly in his blue uniform with the silver buttons, stretched indecorously tight across his belly, removed his helmet. 'If I could come in sir? We need to talk!'

They were seated in the dark lounge, where the windows were small and the walls thick. Jack and Jake still hadn't spoken and sat looking down at their sodden feet, which were both sore and cold. They were still wearing only their socks, muddied and with various bits of debris stuck to them. These they pulled off, throwing them to one side as if resigning themselves to their fate. They were both exhausted, their heads ached and they longed for bed. The exhilaration of the last few hours had long begun to wane, leaving them wasted and dissatisfied as it always did after one of their drinking binges. Their high spirits of the previous evening now deflated and exhausted. Anna wanted to hug them both, but something in their expressions kept her at a distance. She looked anxiously from one to another, but each refused to meet her eyes, continuing to stare dejectedly at the floor. Finally, she braced herself for bad news and faced the policeman who was consulting his notebook. At last, he began to speak, while both Henry and Anna sat on the edge of their seats, digesting his words in dismay.

Following several hours of drinking at the White Swan, the couple were grieved to hear their sons had been escorted off the premises by the landlord, due to their abusive language. Unimpressed the two had staggered to the car, their minds still set on, "finding some fun," as they were later to put it. This, in turn, had led to a charge of dangerous driving, which had culminated in an elderly cyclist being knocked off his bike and taken to hospital with a suspected collarbone fracture. Anna drew a sharp intake of breath as the officer announced this, whilst he was looking towards the pair, with a contemptuous glance. 'Fortunate for Connor, he wasn't killed!' Jake, raised his head to speak in their defence. 'We only clipped his elbow, with our wing mirror and he didn't have any lights on his bike. How were we to know he was there?' Then Jack chipped in. Yeah, silly old coot! Cycling about in the dark without lights; that's asking for trouble, that is! He's the one you should be charging, not us.' The officer calmly began to write more in his notebook, before wagging a finger at them both. 'I advise you two, to say no more, if you know what is good for you!'

'Yes, be quiet, both of you! You've done more than enough harm already!' Anna's face was flushed, a mixture of anger, humiliation and shame. Their sons were not teenagers, but young men in their early twenties. How long were they going to carry themselves like delinquents, denying their upbringing, ignoring their education? The pain she felt appeared to be greater than their own. Moreover, she'd no doubt this was also true of the weighty sense of guilt, which had once again fallen upon her. The twins began to protest their innocence again.

'Silence both of you and show some respect! How much longer do your mother and I have to tolerate your irresponsibility?' Jake stood up swaying erratically; Jack tried to follow, but promptly sat down again. His speech slurred, so Jake spoke for them both. 'You won't have to for much longer daddy dear, because we're leaving! We're going to:' he didn't finish his sentence as he immediately vomited an action which was quickly followed by Jack. The policeman, who had been sitting not more than two feet away from them, quickly closed his notebook and stood, as did Henry and Anna. A splattering of vomit speckled his highly polished black boots and Henry wondered if he'd noticed. 'You haven't heard the last of this, mind!' He nodded towards Henry. 'I expect to see these two at the station tomorrow. There are witnesses both from the White Swan and at the scene of the accident.' He turned towards the twins, both with their heads down, looking into their vomit and waved his notebook at them. 'These two had better be sober by then. I need to take a statement from both of them, do you understand?'

'We do officer!' Said Henry, showing him out. Anna stood, gazing at her sons in anger and disbelief. They had stood to go to bed and sleep off their hangover. 'Oh no you don't!' She said. 'Wait there! This time you're going to clean up your own mess!'

Back at the farmhouse, Megan was sleeping, whilst Phoebe and Mason sat looking into their empty coffee mugs. 'Dad's body will have to be repatriated.' Mason's voice was tense and tired. 'That will be expensive.' Said Phoebe.

'Of course! But it will come out of Mum and Dad's estate. There's no question of him being buried here. New Zealand has always been his home and it is only right that it should be his resting place too.' There was a note of irritability in his voice and Phoebe felt resentful. 'It was only a comment, I wasn't implying anything.' Mason looked at her, his expression inscrutable. So much had changed in their lives in just a few days and it was hard to adjust to the demands, which were being made of him. Of course, he couldn't expect Phoebe to feel the depth of grief which he was experiencing, but he did expect her to understand the impact his father's death was having upon him. Also, the responsibility for his mother, which now weighed heavily on his mind. However, she appeared distant, withdrawn and unable to empathise, adding to his burden. He stood and walked out of the kitchen, leaving her sitting alone.

Phoebe, wandered over to the sink and sluiced their empty cups in a perfunctory manner. She knew that her responses were unreasonable. Of course, Tyrone had not planned to die just before their wedding day, casting the pall of his demise over their celebration of love; overshadowing their beginning with his end. Nevertheless, she felt cheated of time alone with her husband and the closeness with him, which she felt should be hers, especially at this early stage of their marriage. She felt the pressure of his parents' situation separating them. 'What happened to leaving and cleaving?' She whispered to herself, but even as she did so, she knew there was no other way Mason could be expected to react. He was trying to do what was right. Phoebe understood this, but still could not help the resentment she felt. Why couldn't they have taken the doctor's advice, when it was given? Why did they have to take such a risk, jeopardizing not only their own happiness, but also Mason's and her own? Her view was that his parents had both been selfish as well as foolish in leaving her and Mason to pay the price of their stupidity. She chose to ignore the small voice of reason whispering in her ear, telling her Mason's parents had actually risked everything for the love of their son. Their intentions had been benevolent, even though perhaps ill-judged.

Her thoughts turned to her own parents and the tensions she'd witnessed in their marriage. She'd hoped for a better start to her own. However now, Phoebe began to wonder, if after all, they'd made a terrible mistake. Just how well did she know her husband? Had they been wise to rush into such a commitment?

Chapter 7

After leaving the tearoom Frances and Jones walked, oblivious to the quaint shops lining the high street; their bay windows and displays of curious items beckoning to passers-by, to come and buy! Some familiar faces called out a cheery greeting to Jones, in passing, but both he and Frances failed to hear so encapsulated were they in the bubble of one another's proximity. Now, the barriers of doubt and uncertainty between them had been demolished, they were enjoying a new sense of exhilaration. As the reality of their love for one another closed in upon them, blocking out every intrusion, which might threaten their present intimacy. Neither of them realised they were walking in the direction of Jones's house until they arrived. It had been an automatic, yet subconscious, sealing of their newfound closeness. Now, standing before the newly painted front door, they looked at one another, suddenly both a little coy and uncertain. Rather bashfully, Jones asked: 'Will you come in, Frances?' She nodded and so smiling he turned the key, gently ushering her in first.

Frances found herself in a light, spacious room. She blinked in the bright, golden fingers of sunlight, which seemed to reach out to her, in a warmth of welcome, as they stretched in dazzling displays through the large French windows, patterning the carpet with their light. At a glance, she took in the eclectic mix of furniture, both old and modern. The walls were white and the doors of honey-coloured oak. It was clean, cosy and solid, a bit like Jones himself. 'It's lovely Jones!' She exclaimed, her delight evident.

'Davyd!' He corrected her. 'It's Davyd I am!' She smiled as he drew her in close and kissed her. 'Would you like to see the rest of the house, would you?' Frances hesitated, unsure why and glanced out into the garden where a small bird fluttered in the birdbath, spraying the grass with glistening droplets of water that sparkled, as they fell through the sunlight. Perhaps, it was the memory of the previous night, which made her hesitate. Jones felt awkward, he'd meant what he said. He simply wanted to show her his house, not lure her into his bed. Again, he proved he knew her, much better than she knew him. 'I'm Davyd, not Roger!'

He spoke softly, yet with an edge of gentle rebuke. Frances coloured. 'That wasn't what I was thinking.'

'Yes, it was!' His statement was simple and direct, as he always was and suddenly Frances felt ashamed. 'I'm sorry! I'd love to see the rest of the house.'

'No need to apologise, is there?' He said, holding out his hand and leading her into the kitchen, which was modern and well-equipped. She was surprised how clean and tidy everything was, not quite what she'd expected. 'It's lovely!' She repeated, still lost in her surprise. Off the kitchen was a small dining room, with an adjoining study. She was again surprised to see the books lining the walls and the mahogany desk, with a green reading lamp. 'You like to read?'

He looked slightly injured, yet laughed it off. 'Why would anyone not like to, why would they not?' She walked to a shelf and ran her finger along the titles. Most were related to the natural world, in one aspect or another. There were farming manuals and books on various cattle and sheep breeds. Books on agriculture, botany, biology and physics. She turned to him and again he met the surprise on her face, with a shrug. 'I'm interested in all that's living; the natural world has always filled me with wonder and a fascination to learn more.' They went on to view the bedrooms of which there were three, two double and one single. The master bedroom had an en-suite and there was also a family bathroom, with a large walk-in shower. But, it was in the garden they finished the tour. Here, Frances spotted a large, vegetable patch neatly tended, as well as a lawn fringed with early, summer flowers. There were high hedges beyond and Frances thought she heard a horse whinny. She looked at Jones enquiringly and he smiled, taking her hand and leading her to a gate, hidden deep within the hedge. 'Close your eyes.' He said. Frances heard him open a gate, simultaneously opening her eyes, to be greeted with an entrancing view of a spreading meadow, bordered by woodland. The two greys which had so delighted her on her first visit to Jones's farm, came cantering up to her as if they also were remembering the last time they'd met. They nuzzled into her as she gently stroked the softness of their noses. 'They're beautiful!' She said, smiling at Jones. Eventually, they'd returned to the garden. Where everything bore evidence to the care lavished upon it. A small patio area spread just outside the French doors, where Frances had seen the sparrow bathing. Close by, a small wrought iron table and two garden chairs stood opposite a wooden bench. He sat down on it and beckoned for her to join him. Without speaking they sat for some time, enjoying the sunshine and birdsong. Content, just to be in one another's company. However, after a while, Jones spoke, breaking open the moment, with the sound of his voice, as if allowing its magic to evaporate. 'Well?' He asked questioningly.

'Well, what?' Asked Frances, feeling relaxed in the warmth of the sun. Jones hesitated, but only for a moment, as he rubbed his chin. 'Well, do you think you could live here?' Frances looked at him blankly; she'd a house of her own, in which she was very comfortable, was he really expecting her to give it up and come and live with him? He moved closer to her, sliding his arm across her shoulders. 'What I'm really trying to ask, Frances my dear one, is: will you marry me, isn't it?' For a long time, Frances looked into his face, his expression full of sincerity. She'd been pleasantly surprised to see his home and the care he lavished upon it, but his proposal had been an even greater surprise. 'Well will you?' Frances stood, shivering slightly as the sun seemed to disappear behind a cloud. 'This is unexpected! I don't know Jones, I really don't know!' He sighed, patting her hand. 'The name is Davyd! Davyd it is!'

The four of them filled the small area of the police station. The policeman who had visited the house yesterday stood behind the reception area. He interrupted his writing as they entered, placing his pen behind his ear. 'Glad to see you decided to keep our appointment; you're both in enough trouble already, without creating anymore!' His words were directed to Jack and Jake, who no longer wore the indolent expressions of yesterday, but rather stood looking sheepish and uncomfortable. They'd pleaded with Henry and Anna, not to accompany them, but the trust, once complete between them, was now broken. Henry had doubted their ability to walk the distance and certainly was not about to let them take the car. He insisted on driving them and Anna, not wanting to be left alone pacing the floor, had insisted on joining them.

Henry, began to ask what the charges were and what they would amount to? But the officer raised his hand to silence him. 'Your sons are not minors sir; and my business is with them, not you!'

'Well you made it our business last night officer, didn't you? Bringing them back in the state they were, to vomit all over the carpet!' Anna was angry; she and Henry had been awake most of the night, filled with anxiety and dread of what lay ahead for their boys. They felt what all parents feel when the reins of their childrens' welfare are torn from their hands. Guilt and frustration! The policeman cleared his throat. 'Not only over your carpet Madam, but my boots too!' He looked down at them, now brightly polished once again and wrinkled his nose. 'Would you rather I'd thrown them both in the cell for the night? Seems to me they might have many such nights ahead of them, if I know anything!' It was as if an unseen hand twisted in Anna's gut and she felt a pain turn within her, almost as severe as the contractions, which had rhythmically expelled her sons into the world. Henry too, had felt his heart rate quicken, but the impact on their sons was more apparent. Suddenly, the policeman had their attention. 'You don't mean we might go to prison, do you?' For a few moments he officer failed to answer, rather he took the pen from behind his ear, continuing to write in the huge ledger in front of him. Then, putting the pen slowly down, he slammed the book closed, holding it up, as if to throw it at them. Henry thought he looked like an actor rehearsing a performance well practised over many years. 'See this! I could metaphorically throw the book at you! You were both well over the alcohol and speed limit. You knocked a man off his bike and he's broken his collar bone! I have enough witnesses from both the pub and the lanes to charge you with dangerous driving! Which means you might, not only be disqualified from driving for up to a year, but also face a prison sentence of one to two years!' Anna, let out a gasp and Henry groaned. Jack and Jake looked at one another in shock. Their faces already pale now turned an unhealthy pallor. 'Surely not prison, officer?' Asked Anna, her words trembling as they fell from her lips.

'I don't make the laws Madam! I just try to make sure others keep them!' Then he turned his attention back to the boys. Now what I want to know is: which one of you drunkards was driving the car?' Jack looked at Jake and Jake looked at Jack, each pointing a finger at the other, simultaneously stating: 'It was him, officer!' Smirking as they spoke.

'I see you still don't appreciate the gravity of your situation. Do you want me to add a false statement to your list of crimes? I advise you to call a solicitor asap. Because, I'm telling you now, you're going to need one!'
'Will that be all, officer?' This was Jake speaking and for some reason known only to him, Jack seemed to find this hilarious. 'No, I will need your home address and other details. For, young men, you're going to find yourselves up in front of the magistrate. You may return home, if bail is paid, however, you are still going to have to go to court in a few months' time, which will mean you'll have to return here, to the county where your crimes were committed to face sentence.' Suddenly, the laughter ceased as silence fell on them all. Neither parents, nor sons had fully realised the implications, which now threatened them.

Phoebe was stunned. Mason had just announced he was going to accompany his mother back to New Zealand for the repatriation and burial of his father. She'd not anticipated this and wondered at Mason's judgement. 'You can't leave now with guests arriving in a few days' time and work still to be done. Besides, we can't afford it, in more ways than one.' Mason sat down, at the table, resting his head in both hands.
'I know. I'll have to borrow the money.' Her patience suddenly gave way to fury causing Phoebe to shout.
'How can you say that when we're already in so much debt?'
'Phoebe try to understand, please! I have to do this; there is no one else who can. I can't let my mother cope with this on her own. You've seen how she is, barely functioning! What other option do I have?' Phoebe was astonished at his words. 'You have me and Lucy to consider as well as the farm and the start of our new business. How do you think I'm going to manage on my own?'
'I'll make arrangements!'
'What arrangements? Who is going to be able to step in at this late hour, with the right knowledge and experience?'
'I don't know immediately, but I'll think about it. There's bound to be somebody.' Phoebe was pacing the kitchen the hard soles of her slippers, drumming a war dance rhythm on the cold, slate tiles. Mason sat, his shoulders slumped, still holding his head in both hands. His head as well as his heart ached. He felt he was letting Phoebe down. After all, on their wedding day, he'd promised both Phoebe and himself, he would never

leave her again. Now however, he also felt the responsibility to be there for his mother, whose mental health he feared for. She still would hardly speak or eat, but rather sat staring into space, lost in a world which had no connection to the one they were living in. He looked up disturbed by Phoebe's pacing and the anger in her voice. He'd never seen her like this before and it unnerved him.

He stood and slowly walked over to her, catching both her shoulders in his bands and roughly turning her to face him. 'Look Phoebe, please try and understand. I really have no choice. Why can't you understand? It is not as if I'm running off with another woman. This is my mother!'
'She may well be your mother, but she is also the other woman in our lives! Surely as your wife, I should come first? Your parents have ruined our wedding, honeymoon and are now about to wreck our new business venture too! Why can't you make other arrangements for your mother? She has no right to heap all this on you, especially at this time in our lives!' Then, she raised her arms, knocking Mason's hands away from her shoulders and stormed out of the backdoor. Leaving it swinging to and fro on its hinges, a little like their marriage, as well as her frame of mind: in danger of becoming unhinged.

Unknown to both of them, Frances had walked in at a key point in their argument and retreated not wishing to interfere. Also, unknown to them, Megan overheard their raised voices, carrying to her room above. Their anger had roused her from her reveries awaking her to the implications of all that had occurred. Megan wasn't a self-obsessed person. She'd simply been overwhelmed by loss and grief. The trauma repeated itself with frightening clarity in which painful images were repeatedly played over and over in her mind. More than this, she was angry with Tyrone! Angry with him for not listening to either the doctor or her. Angry for his misplaced confidence that everything would be alright. She was also angry at his unjustified irritability towards her concerns. Despite the fact, they had now been proven to be justified, which brought her no comfort at all. But most of all, she was angry with him for leaving her alone to face the consequences of his stubbornness. Now, as she listened to the angry tones rising from below, Megan began to feel the responsibility of her position and the realisation of what she and Tyrone had brought upon Mason and Phoebe, began to sink into her consciousness. Neither of them, had ever intended to cause such distress and this new appreciation of the suffering their decisions had brought, swept over her with a brutal awareness, galvanising her into action.

Frances had been shocked to hear the anger in Phoebe's voice and the violence with which she'd broken Mason's embrace, before storming out. She wanted to help but understood there was a fine line between this and interference. She needed time to think.

Megan also felt the need to reflect. She'd been grateful for Mason's support at a much-needed time, but now the first shock and disorientation of Tyrone's death had begun to wane. She still felt the gnawing pangs of bereavement; however, overhearing Phoebe's tirade, had been like a bucket of icy water, thrown over her self-pity and grief. She was not the selfish woman Phoebe suspected her of being. Conversely, Mason's welfare had always been both her and Tyrone's main consideration in life and the series of tragic events surrounding his wedding day had culminated in a catastrophe, which neither she nor Tyrone, had ever anticipated.

With hindsight, she could see they would have been wiser to have stayed in New Zealand. Nevertheless, bad news is usually met with unbelief and this, sadly, had been the case with Tyrone, who felt well able to extend the death warranty, which his consultant had issued him. His motivation had primarily been to attend his son's wedding, but also having only left New Zealand once before, the temptation to visit other countries, whilst he was still able to, had been his undoing. However, in that moment of acceptance, Megan decided her husband's death would not be the undoing of their son's marriage. She took a few moments to gain her composure and taking a deep breath, resolutely opened the door, to see Mason still slumped at the table. She felt mortified to think of the weight their thoughtlessness had heaped upon their only child. Walking over to him she placed a hand on his shoulder. He flinched, not having heard her approach and looked up, his face strained and tired. Megan, placed the palm of her hand, in a gentle caress, on his cheek. She spoke softly, her heart recognising his inner turmoil and aching at being part of the cause. 'It's alright Mason, I know I've been absent for a while, but I'm back now!'

The sun was high and Frances's mind full of crumpled thoughts, which gradually began to straighten in the warmth of its rays, like linen smoothed beneath a hot iron. In that moment, it occurred to her, she could accompany Megan home. Why not? She could afford to; she had the time and perhaps the distance would help her to clarify her feelings for Jones. More importantly, it would provide Phoebe and Mason with a better start to their married life. If only she would be able to persuade everyone this was a sensible solution.

Chapter 8

It was a subdued Henry and Anna, who returned home. Jack and Jake's car had been left with Phoebe and Mason at the farm and the boys had returned by train, the tensions between parents and sons being somewhat taut. It seemed to everyone to be the wisest decision. The twins were in their last term at university, having returned to resit their final year; nevertheless. both had been advised they were still on course for a third-class degree, which had been a further blow to both Anna and Henry; who knew, if only their sons hadn't been drawn into addiction and side-tracked by the social distractions of student life, their results could have been much improved. It had also been a costly experience, not just in terms of finances, but also emotionally as well as relationally, between the four of them.

So, it was a subdued Henry and Anna, who drove home with heavy hearts. Their newfound bubble of a romantic relationship, having burst; leaving them deflated and uncertain of the way forward for them all.

Henry dropped Anna off at her flat, his disappointment obvious at not being asked in. Anna had paused before leaving. 'I need more time Henry, so much has happened and I need to be alone to process it all.' He nodded as if in agreement, but in truth he felt his own need for Anna to be greater than ever. As he drove away, he noticed her reflection, in the mirror, just standing, watching the car disappear. He raised his hand to wave, but apparently this gesture remained unnoticed, as Anna had already turned away.

On returning from her walk, Frances asked to speak with Mason, much to Phoebe's surprise as she saw the two of them disappearing into the snug. Unknown to Phoebe, Megan had already told Mason, she wished to return alone. 'It is what I want and also what your father would have wished.' She said her eyes blurry with tears. 'He'd want you to remain and continue with the work here. To be successful in the same way, he was. Farming is in your blood, as it was in his. You're married now, with both Phoebe and Lucy to consider. As well as this new camping project. The yurts haven't arrived yet, have they? And your first guests will soon be arriving!' Mason had felt the pressure upon him ease as her words seem to pour over him in a wave of relief. Nevertheless, he still felt it would be better for his mother to have company on her return journey. It was still early days following his father's death, and although apparently stronger, he knew she was still emotionally vulnerable. However, he realised it would be futile to express his concern, as she seemed so determined. He knew better than to try and argue with her in this present mindset, but promised himself he'd find some solution. Therefore, when Frances made her proposal, he saw this might be an answer to suit everyone.

Megan knew her son well. So, although he appeared to accept her decision without argument, she knew he was still troubled by her decision and was expecting him to try and persuade her once again to let him accompany her on the long journey home, which she was not looking forward to, and found herself wondering if she would be able to keep her resolve, in the face of another counter-argument. Nevertheless, she'd seen the relief, which had flooded his face and frame, at her words. The dark shadows following the contours of his cheekbones had seemed to lighten and he looked taller gaining stature as the slump of his shoulders straightened. Megan smiled; she was proud of her son and promised herself there would be no going back on her decision. Very few mothers would want to be a burden on their children or a strain on their marriage, and Megan was certainly not one of those few.

Therefore, when Frances had approached her with her offer, Megan had promptly accepted offering to pay Frances's fare. An offer immediately refused; for as Frances explained she had her own reasons for making the journey, which were not all as altruistic as they might appear. Frances was surprised at the alacrity with which both Mason and Megan had received her offer. Nevertheless, she'd seen the gratitude in Mason's eyes and felt it in the warm squeeze of Megan's hand. This was enough for Frances, who always found fulfilment in the need to be needed. It always brought out the best in her as she drew on her inner strength, often hidden, yet always present. However, for both women, their reward was the obvious relaxing of tensions between Mason and Phoebe, as domestic equilibrium was restored.

However, this was not the case for Jones, who at the same time as Frances was offering to accompany Megan to New Zealand, was digging vigorously in his garden. Manual labour usually relieved his stress, but despite his best efforts and the need to wipe away the dripping perspiration from his forehead, Jones was inwardly still berating himself for what he considered to be his pig's ear of a marriage proposal. He felt he'd badly misread Frances. He'd thought himself on safe ground, following all that had passed between them in the last forty-eight hours. He knew he was in love and had believed she felt the same way. To him, their marriage would only be a natural progression of what had already passed between them, but it looked as though he'd been completely mistaken. Could it be, he wondered, that Frances still had feelings for Roger? What an idiot he'd been! Was he simply a card to be played in their competitive game? Immediately, he rebuked himself, ashamed for doubting Frances in this way. Nevertheless, maybe he had played his hand too early. It would have been wiser to wait until he could have been sure of her hand too.

But more than two years had passed since he first saw Frances, leaning on the paddock fence, mesmerized by the two greys, cantering and whinnying for the sheer joy of being alive; a complete antidote to the desolation he was experiencing at that time when Henry had unexpectedly stopped by. Those times seemed an age ago now and he wondered if that first sight of her had been the beginning of his love or if it had all begun with her distress in the orchard, causing him to follow her to the mouth of the crevice. He'd saved her life and in so doing had also saved his own. Frances had given him a reason to live; a reason that had gradually blossomed into a love, which continued to grow. He realised they were very different people, but surely this was a positive in that they complemented one another. Of course, Frances had wanted nothing to do with him at first, but he knew her tolerance of him had grown until there had been definite signs, his feelings were reciprocated. Had he totally misunderstood? Or was it that Frances still had feelings for Roger? Angrily he thrust the fork into the turned soil and left it there. A metaphor perhaps, of the pain piercing his heart, before grabbing his cap off the bench and heading for the White Swan.

There was only one day left before Frances had to leave the holiday let. So much had happened in such a short time! She ought to return and collect her things, before Henry's family left, not realising they already had. Therefore, she was surprised to see the car park empty and the door unlocked. She called out in the narrow hallway, but it was only her echo that replied. She assumed they were making the most of their last day there and hoped this was a positive sign. They'd all been through so much during the last two years and the boys' behaviour at the wedding had been an embarrassment to them all. Their family life had once been the ideal model to build her own hopes on. But standing in the hallway, listening to her echo she felt as if she was imbibing this emptiness into her soul and that instead of the reunion she'd hoped for, this holiday had been another disaster. She sighed; mounting the steep stairs for what she hoped was the last time.

As she was repacking her suitcase, she heard a car pull in below. Perhaps, after all, it was Henry and family; she hoped it was and moving to the window raised her hand to shield her eyes from the sun. Her hope quickly dissolved as she realised it was Roger's car and the man himself was already approaching the house. Frances panicked! She hadn't anticipated ever being alone with Roger again and became unnerved. Quickly, she piled the rest of her clothes into the case, snapping it shut. Her first thought was to hide, but too late she heard his footsteps on the stairs and before she could close it, he was there standing outside her door, looking in. Frances froze.

Roger looked as surprised to see her, as she to see him. 'I came back for my things.' He said staring at her. Silently, Frances stood grasping her case close to her body like a shield. 'Well, go and get them!' She said: the bitter nervousness in her voice evident to them both. But, Roger remained standing where he was. He realised they were alone. 'Can we talk Frances?' His tone was not confident, as though he anticipated her answer.

'I've nothing more to say to you!'

'I know, but if you will let me, I have things I need to say to you.' Frances knew it would be wise not to anger him and so replied. 'You can say them from where you are Roger and you'll need to be quick because the others will be back again soon.' He obviously hadn't expected this and flinched looking over his shoulder, as if expecting them to materialize behind him. For one mad moment, Frances thought about making a dash for it. However, he turned towards her again and she retained her stance, her heart thumping. 'I want to apologise. I'm sorry! I'm truly sorry Frances!

I'm sorry about everything!' Anger rose within her, both towards him and towards herself. Anger that he'd married her sister, breaking their engagement. Anger with herself she'd betrayed Cynthia, by sleeping with him. She knew in her heart it hadn't been a case of wanting revenge on Cynthia, but rather a mistaken belief she still loved this man. How wrong she'd been! There was also anger for all those years their shame and guilt had sullied three lives causing a rift between her and Cynthia, preventing herself from forming any longer-term relationships, as she'd imagined herself still in love with this reprobate. What a pathetic fool she'd been! 'Can you ever forgive me?' There it was again, the same note of pleading in his voice, reaching out to entrap her in self-denial.

'Never!' She spoke with vehemence and her anger gave her courage. 'Get out of my way! I abhor you! I despise you! I feel nothing but contempt for you! Have I made myself clear?' And with that she pushed passed him, causing him to step back, his face full of pained surprise.

Frances flew down the stairs, her footsteps echoing throughout, as she loudly slammed the front door behind her. 'Good riddance!' She thought as she sat in the driving seat and hit the central locking button. Her heart was racing and her breath short, but looking anxiously in her mirror, she saw no sign of Roger. Relieved, she took time to regain her composure, more confident now she felt safe again and as she turned the ignition, she promised herself never to return to that place again.

Phoebe was relieved to know Mason was going to be home for the start of their new venture. Her resentment towards Megan had diminished and she felt guilty for her anger towards Mason. Nevertheless, she believed it was only Frances's intervention, which she realised had been solely on her behalf that had changed the situation. Therefore, a sense of injustice still harassed her with antagonism, ever-widening the rift between her and Mason.

Megan was conscious of tensions filling the home with the silence of unspoken words, which chose to voice themselves in grim expressions and cold attitudes. She felt responsible, and so retreated again to her room, feeling the need to hide away as the intruder: she knew Phoebe thought her to be. Because of this, she tried to quicken the whole process of repatriation, enlisting Mason's help. He was a willing helper, still feeling he should be the one accompanying his mother home and so gave generously of his time to assist as much as possible, taking time away from his work on the farm, still needing completion, leaving more work for Phoebe, which she resented.

Frances had driven back to the farm; she was staying on until she and Megan left for New Zealand. It had seemed the obvious thing to do and Phoebe was grateful to have her there. Therefore, she was concerned to see Frances looking shaken and pale on her return. She'd dumped her cases in the middle of the kitchen and seated herself at the table. Lucy was in her highchair, kicking her chubby legs rhythmically against the foot support. 'Hungry, mummy!' She cried and Phoebe smiled, placing a slice of bread in the toaster. 'Cup of tea?' Phoebe asked. Frances nodded grateful for the offer. 'Hungry, mummy!' Lucy's plea was more insistent this time. Phoebe placed the toast on a plate and reached for the butter dish. 'No mummy, Lucy like honey!' The little girl called, kicking her legs more furiously as her hunger grew.

'But you like butter too?' The little girl shook her head, causing her blonde waves to turn and tumble over her tiny shoulders. 'Lucy wants honey! No butter mummy!' Phoebe looked at Frances and both stared at the child in wonder. Both heard their mother's words in the little girl's mouth, but neither spoke. Phoebe spread the honey thickly, cutting the slice into four. Her eyes full of love, as she watched her little daughter laugh, cramming the sticky sweetness into her mouth. She then joined Frances placing two mugs of tea between them. 'Has something happened?' She asked, taking a sip of tea.

'No, of course not! It's just the holiday let has so many unhappy memories and I never want to go back there ever again! I was stupid to have organised it! Just look what's happened!' Phoebe remembered how she had felt, following their first holiday there and herself repeating the same words, Henry had spoken to her on that occasion. 'You can't take responsibility for other folks' choices Fran, you know that. People came for the wedding, they could have stayed somewhere else, if they'd really wanted to, but everyone understood you were trying to bring the family together and create happier memories, both of the place and of what happened there. Nobody blames you! Life happens and everyone has to take responsibility for their part in it. No one is perfect!' Frances began to calm; her reason agreeing with Phoebe's words, but she was still left with a sense of her own responsibility for what had happened, which was difficult to assuage. 'I know, but so much has happened in such a short time; I suppose I'm still trying to process it all.' Impulsively, Phoebe hugged her. 'Give yourself time Fran and stop being so hard on yourself. Sometimes, we find it easier to forgive others than we do ourselves!' Frances felt her inner dragon rise; she was thinking of Roger. 'That's easy to say, but so much harder to do!' Phoebe heard the exasperation in Frances's response. She understood and so remained silent. Many things in life were easy to talk about and even plan, but to put those words and plans into action was always so much harder, especially if it meant lowering your defences in some way. Her thoughts turned to Mason and the pain in his expression when he looked at her lately. It was a look she'd come to recognise and it hurt her too. She'd failed him at a time when he'd needed empathy, understanding and comfort. However, she'd found herself devoid of these and had remained cold and distant, in the face of his need; because she had been so painfully aware of her own, which he, in turn, had failed to meet. It was only as she now thought about this, the realisation of having done exactly the same to him, fell upon her. How could they be there for one another she wondered, when they were both so self-absorbed? 'Perhaps forgiveness and love are both parts of the same process Fran.' Phoebe, felt startled by her own words; it was as if she'd been thinking aloud. Yet somehow, it seemed to make sense. 'I don't see the logic in that! I don't feel love towards somebody, I can't forgive!' Frances's tone was bitter and the reality of years having felt wronged, threatened to overwhelm her. Phoebe saw this and searched within herself to find words of comfort. 'Perhaps, we need a love capable of reaching beyond our own feelings, before we are truly able to forgive?' Phoebe spoke quietly, her thoughts still focused on her husband. Frances's eyes narrowed and she replied, her words full of cynicism. 'So, as well as being the injured party, you expect the victim to sacrifice their dignity too?'

'Well, I suppose there needs to be a willingness to do whatever it takes, whatever the cost. For, if we don't forgive, in one sense we condemn the unforgiven to live in the consequences of their failures, mistakes, imperfections, whatever we like to call our wrongdoings. Thereby, depriving not only them but also ourselves of the opportunity to change and move on. Because, without forgiveness we lock both them and ourselves in a prison of pain! Don't you see?' Frances looked angry. Nevertheless, Phoebe felt she was on the brink of a discovery. It was as if something she'd been searching for all her life, was about to reveal itself and in the face of this, she was unable to contain her thoughts. Consequently, she continued speaking. 'But don't you see Fran, forgiveness is *for giving*! It's a generous choice which begins with the will, but it takes time to reach our hearts, changing our thought patterns and eventually our lives. It is the only way to bring release!' Frances looked incredulous. 'So, you're telling me, if someone injures me or my reputation in some way, I should let them get away with it, by simply forgiving them? Are you mad? Where's the justice in that?' Momentarily, Phoebe looked defeated and she sighed. How could she explain, both the simultaneous conflict and yet elation of that which she was still struggling to grasp herself? She paused to reflect for a moment, before continuing. 'In releasing the other person from their debt towards us, we are also releasing our inner pain, injury, sense of injustice, whatever you wish to call it. Don't you see Fran, potentially you change a situation in which everyone would otherwise lose into a win-win!'

'But the other party might never know they've been forgiven! So how can they benefit?' Replied Frances. Phoebe heard a slight softening in her tone. 'That's true! Nevertheless, the one who forgives finds freedom from their bitterness. I call that winning, and in my heart, I believe there is a principle in which the other is released too!' Frances looked unconvinced.

'I expect you also think there is a spiritual law of reconciliation built into the DNA of the universe?' At that moment, Lucy cried out. The two women had momentarily forgotten her presence so deep was each in the turmoil of their memories and unresolved pain. 'More honey mummy! More honey!' The little girl called, her dimpled face full of smiles as well as a gooey mess of breadcrumbs and honey. Phoebe popped another slice of bread into the toaster as if finding sudden inspiration from those early days of childhood. 'Fran, do you remember when Mum would spread honey straight onto burnt toast when we ran out of butter.'

'Of course! How could I forget?' Said Frances, wrinkling her nose. 'I hated the stuff, but I ate it rather than going hungry.' Both her looks and her retort informed Phoebe her sister was in no mood to be mollified. She hesitated, wondering at the wisdom of continuing. However, she obviously felt the need to do so, as she ploughed on, conscious she was ploughing a deeper philosophical furrow than she intended. 'Well, the sweetness of the honey, cancelled the bitterness of the burnt bread, by covering it completely; thereby, changing not only the substance but also its usefulness. Without the honey, the toast would have been indigestible. So, in a way, the honey enabled it to fulfil the purpose for which it was kneaded!' Frances's eyes narrowed even further.

'Phoebe just quit on this forgiveness thing, will you? What about the pain of the injured party? Forgiving someone doesn't take that away.'

'But don't you see, that's part of the process. Honey is a metaphor for love and in one sense, the one who forgives absorbs the bitterness of the injury into themselves, and in so doing, they cover it with their love. Frances now looked askance, her expression incredulous. 'I suppose next you'll be telling me that, forgiveness brings restoration!'

'Potentially, that's it!' Phoebe replied excitedly; pleased Frances had found the very word which had eluded her. She continued. 'Love is sometimes painful! It makes us vulnerable. Nevertheless, it also brings hope and facilitates change. Love is powerful: bringing release and freedom to both parties. It enables us to move forward, as love brings healing in its wake. Just like honey!'

'Whatever, do you mean?' Asked Frances this time her enquiry laced with genuine interest. Encouraged by this Phoebe continued. 'Bacteria can't grow in honey, just like hatred can't continue to grow when covered by love. Both honey and love bring healing!'

'Hmm!' Said Frances. 'Healing takes time, depending on the extent of the injuries!'

'Of course, but don't you see, without forgiveness the process of healing can't begin!' Phoebe's reply was rushed for suddenly she seemed in a hurry to leave the room. However, Frances was reluctant to end the conversation. 'So then, tell me! What is the lowest common denominator of love then?' Phoebe's thoughts appeared distracted. However, despite this she answered. 'Well, I suppose it is to do no harm!'

'Quite the philosopher, aren't you?' Said Frances. Although, Phoebe didn't hear for she wanted to run and find Mason. She wanted to say sorry, to hold him close; to see the tension disappear from his face and for her own pain to dissolve within her, leaving more room for the love they both needed. It was going to be hard and they would both have to work through the experiences of the last few days, but they had a future together and a lifetime in which to try!

Impulsively, she picked Lucy up, hugging her tightly; the stickiness of the honey cloying to her cheek. Then placing her little daughter in the arms of her bemused auntie; she ran off without explanation in search of her husband.

Mason looked up as Phoebe entered the room. She noted the same pained expression on his face. He was sitting at his desk looking through some paperwork and she knelt beside him, pulling his face down to hers, covering it with kisses. 'Forgive me?' She whispered. For a moment he held her away from him, his eyes fixing hers with a look of incomprehension. This was the Phoebe he'd fallen in love with. 'Forgive you?' He asked. 'After all I've put you through? Phoebe darling you've already forgiven me so much! Why do you think you need to be forgiven?'

'I see the pain in your face and I've noticed the way you look beyond me, even when we're close.' He stood and raised her to her feet, pulling her in close again.

'I'm sorry Phoebe, nothing was ever your fault. It was just the circumstances, which have been so difficult to come to terms with and also to try and resolve. They just seemed to take over both my thinking and my life. I'm sorry if you've felt left out! I should have drawn you in and not excluded you.' Again, Phoebe realised, this was exactly what she'd done, by not letting him know about Lucy. He continued. 'I'll never shut you out again, I promise.' Phoebe smiled through her tears, noticing the traces of honey, her rush of love had smeared across his cheeks!

When Phoebe eventually returned to the kitchen; she found Frances playing with Lucy. The tell-tale signs of honey on Frances's cheek betrayed Lucy's kisses. Certainly, the child's spontaneity and innocence had left their marks on her sister, who seemed more relaxed. Frances, smiled as Phoebe entered. The heavy lines of weariness had vanished from her face and Phoebe was in no doubt Lucy's kisses were responsible. She walked over to her sister and held out her arms; as

Frances relaxed into her hug; both sisters stood quietly as they wrapped one another in a sisterly embrace, warmed with a newfound understanding and appreciation of one another. They both looked at Lucy and laughed. Her chubby face was covered in honey, as she held the toast close to her mouth, unashamedly licking the golden offering with obvious pleasure. 'More honey, mummy! More!' She exclaimed, holding out the soggy mess for Phoebe to spread. Phoebe felt overwhelmed with love as she looked into Lucy's cherubic face. Knowing she was going to need a similar supply of honey, to last a lifetime. 'Mum would be proud of her little granddaughter!' Frances said. 'I know Mum would be proud of us all!' Replied Phoebe. 'For I believe each one of us, has the capacity for spreading a covering of honey; wherever and whenever it is needed!' 'Possibly;' said Frances.

The old familiar saying, which they'd both heard repeatedly in childhood, seemed to resurrect itself both in Lucy's chatter as well as their hugs, wrapping itself around them both, like the comfort of a soft blanket; swaddling them both in love and a newfound hope, not only for their own lives, but also for their shared family. When they parted, they were both smiling as suddenly the prospect of a brighter future suddenly became a real possibility for both women.

Chapter 9

Loose Ends Tied

Frances and Megan were at the airport, waiting to have their luggage checked in. They were travelling economy class and as Frances watched the endless, serpentine queue of heavily laden travellers in front of them, she wished she could have splashed out on business class. However, she was booked onto the only available seat left, which sadly, had once been Tyrone's.

Since they'd arrived at the airport, Megan had become quiet and withdrawn. It was almost inevitable this would happen and Frances understood. However, she was concerned about the hours stretching before them and how Megan would cope, once she arrived home. Frances, hoped it would help her to be once again in a familiar world, except it wouldn't be familiar; how could it be without Tyrone's presence? Not for the first time Frances wondered, if her need to be needed, had tempted her into circumstances beyond her ability to cope?

Her thoughts turned to Jones. For some reason she still couldn't think of him as Davyd. They hadn't been in touch since, that last memorable occasion when Jones had proposed to her. She'd expected some form of contact from him, a phone call, a letter, a text even, but there had been only silence, a silence almost deafening, due to his absence. His proposal had been too soon, leaving Frances confused. Wondering, if she really could give up her independent life-style, blending and bending it to suit another. She'd lived alone for too long. Would it be right to risk so much at this time in her life? Although, the real problem was that, Jones had already become a part of her life. True it was a tentative and uncertain part, but one which had changed her in so many ways, hopefully for the better. She felt her time in New Zealand would give her a welcome space and interlude in which to assess, what this man really meant to her and to know if she was willing to make such a profound commitment. She'd seen the love in his eyes and had felt the response in her own, but how could she be certain this would last?

They were somewhere in the middle of the slow-moving queue. The check-in staff seemed to be stressed and overworked. Megan looked morose and had once again hidden within herself. Frances felt abandoned, but by whom or what, she couldn't say. Suddenly, she heard murmurs of disapproval and protest rising from the weary travellers behind, as she heard a familiar voice apologising. 'It's sorry I am, really! But I'm looking for someone, who I need to find, don't I?' An incredulous Frances turned to see the figure of Jones, squeezing past the annoyed line of people; apologising to each angry or bemused face confronting him. Then he noticed Frances and waved, pressing forward and causing more commotion as he did so. Then he was standing breathless in front of her. His face was red with the exertion of hurrying. 'I only heard this morning you were leaving, and I had to know Frances, didn't I?' Frances felt herself flush. In truth, she was delighted to see Jones and her feeling of abandonment had suddenly evaporated. However, Frances wasn't a public person and this was so very public! 'Jones, what a surprise; have you come to see us off?'

'More than that my darling! I know I made a pig's ear of it last time, didn't I? But Frances, my love, my dearest one.' At this point Jones paused and to Frances embarrassment, went down on one knee, producing a small jewellery case from his pocket. He flipped the lid open revealing a cluster of sparkling diamonds. The queue had fallen silent. Even the check-in staff stopped weighing the luggage and paused to watch. Also, Megan had been roused out of her reverie and was intently watching, with the hint of a smile beginning to appear. Jones continued. 'Frances my darling, will you do me the very great honour of becoming my wife, will you?' Silence prevailed, all eyes were on Frances, but hers were only on Jones. She saw the love in his face, heard the tenderness in his voice and felt the corresponding love in her heart for this infuriating man, who always ended both his questions and answers, with another question. Nevertheless, on this occasion, there was no rebuff from Frances, only the following words. 'I will. Jones. I will!' He was quickly on his feet as loud applause broke from the queue both before and behind them. Even the check-in staff were clapping and cheering as Jones placed the ring on her finger. 'Davyd it is, Davyd I am, isn't it?' He said, bending forward and kissing her lightly on the lips. Frances blushed, before gently pushing him away. For suddenly the staff were working again and the passengers moving forward. They had a flight to catch, after all! Jones moved with them. 'Marry me when you return Frances?' Again, she replied, but this time with certainty and confidence. 'I will Jones, I will!' Before adding with a wry smile: 'Won't I?'

Henry and Anna are still living apart. They've revisited a time before the birth of their sons, before their marriage, before their engagement. They're enjoying the delicious wonder, not of young love newly found, but rather a mature love rediscovered. They're taking things slowly and beginning the journey of finding one another all over again.

Jack and Jake, after standing before the magistrate, have a one-year suspended jail sentence hanging over them. However, due to their earlier addiction records and relative youth, the magistrate declared the prison sentence would be replaced by six months in a rehabilitation centre for young offenders with addictions. If they failed to attend for any of those six months, then the sentence would revert to imprisonment. Henry and Anna were relieved to hear this and hope their sons will now find both the motivation and ability to take more seriously, the responsibility for their decisions and destiny. As parents, they are now more hopeful of rebuilding their family life together.

Phoebe and Mason, have found the farm and camping enterprise demanding, but also fulfilling. Their business is a success and has brought them closer together through the united effort of their hard work. They will soon be in a position to take on extra help, which will free up their time a bit more. Allowing them the opportunity to not only extend their family but also the possibility of potential visits to New Zealand and Megan.

Megan was so grateful for Frances's support in accompanying her home. It made all the difference, during the long, gruelling flight and even more when returning to an empty house and making the necessary adjustments to her great loss: Tyrone, her husband of 47 years.

The farmhands, who had been hired before the couple had left for the UK, have stayed on and are still working for her. Megan has decided to wait a year, before making any longer-term decisions.

Jones was waiting at the airport when Frances arrived home. The love in his eyes and his bearhug of a welcome, the reassurance Frances anticipated. They're currently planning their wedding. The love of Jones and Frances's love for him has not only changed her heart, but also her outlook on life. She has become stronger, yet also more tolerant, more understanding, flexible and willing to make allowances for the faults and mistakes of others. Love has changed Frances to a remarkable extent.

Therefore, when a letter arrived for her from Roger asking again for her forgiveness, Frances was able to find the grace to give it. As a result, Roger has found a new lightness of spirit. He still regrets his past actions and although he knows he can never undo their consequences; yet he feels released from his despair and able to face the future with new hope. For, everything has the potential to change for the better, including ourselves. In other words, to spread a covering of honey is always the best we can do in every situation. For Love really does cover a multitude of faults.

A Christian Perspective of Love.

Dear Reader,

A Covering of Honey is a metaphor based on the premise: "Above all, love each other deeply, because love covers over a multitude of faults."

Such love is very practical; providing us with the opportunity, as well as the ability, to offer Love. For the following are all things we can do. Be patient, be kind, don't be envious or jealous, boastful or proud, rude, or easily angered. Keep no record of wrongs. Don't be pleased when others face misfortune. But rather, be happy when things go well for them. Always, protect, trust, hope, and persevere with everyone. For love never fails!

The characters in the story demonstrate attitudes, we all experience, in differing contexts. Like us, they too, also struggle to forgive others, as well as themselves. They found as we do, forgiveness is no easy matter! It is often a process, which takes time and begins with our will. Nevertheless, at the very least, it provides a less bitter way forward and at the very best, leads us to a place of reconciliation, wholeness and even restoration!

I write, not as a forgiveness expert, but simply as one who has struggled many times, in many ways, to forgive. I understand it is not easy, either in forgiving others or one's self! Nevertheless, many times, the act of forgiving, has steered me away from the abyss of either self-loathing, which confronted Frances; as well as the loathing of others! It is much better to love than to loathe. Loathing may last for a day, but love is eternal. And, I hope, in finding the love of Jones and the ability to eventually forgive Roger, Frances won't have to find herself in danger of slipping over that precipice again. For, when we know we're loved, then we find ourselves in a safe and spacious place!

Phoebe began to understand, that forgiveness involves a kind of dying to self, in terms of our pride and dignity. It is painful! Perhaps even more so, when we are the ones who need to take the first step in saying sorry. Yet, in such a dying to our perceived rights, we find the real possibility of a new beginning, as well as a new hope for the future. For as we tread the pathway towards forgiveness, we at last discover a spacious place of healing, where we are invited to lay our burdens down and rest.

Jesus said: "Greater love has no one than this, that one lay down his life for his friends." Jesus was one who walked the talk! Moreover, He spread his love for the world widely, by dying on Calvary's Cross. A demonstration of love, which makes the gift of forgiveness a real possibility for us all.

In doing so, he covered our darkness, by inviting us to taste the sweetness of the honey He offers. A covering of love, which helps us to not only forgive others, but in turn to acknowledge our own need for His forgiveness. For when we know we are loved and find our faults covered, then we in turn, are able to offer a covering of honey to those in need, which of course, also includes ourselves!

References

1.   "Above all, love each other deeply, because love covers over a multitude of faults." | Peter 4: 8.

2.   "Love is patient, love is kind. It does not envy, it does not boast, it is not proud. It is not rude, it is not self-seeking, it is not easily angered, it keeps no record of wrongs. Love does not rejoice in evil but rejoices with the truth. It always protects, always trusts, always hopes, always perseveres. Love never fails." 2 Corinthians 13: 4-8.

3.   "Greater love has no one than this, that one lay down his life for his friends." John 15: 13.

4.   "The heart has its reasons which reason knows nothing of... We know the truth not only by the reason, but by the heart." - Blaise Pascal

5. "...love is as strong as death..." Song of Songs 8: 6.